Where the Lies Begin

Other Five Star Titles
by Robert S. Levinson:

Ask a Dead Man

Where the Lies Begin

Robert S. Levinson

Five Star • Waterville, Maine

This novel is a work of fiction. Names, characters, places and incidents are either the product of the author's imagination, or, if real, used fictiously.

First Edition
First Printing: May 2006

Published in 2006 in conjunction with Tekno Books
and Ed Gorman.

Set in 11 pt. Plantin by Christina S. Huff.

Printed in the United States on permanent paper.

Library of Congress Cataloging-in-Publication Data

Levinson, Robert S.
  Where the lies begin / by Robert S. Levinson.—1st ed.
     p. cm.
    ISBN 1-59414-432-X (hc : alk. paper)
    1. Los Angeles County (Calif.). Board of Supervisors—
Fiction.   2. Police chiefs—Fiction.   3. Terrorists—Fiction.
I. Title.
PS3562.E9218W47 2006
  813′.54—dc22   2005034658

ALWAYS FOR SANDRA
LVY
(No lie . . .)

and for

ED, JOHN, MARTY,
BILL, TIFFANY & MARY

Who Helped Make It Happen
(Also the truth . . .)

Chapter 1

The name's Marion.

Daniel F., for "Francis."

Generally called "Duke" most of my adult life.

Called a lot worse by some.

I used to be L.A.'s chief of police.

Last year I became a member of the Los Angeles County Board of Supervisors, elected in what the press called a landslide victory to fill a seat vacated by the death of a supervisor whose distinguished career in public service was cut short by a heart attack in the middle of a routine liaison with one of a half dozen mistresses he kept stashed around the city.

I got talked into running by people I respect, who had more faith than me in the kind of good work I might achieve as one of only five supervisors who, to put it bluntly, run this earthquake-prone area of ten million and are ranked among the most powerful public figures in the nation, not just L.A.

Why'd they pick me to be one of "The Five Kings"?

Because at the time I was doing better than okay in the popularity polls. I was coming off a general reorganization of the department that had resulted in a substantial reduction in major crimes and, specifically, my part in a headline-grabbing Murder One case that had come close to costing me the one thing I value most in my life—

—my family.

Close, too close, but my aim was better.

I didn't want the supervisor's job.

That kind of power has never been my thing.

The kick in salary was no selling point, either.

Like my Pop before me, I was a professional cop, almost twenty years on the force, the last three as chief, but the power brokers were a persuasive bunch, skilled at showing me how much more I might be able to achieve as a supervisor and, as it turned out, skilled at raising the couple mil it took to negotiate a winning campaign.

My wife, Anny, made me listen to them when I seemed to be wavering, the way she can talk me into anything. She's one persuasive lady that one, and people don't have to check too closely to see she's the love of my life.

"Your Pop would be proud of you," Anny said, capping a bunch of other reasons she quietly drew from her storehouse of basic intelligence and common sense logic when the idea was raised. "For all the good you've done as chief of police and all the good you could keep on doing, think of how much more and greater good you'd be in a position to accomplish on the Board of Supervisors."

She was right.

No surprise there.

The only dumb thing Anny may ever have done was agree to marry me.

She's too good for me.

Always has been.

She doesn't think so, but that only proves nobody can be right a hundred per cent of the time.

Anny is my cornerstone, my foundation, my Rock of Gibraltar.

When we first met, I was a Detective One, having set some kind of speed record making the grade, and working the down-and-dirty stuff out of Parker Center. Anny was running an executive job placement agency in the mid-Wilshire area and living in a three-story apartment building built in the thirties, in a fractured neighborhood behind the old, shuttered Ambassador Hotel.

The area had never been high fashion and lately was becoming as low grade as a part of the city might get, full of transient foot traffic that included an increasingly large assortment of street bums, beggars and junkies mining the legit population for handouts when they weren't breaking the law going after bucks or booze or whatever it took to get them to the next hour of their life.

Lately, there'd been a series of residential break-ins. Usually, it was hit-or-miss hit-and-run. Get in. Get your hands on something valuable. Get out. Get headed for the nearest pawnshop, fence, or fix.

Sometimes, it was worse than that.

It was one of the worst of the worst that brought Anny and me together.

Following a business dinner, she had walked into the second floor two-bedroom she shared with a co-worker, Carolyn Keener. Carolyn Keener was dead in bed, a body under the bloody mess left by the junkie rapist who was still there and sprang after Anny the minute she shut the front door and clicked on a light.

Anny was fit, knew her karate, and had the reflexes of a panther. The rapist got the worst of it, but managed to get away. It was then Anny discovered Carolyn Keener's body. She kept her peace of mind until she'd dialed nine-one-one, then proceeded to fall to pieces. That was her state when I laid eyes on her at the crime scene.

I felt the kind of connection that defies words and gravity.

I began the process of helping her put the pieces together.

She let me, otherwise it never would have happened for us past the kinds of basic statements you make to a traumatized civilian mired in stress, disbelief, sadness, and a growing understanding of what the word "revenge" can mean.

The bond between us grew into happier areas of coexistence, especially after she said, "If you think this is all about me expressing gratitude, Duke, it's time to turn in your Dick Tracy badge."

Then, Anny used the L word.

She said, "I think I love you, Duke."

When I found my breath, I said, "I know I love you, Anny."

"Okay, then," Anny said. "I know it, too. I knew it before you."

It's impossible to miss Anny's outer beauty. She's movie star pretty, although she can't see it herself. She has a face a movie camera would love to caress if it ever got the chance, Reese Witherspoon's kind of perky freshness and innocence in a taller and sexier package. The privileged people are the ones who get close enough to see, experience, and recognize her inner beauty.

We'd been seeing each other six going on seven weeks when we eloped to Las Vegas.

We've been honeymooning almost ever since.

According to Anny, since getting elected a supervisor, I've achieved some pretty good stuff, stuff I can be proud about, stuff Pop would be proud of if he were still living, the same way—had he lived—my Pop and not me might have replaced Charlie Temple as chief of police, the job Charlie beat him out of years earlier.

Not so good yet, but maybe in time, is how I've been getting along with the four other supervisors, who don't agree with most of my methods, more often with what they deem my lack of manners and I consider an incurable inability to kiss anybody's ass.

Until then, a lot of what the supervisors call my personal agenda and I see as part of my vision for a bigger, better, safer L.A. lingers in limbo for lack of the votes I need to get any part of it on the table, much less enacted.

Tonight, though, that was incidental, insignificant petty politics compared to what had brought Anny and me to the Coventry Arms Hotel in Century City, where a Lifetime Achievement Award was being presented to the great Nell Fontanne by the National Motion Picture Assembly of Artists.

Tonight, I'd be playing a crucial role in preventing a national tragedy that could result in death for hundreds of thousands of people.

The person who reached me the previous week in a phone call that rang through on the private office number he had no business knowing said the Feds were calling it "Operation Pay Day."

"It's a damned nuisance having to come up with a cutesy code name for this sort of thing," he said, bustling with conviviality. "Easy to blame Hoover or Dulles, but it was a fact of life in all your government's agencies before either of them came onto the scene. Wild Bill Donavan, I believe it was, started it in the dark days of the OSS, which became the CIA. Initials, also a damned cutesy nonsense."

"And what agency are you?" I said, the sarcasm rumbling at the base of my throat, having quickly figured out this was somebody set up by my old sidekick at Parker Center, Fuzz Todd. "Avis Rent-A-Car?"

"We do try harder, Supervisor Marion, but, no, that's not

it at all." He hmmm-ed into my ear. "You believe this is some kind of prank, don't you? I hear it in your voice."

"If you were here you'd also see it on my face. Who did you say this was?"

He hadn't.

He had ducked the question the first time I asked and launched straight into his Operation Pay Day pitch.

"I didn't," he said, with less humor than before. "If it should make a difference, however, my name is Bachman. Rupert Bachman. Perhaps you know it?"

He knew that answer by the way I sucked air and said nothing, taking a minute to let the ID sink in. Yeah, right. You bet. Of course. Now I was absolutely, totally certain it was one of Fuzz's practical jokes.

"*The* Rupert Bachman?"

"Suffice it to say, Supervisor Marion, there are only fourteen Bachmans in the contiguous and continental United States, two more in Alaska, none in Hawaii, none who carry the name Rupert, and none even approximately related to me, living that is, unless the Vietnam government one day opts to reveal otherwise about my brother, Romaine."

Okay, enough of this. "Is Fuzz there with you?"

"Begging your pardon?"

"Fuzz Todd. Put him on, okay? Enough is enough and this is already too much of a not-so-fun thing."

The voice on the phone exhaled. "Are you wearing a watch?"

"If you were calling for the correct time, you definitely have the wrong number, Mr. Bachman." I said his name so he'd know what I thought.

"Supervisor Marion, I have the right number and also the right person. If your watch reads the same as mine—" He mentioned the time. "—any moment you will be informed about two unexpected visitors downstairs at lobby security who would like a few minutes of your time."

Whereupon, as if on cue, a voice over the intercom system: "Chief, Security just called up to say there are two square jaws to see you, but they're not on the clearance log and I don't have them on mine, either."

The caller heard something going on in the background. He said, "I expect that is your extremely efficient Miss Gossage so advising you, Supervisor Marion?"

"Chief, Security says they just flashed badges and IDs. Feds out of Washington."

The caller was humming some personal melody in my ear.

I didn't know whether I wanted to brain Fuzz for this one or applaud his initiative.

This gag of his was better than the bull he bought and had Air Expressed from Billings, Montana, after my election, with a note that said, "In case you ever have any problems telling your political bullshit from the real stuff."

"Look, here's the deal," I said into the phone. "Two seconds to tell me what this is all about or it's a click in your ear and your playmates downstairs get sent back to Central Casting."

"I can do it in two words, Supervisor."

"Yeah?"

"Bruno Guy."

I hadn't had the feeling that hit me then since the last time I was cold-cocked.

I couldn't remember how much I'd ever said to Fuzz about Bruno and me.

"What about Bruno Guy?"

"My associates will tell you."

"You tell me first."

"I don't think so, Supervisor Marion." This was not a man

who liked to lose. You could hear it in his voice. "But I will give you the message Bruno asked us to convey to you: Green Peace. He said you would know."

I didn't and was about to say so when the light bulb over my head lit up.

"Do you mean *green pee? Pee* as in *piss?*"

The caller made a buzzing sound.

"Correct, Supervisor Marion! You get to advance to the next square . . . Peace, that was my little test, you see?" he said, sarcastically. "Just to be certain you are who you say you are. Green Peace. Green Peas. As foolish as Operation Pay Day, but lacking the same potential for wide-scale death and disaster. Unless, of course, you continue to think this is a prank." Turning too hard-voiced serious for that. "It is not, Supervisor Marion. It is not, as God is my witness."

Five minutes later, Bachman was off the phone and two men wearing identical charcoal gray Brooks Brothers suits and dark druggie-style glasses, looking like fugitives from one of those old Blues Brothers skits, were settling at attention in the visitors' chairs across from my desk.

As they re-pocketed their IDs, the taller and bulkier of the pair said, "Affirmative, sir. Rupert Bachman. And all of us to a man proud to be serving on his watch, Supervisor Marion."

" 'The Bug Man.' "

"Yes, sir, correct, sir. The Department of Domestic Terrorism."

"DDT."

"Yes, sir. Correct, sir. DDT's mandate has to do with homegrown terrorism and identifying and defeating any and all the anti-American elements working to undermine our democratic structure, you understand who I mean?"

"Like the Branch Davidians?"

"That was an FBI matter, sir, although we did consult early in the game."

"The Olympic Village bombing?"

"Also, FBI," he said, not entirely convincingly.

"Like Ruby Ridge?"

The Brooks Brothers looked at one another but neither replied, until the shorter one, who toyed with his nose like he was trying to keep it from running, said, "Apologies, but it's still too classified to discourse on yet, sir, without the express authorization of Mr. Bachman."

"Like Bruno Guy?"

"Closer to the situation at hand, sir," he said, taking short snorts as his fingers plugged one nostril and then the other. "Ralph and I are here expressly for that discussion." He made a deferring motion.

Ralph looked around the office and, satisfied, clasped his hands on the desk, leaned forward, and said, "Bruno Guy wants to come home," so quietly it was almost a whisper. He nodded to the disbelief he read in my eyes. "You, sir, are his designated safety."

When I was sure of my voice, I said, "Exactly what the hell does that mean, designated safety?"

Out of the side of his mouth he muttered to the other Brooks Brother, "Paul?"

Paul's turn now, like they were a pair of performing seals.

"As far as we can advise, sir, the prick traitor does not trust his country's word of honor in a sufficient amount to believe entirely in the agreement reached with him," Paul said. "It includes a guaranteed safe return, but Guy fears he'll be terminated upon contact, unless he surrenders in the presence of a collateral safeguard. He specified you."

"Are you saying he wants to surrender to me?"

They harmonized the answer: "Yes, sir."

I was too amazed by what I had just heard to respond to the fact Paul Brooks Brothers had called my oldest friend a "prick traitor." Bruno was no saint, but he was better than that. Always had been.

"He wants to turn himself in after seventeen years of hiding from people like you?"

"Yes, sir," Ralph Brooks Brothers said.

"To go to prison for the rest of his life?"

Ralph looked at Paul before speaking. Shook his head. "No, sir. I'm at liberty to say Bruno Guy will receive a full and complete amnesty under the agreement worked out with Mr. Bachman."

Paul said, "Besides, the prick traitor's only been a *fugitive* from charges over the course of the past seventeen years. Under our legal system, he's not guilty until a court of law finds him guilty, as he most assuredly would be without the amnesty agreement."

"When is this supposed to take place?"

"Next week, sir."

"Where?"

"At a special awards dinner we understand you're going to at the Coventry Arms Hotel? For some actress named Belle Fountain?"

"Nell Fontanne."

"That's it," Ralph said, and corrected himself.

"How did you know I'm attending the dinner? I haven't sent in my RSVP yet?" I shuffled through a modest pile of paperwork to my left and pulled out from somewhere near the bottom the reply card that should have gone off a week ago. Held it up for them to see.

"We did not know, sir," said Paul. "It was that prick traitor's idea?"

He stopped, as if expecting I'd tell him how that could be.

I could have.

It was another indication there was truth in what I'd been hearing.

Bruno knew how much my wife, Anny, and I loved Nell Fontanne.

When I didn't offer any explanation, Paul shrugged and said, "I suppose it's because of how public Miss Fountain's dinner will be. Big crowd and all. Safety in numbers. So Guy's got that on his side, as well as you." Spoken as if I were a "prick traitor" by association.

"How will the contact be made?"

"That's the part we don't exactly know, sir," Ralph said, as if I'd asked a question he didn't expect. "As we understand it, he'll have someone deliver a message to you. That message will take you and us to him."

"Someone?"

Ralph and Paul shrugged in unison.

"Something else. After seventeen years, why's the government letting Bruno Guy come home? Since Bruno's a prick traitor—" I gave Paul a harsh glance, "—why negotiate an amnesty? Why not just go out and capture the prick traitor once and for all?"

"Too slick and too many fellow travelers to hide with," he said. "Besides, not who he is, sir. It's what the prick traitor knows."

"Fellow travelers? Are you now saying Bruno Guy is a communist?"

"Communism has ceased to exist, sir, but communists still abound on the frontiers of freedom, looking for new opportunities to cross and conquer."

Righteous indignation glimmered in Paul's eyes.

I wasn't about to discuss political theory with either of them. Or, religion. Or, the weather.

I said, "What does he know that's worth amnesty?"

They made eye contact.

Ralph nodded and said, "Sir, we were contacted by Bruno Guy with an indication that the—you know of the Freedom Militia?"

"They make bombs that blow up people. You're not saying Bruno Guy is one of them, are you?"

"Not saying that, no, sir. Saying he contacted us and said the Freedom Militia, before the month is over, plans to explode seven bombs in seven government buildings in seven locations throughout the country. The bombs are already in place, Bruno Guy said. Meaning thousands and thousands of lives are at risk even as we sit here talking. Bruno Guy said he knows where the bombs are and the day and time they'll go off. He said he would give us this information in exchange for complete amnesty."

I got up, shaking my head, looking around the office for— —what?

A truth easier to deal with?

I said, "You're serious, aren't you?"

"Deathly serious, yes, sir."

"What's to prevent you from taking Bruno down once you have the information?"

Ralph thought about it. "You, sir, we suppose."

"And if something goes wrong?"

Ralph threw up his arms and ever so softly said, "Boom!"

The other supervisors also were rolling out for Nell Fontanne tonight, along with the mayor, city council members, other city and county honchos, and the governor, to see Nell receive the Lifetime Achievement Award. The annual

NMPAA gala was one of the perks of officialdom and an outstanding *see and be seen* opportunity for the ones who'd be campaigning next year for reelection.

It was one of those typical Show Biz spectaculars, where you can't find the sky for all the kliegs shooting golden shafts of rotating light upward to infinity.

The Hollywood A-list out in full, fancy, formal dress.

Bodies beautiful coifed and prepped for adulation.

Rows of perfectly-groomed teeth glistening inside frozen smiles aimed at the crush of screaming, wide-eyed fans, scrambling news crews and wild-eyed paparazzi shouting their *Look this way*s behind red-velvet ropes protecting the red-carpeted route curbside to the lobby of the hotel.

Jack Nicholson brushed by me, his dark glasses intact, as usual, his aging bulk on proud, indifferent display stuffed inside a tux with out-of-date lapels almost as long as his rounded shoulders, lapping up every moment of the gushing adoration, scribbling his name in autographs books thrust out by fans who were squealing madly, needing a piece of Jack but not wanting to miss out on Mel or Julia or Tom Hanks. Harrison Ford. Brad Pitt. Denzel. Michael Douglas and Catherine Zeta-Jones. Nicole. Halle Berry. Two of the newer hunks on the fame front, Russell Crowe and George Clooney, trying to lure Johnny Depp into their clowning for the cameras, thumbing their noses at him as he side-stepped their shenanigans.

Anny nudged an elbow into my side, leaned in to whisper, "Over there, don't be obvious . . . Peter O'Toole."

I must have been obvious. Peter O'Toole smiled and waved at me, as if he really knew who I was. I smiled meekly and waved back like it was the most natural thing in the world. Two celebrities out for another night of nights in the City of the Angels, ol' Peter, wearing his celebrity like a crown, me, wearing my rented tux like a, well, rented tux, the sleeves a half inch too short, the old-style collar of the heavily starched shirt a fraction too small, the plain black button studs no match for the ornate diamonds on the ruffled silk shirt stretching across Sly Stallone's sculptured chest.

"He's still so beautiful, Peter O'Toole," Anny whispered. "I'll never forget him in *Lawrence of Arabia, Becket, The Lion in Winter*."

"What about *A Private Romance*?"

"*A Private Romance* was not Peter O'Toole's picture," she said, in that resolute manner of hers. "That was Nell Fontanne's picture. Peter O'Toole was clearly the second lead to Nell Fontanne." Anny invariably referred to movie stars by their full screen name, as if anything less was a disservice to stardom.

Nell Fontanne, of course, was stardom personified, as dozens of handmade signs waved by hyper fans ready for their close-up from the TV news cameras made perfectly, reverently clear:

Welcome Back, Nell Fontanne.

You're Still Our Belle, Princess Nell.

Nell Fontanne—Ever a Princess, Always a Star.

Nell, The Silver Screen Needs You Now More Than Ever.

Just One More Movie, Nell. Just Say Yes.

It had been thirty years since she had run off to become the bride of a prince, the heir to some foreign throne in a rinky-dink kingdom that looked like a dust spot on the globe, hardly as regal or glamorous to us as the throne Nell occupied in Hollywood as "Queen of the Screen."

Nell Fontanne before her marriage and retirement was a last link between the Golden Age of Motion Pictures and all the decades that followed, who became a star opposite the likes of Gable, Bogart, Stewart, and Grant and by her mere presence stole scenes from Tracy, Clift, Powell, and even Brando, who explained how she did it in the years he was still talking to the press:

"I don't know," Brando said. "That's how."

Even Fred Astaire, who'd routinely answer "Gene Kelly" when asked to name his favorite dancing partner paused whenever Nell's name was mentioned and, finally, in a self-effacing manner would mumble, "Oh, brother! She reminds me of my sister." That was Adele, who the critics considered the more talented of the Astaires before she went off to England, marriage to royalty, and her own retirement.

Nell Fontanne in her day was one of the few stars and certainly the only actress besides Davis and Crawford who could demand and receive sole billing above the title, because the moguls knew Nell's name on the marquee was enough to fill movie theaters everywhere in the world.

And Nell Fontanne was one of the few stars who got a million bucks a picture, this at a time when the likes of reigning box-office champs like Newman and McQueen had not yet broken into seven figures.

With the passing years, all but Nell's diehard fans—like Anny and me—seemed to forget about her, moving on to newcomers like Ali McGraw and Faye Dunaway and, of course, Streisand.

Videocassettes and cable television changed that again as Nell's performances became more accessible, even though she didn't. She chose to stay at home, performing the charity work and good deeds that had made her much loved among her countrymen.

Year in and year out, there were published news reports about movie offers from a Hitchcock or Wilder; more recently from Spielberg and Oliver Stone, who supposedly wanted her for the Queen of England in some fanciful fiction about the supposed political assassination of another princess.

The legitimate offers, the ones not made for the publicity windfall they usually guaranteed, were met with a reply from a social secretary at her seaside castle, always to the effect that Her Royal Highness Princess Nell was flattered by the invitation, but was not able to take time away from her responsibilities to His Royal Highness Prince Jean-August and her domain.

She even sent gracious thank yous—and regrets—every year the Motion Picture Academy invited her to come back home for the Oscar ceremonies. That was just about every year, so it came as a major surprise to all who knew her history when the National Motion Picture Assembly of Artists told a hastily convened press conference that Nell Fontanne had agreed to accept the NMPAA's prestigious Lifetime Achievement Award and would return to America to personally receive the honor.

I was on the lookout for someone with a message for me as Anny and I passed a reporter with flowing red hair and over-painted lips, who was gushing into her handheld mike, "The last star-studded turnout like this was for Britain's Royal Family. But, tonight, the royalty of Hollywood honors a true princess of its very own . . ."

Honking horns grew louder, shriller, emphasizing what was already clear to a glance. The traffic wasn't moving in either direction on Avenue of the Stars. It's what happens when everybody is too important to arrive on time or, heaven forbid, a little early from their Beverly Hills homes next door to Century City.

Uniformed cops on casual foot patrol, alert but not aggressive, mingled with the crowd. One of them was tucked in a corner with a good sight line to the arrivals lanes of the circular driveway, responding to something he had just been asked by a blond-haired man in a classic Brooks Brothers suit and designer shades, who at once transmitted what I guessed was the answer into a miniaturized two-way.

I figured him for one of Rupert Bachman's people, not part of the regular security setup, although there never can be enough security on nights like these, not with more Nutso McGonigles out there than MGM ever had stars in the heavens, or whatever the slogan was in the days of Garbo, Gable, the Barrymores, Tracy, Hepburn, Crawford, and, of course, a young Nell Fontanne using her pigtails to steal scenes from Mickey Rooney.

A blue-jacketed parking attendant carelessly let the passenger door of a late-model silver Rolls bang into the side of a sleek Lexus with new owner paper Scotch-taped to the window.

I winced loud enough for Anny to glance at me questioningly.

"You should have let me park Red Rider by myself, next door at the mall," I said of my beloved, classic '62 Porsche Roadster. "See over there?"

She followed my traveling thumb to the Rolls, just as Travolta emerged and, with a grin good enough to end wars, raised his fists to the roar of the crowd.

"God, he's beautiful!" Anny said. "I'd almost wet my pants if I were wearing any." She was quite beautiful herself, of course, in a black silk strapless gown she'd copied out of *Vogue*, *Vanity Fair*, one of those magazines. "Duke, I think John Travolta is hugging Tom Cruise. Yes! Tom Cruise was in the limo behind him. All by his lonesome tonight."

I made a face. "Did you hear what I said about Red Rider?" I asked over the din, pressing my mouth closer to her

23

ear. "They still haven't moved it from the parking lanes. I'll go drive it to the mall. Park it myself. I don't do something fast, one of those parking kids is sure to strip my gears."

Anny gave me one of her bedroom looks. "Don't be silly, Sailor. You know that stripping your gears is my job."

She has this flair for raunchy humor, Anny.

I ignore it when I can.

I said, "I'm gonna get the kid who never saw a stick shift before tonight."

"Love your stick shift."

I said, "Probably the son or the nephew of the parking concession owner."

Anny said, "Everything is relative, Sailor," and steered me ahead.

At about the same time, an early model white Mercedes slipped out of the traffic flow, descended into a low level of the Century City mall's underground garage, and slid into an empty space against a distant wall. The driver who emerged and clicked his door locks was wearing a tux that added to his distinguished appearance as much as his head of thick white hair and a neatly manicured white beard.

He walked around to the trunk, popped it open, and in a moment had pulled a .22 caliber automatic from the toolbox. He checked the clip and, satisfied, he pocketed the weapon and slammed down the trunk lid. He clicked the locks one more time and headed for an exit in a soldierly stride, back straight, shoulders erect, like a man on a mission.

A minute or two later, the Driver crossed the side street, angling through the maze of cars trapped bumper-to-bumper and joined others who were using a side entrance into the Coventry Arms Hotel.

A dark-haired, olive-skinned man in a Brooks Brothers

suit and dark glasses, unquestionably a security person, casually studied the foot traffic while talking into a com phone and gave him no more attention than anyone else as he passed by.

Why should he?

Unless, of course, he were a mind reader.

Then he'd also know to stop him before he murdered—

Ah, but it won't be murder, will it? the Driver thought to himself, smiling at no one in particular.

Death takes many forms, he thought, *as it will again tonight, not too many hours from now.*

He patted the .22 for reassurance.

Chapter 2

"Duke! Anny! Over here!"

Fuzz Todd was calling up to us from the base of the escalator landing, working a pocket handkerchief for his damp forehead and a hand for the beads of sweat forming on his upper lip. The velvet button of his tuxedo jacket strained to contain his gut inside his cummerbund.

As we stepped off, he ignored me like some invisible man and greeted Anny with a bear hug and an exaggerated kiss.

"It's still not too late for us," he cooed at her.

"Easy, police man, get yourself under arrest," I said. "You didn't get my old job, so you don't qualify for my old wife."

Anny said, "Hear the man, Fuzz? *Old*, as in *antique*, he means." Then to me, positively dripping sarcasm, "Now—I am most definitely rooting for the parking kid."

Fuzz released his hold on her. Burying my extended hand in both his oversized mitts, he wondered, "What the hell you doing here anyway, Duke?" He knew the answer but was never one to let a playful opportunity pass without taking a few swipes. "This elected official stuff done you some brain damage? Certain business aside, in your last life not even Clydesdales could-a dragged you to a circus like this here."

"Tonight's also a stroll down Memory Lane, Fuzz, with or without any business. When we were kids, Anny and I did a lot of hand-holding at every Nell Fontanne movie."

26

"Sometimes we even French kissed, Fuzz."

"Anny . . ."

She stuck out her tongue at me.

Fuzz pounced on her teasing vibe. "Jeez, Duke, and here I always thought your tongue didn't start getting you into trouble until you became a cop."

Anny poked his chest playfully. "Trouble is my middle name," she said.

"In that get-up, it's also your first and last name, you beautiful creature."

"Thank you, kind sir," she said, acknowledging the compliment with a gracious smile. "I made the gown, Fuzz, with my own two little . . . about two or three months ago. This is the first time I'm testing it out in public."

"In that gown, that's not all you're testing out in public," I said.

Fuzz said, "And you're the one thought he'd drop his antisocial behavior when he got elected a civil servant. Nothing civil about your man, Anny. Face it, Duke. She's too good for you. Come to think of it, she's too good for me, too."

"Is your illustrious Chief Crescent here?" I said, changing the subject.

Crescent, the better politician, had scored my old job as chief after my election, beating out Fuzz—probably the best-qualified and most deserving candidate—and four other deputy and assistant chiefs.

Fuzz rolled his eyes and took another hanky swipe at his face.

"At this dinner? You know the only thing your unworthy predecessor needs to eat is toilet paper. In fact, the old gang is taking up a collection to buy him a roll or two as a birthday present." Fuzz checked over both sloped shoulders. "But the government buddy you need to see? He's been on the premises for hours. He's wanting some face time now for your official meet-and-greet brainwash."

I glanced toward Anny.

She understood.

"Why don't I go ahead to our table?" she said, and held a hand out for her dinner ticket. I fished the ticket from a pocket and sent her off with a flying kiss, watching as she rounded the corner and sashayed through the crowded reception area toward the ballroom entrance to a chorus of admiring stares.

Fuzz was also tracking her.

He made a clucking sound and said, "You are one lucky son of a bitch, Duke," then turned, eased a few feet away, and signaled for attention from a pair of Brooks Brothers observing the guests stepping off the escalator and out of the elevators.

The Driver had no reason to notice them as he moved off the escalator and joined one of the thick groups of people aiming for the ballroom.

He flashed a ticket at the ushers at the door, too quickly for them to understand it wasn't a real ticket, and half listened to a greeting that included an offer, declined, to help him locate his table.

A few feet away: a beautiful woman in a strapless gown held up by willpower, blonde, somewhere in her middle thirties, the kind of woman who always appealed to him when he was in his middle fifties. She was trying to relate the number on her ticket to the large numbered cards on stands rising above floral centerpieces on all the round dinner tables set for twelve.

The ballroom was exquisitely, expensively decorated, and strolling violins added to the ambience. An empty dais ran the full length of a stunningly decorated and draped stage and the podium stage left.

Drifting down the steps and heading for the front, the Driver supposed he should recognize some of the people already in their seats. Movie and television stars. He knew Gene Hackman and, nearby, Michael Caine was holding court. The loud fellow heckling Hackman from an adjacent table looked like an older version of Warren Beatty.

The Driver chose a table almost dead center of the stage, near steps leading up to the dais. He settled in a seat with a view of the stage and the audience, returning a tight, twitchy smile to the six people already there. He reached for the napkin setting, then had second thoughts. His eyes swept the ballroom until they came to the vacant podium, and his mind began to play with the future that would become the present less than two hours from now.

When he looked back at the ballroom, fast filling up, he saw that the beautiful blonde had found her table. It was also an excellent central location down front, within hailing distance of his own table.

She turned in his direction and seemed to study him, as if he looked familiar. He turned away, back again a moment or two later. She was still staring his way, yes, at him, and seemed embarrassed to have been trapped by his eyes.

"So there you are, Mr. Marion."

I heard him before I saw him—

Rupert Bachman.

I knew it was him by his voice. It was sharp and static as it had been in our brief conversation last week. Turning, I saw he looked the voice.

Bachman was about six inches shorter than me, putting him in the five-six, five-seven range, with an outsized head that contributed to an air of command he'd probably built over years of giving orders and having them obeyed.

He wasn't particularly attractive, eyes almost smaller than a squint, rubber lips and a gutted complexion his deep tan couldn't hide. The offset was a casual elegance he now capitalized on with a maroon dinner jacket and a matching bow tie, along with an empty ivory cigarette holder about four inches long that he used as a speaker's prop.

"I am Rupert Bachman and I thank you keenly for coming," he said, locking his eyes onto mine. "You look in person like a much, much younger edition of that Paul Newman actor fellow as you do in your photos. I suppose you hear that all the time."

The two Brooks Brothers Fuzz had signaled were behind him, obviously his men. Bachman sensed their presence and dismissed them with a whisk of a hand. They moved quickly.

I shrugged as I took Bachman's hand and said, "I've heard it once or twice, yeah. Same about you. I recognize you from your photographs."

"Surprising," he said, surveying the cigarette holder. "Usually, I photograph quite badly."

Fuzz, who'd been ignored to now, said, "I don't think Duke meant to say you were movie star caliber, Mr. Bachman."

Bachman didn't find the humor in Fuzz's remark. He shot him a look somewhere between pity and contempt.

Fuzz turned away with a shrug as Bachman moved nose close to me and began speaking in a conspiratorial whisper.

"Mr. Marion. Duke. May I call you Duke?" I had no sense that the concession included my calling him Rupert, but I turned over a palm that said *Go ahead* anyway. "I do sincerely wish to thank you for agreeing to involve yourself in some potentially nasty and dangerous business."

"I'm only here because Bruno Guy asked for me, Mr. Bachman. I've already told you—Bruno is my friend."

The fact he didn't like that flashed across Bachman's eyes almost too quickly for me to notice. The corners of his mouth flickered then drew into a patronizing smile.

"Yes, of course. Certainly. But, be that as it may, we were advised he plans to make the first contact with you tonight, here at this gala celebration for Miss Fontanne. So, here we are, imposing on your privacy." He pronounced "privacy" with a soft *i* like the English.

"I told your men when they came calling—I planned on being here anyway. Me and my wife."

Bachman gave me another once-over and sighed. "Ah, yes, we public servants do come to recognize there is no time off for good behavior."

"Not that at all."

"Duke, is it something Bruno Guy already knew that we did not know, about your planning to be here anyway?" He tilted his head and raised his eyebrows, almost but not quite making a joke of it.

I tried not to show my irritation. This guy could get under your skin faster than dust lice. "Maybe." I wasn't fooling him. He knew we weren't destined to share any lottery tickets.

"Suffice it to say, Duke, only you can perform this mission for our government and we appreciate it. Also, I appreciate it. Personally."

"Mr. Bachman, don't pull my dong."

"Hardly," he said. His eyes shuttered and his lips squeezed into his mouth.

Inside the ballroom, the overhead chandeliers had been dimmed and the strolling violinists had been replaced by an orchestra that stretched across the full upstage area. Sean Connery was at the podium, chatting up the audience, and the Driver was pleased to remind himself that Connery's bald head hadn't intruded on his stardom or his popularity. It would have been different years ago. Stars of Connery's magnitude could not go out in public without a hairpiece, anymore than they could appear on a movie screen with their head as naked as a bowling ball. Except of course, Yul Brynner, but that had been part of Brynner's costume, his mystique.

". . . so thank you, Milton Myrowitz, and the lovely Mrs. Myrowitz . . . Essie," Connery was saying, with a dripping charm that nevertheless played as sincere.

The Driver followed the travel spot to Milton and Essie, who waved in response to the introduction and the applause and shifted back into their dais seats.

"To think," Connery said, "that's the man that produced some of Nell's greatest movie triumphs in the glorious decade none of us will ever forget . . ."

The Driver stole a look at the blonde. She was checking her watch. Then, she took an unused napkin and covered the salad bowl at the empty place next to her. He observed that her own salad bowl was empty.

"*Dancing in the Wind, The Melody Lingers On, Forever Yesterday,*" Connery recited to ongoing applause.

A tap on the Driver's shoulder.

It was a dinner captain, trying not to be too obvious, as he wondered if perhaps the Driver had settled at the wrong table. Alongside him was a couple, tickets in hand, visibly irritated, especially the man, whose mouth kept moving in silent aggravation.

"*The Tap Dance Kid,*" Sean Connery said. "Gad, by Jesus, what a bloody remarkable lady we honor tonight."

The captain explained that the other guests at the table seemed to belong there, and perhaps he might also show his dinner ticket and, maybe, he also held one for the empty seat next to him?

The Driver pretended he couldn't locate his tickets.

The captain requested anxiously, hopefully, politely, that they might step outside to resolve the matter. The Driver knew it would be the wisest thing to do, rather than call more attention to himself. He rose and smiled at the couple, then followed the captain away. The couple, instead of joining the march out, quickly commandeered the empty seats.

"*London Days, Paris Nights*," Connery said, almost reverently.

The Driver passed the blonde's table as her date slid into his seat and lifted the napkin from his salad while acknowledging her inquiring look.

"All this and Bruno, too," I said, checking under the linen napkin Anny had covered my salad with and discovering the usual combination of soggy lettuce and tomatoes and two thin slices of cucumber.

"Did Rupert Bachman actually put in an appearance or was it another round with his messenger boys?"

"Super Spy himself," I said. That's the nickname he had been given years ago by *Time* magazine, and it had stuck. "See for yourself."

I discreetly thumbed her attention to the back of the ballroom. She performed one of those look in every direction maneuvers.

"Extreme right? Stupid jacket and playing with—a stick?"

"No, that's a cigarette holder. The stick is up his ass."

"You didn't get along, huh?"

"This is a go-along I'm doing, not a get-along. I thought I trained you to know the difference."

She raised her arms and twisted her wrists minstrel-style. "That was before we wimmen folk was emancipated, Massah Duke . . ."

I answered her in kind. "And we men folk was emasculated."

The woman two chairs away from Anny, a short-haired brunette in her mid-twenties who was dressed for aggression, had eavesdropped on our horseplay.

Thinking it was serious, she shot me a sour look that turned into a supportive expression for Anny, who acknowledged her with a wistful smile. I acknowledged her with a wink. Her lip curled and she turned away.

"Brute," Anny whispered.

"Keep 'em barefoot and pregnant, I always say."

"You say that to Super Spy?" she said, keeping her voice low.

"I didn't get a chance. He did all the talking."

"About Bruno?"

"About Bruno."

"Who hasn't shown up or sent you any sign yet."

"That Bruno, yes."

I quietly repeated our conversation, pausing only to wink at Ms. Mid-Twenties and send her fleeing anytime she edged her purple-shadowed eyes in my direction.

At some point, I slid a look at the back of the room and caught a Brooks Brother perched at Bachman's earlobe.

Bachman showed no emotion before he gave him a consenting nod and followed the agent out to applause, only it was for Steven Spielberg, who a few minutes ago had supplanted Sean Connery at the podium.

Spielberg was saying, "—The Oscar, thank you . . . So,

take a singer, a dancer and—what?—and she turns into a magnificent dramatic actress? Surprised? Not me. Not when it's the remarkable woman we honor here tonight— who I would have cast and happily so as either Indiana Jones, no offense Harrison, or E.T., knowing she would have been great in both roles." He waited for the laughter to subside. "So, dear friends and distinguished colleagues, without further adieu, let us show her how much we still love her—"

I was already applauding, along with most of the other guests.

Anny tugged at my shoulder and delivered a loving look, unnecessarily reminding me about the shared memories we have of Nell Fontanne.

I leaned over and grazed her cheek with my lips.

Ms. Mid-Twenties stared at us in disbelief, as if Anny were a traitor to the cause.

Spielberg was saying, "—Ladies and gentlemen—The princess! Our queen! Miss Nell Fontanne!"

The applause grew.

Thunderous.

Some guests were already on their feet.

The orchestra had launched into one of her biggest hits, the "Loving You is a Sin" ballad from *Times Past*.

But where was Nell Fontanne?

A spot held on the wings, stage right, but—

No Nell emerged from behind the curtains.

Crowd murmur began to intrude on the applause, and the applause seemed to be subsiding, and—

—now—

—as every light in the room disappeared, except for the spotlight that popped center stage—

—there she was!

As if she had materialized from air like some goddess of divine light, a mystical experience beyond any magical trick ever devised by David Copperfield.

And the applause was deafening, the thousand or more people packing the ballroom on their feet as one, the ovation exploding all around Nell—

—who took the welcome graciously, beginning with one of those feigned surprise expressions a Helen Hayes or a Gertrude Lawrence would always make on first entrance.

Then she accepted it as her rightful reward.

And she was beautiful. Beyond age. Beyond memory.

As if time had stood still for Nell Fontanne.

While the response grew louder, stronger, and became a blanket of love I couldn't recall ever experiencing before for anyone.

Not Elvis.

Not Streisand.

Anny, yes, but that was never out in public.

Even before Nell Fontanne appeared, the Driver had managed the .22 onto his lap and checked the clip. He felt the sweat on his forehead and the tiny water trails down, one into his eye, stinging, another close enough to his mouth for his tongue to reach; salty. He rose with the crowd and, as Nell extended her arms to embrace everyone and curtsied, strode purposefully from his table in the rear and up the four steps to the stage. His gun hand was hidden inside his tux jacket, like he'd learned the trick from Napoleon.

Ignoring Spielberg's surprised, curious look, the Driver passed behind the director with cool calculation.

He pretended the dais didn't exist.

He knew he was nothing more than an invisible ghost to the audience, which only had eyes for Nell.

Nell Fontanne sensed his presence when he was about ten feet from her.

She turned to look at him, her smile masking annoyance at this person stealing her moment.

The Driver removed the .22 from his tux.

It was an upstage move, and the celebrities on the dais saw the .22 first. Their audible responses were lost in the applause.

When he was barely two feet from her, the Driver stopped.

Adjusted his body.

Sighted the weapon down his right arm, legs apart for balance, both eyes open, adjusting his aim at her chest by an inch.

And all the noise in the ballroom quit.

Like that.

The orchestra had already, abruptly stopped.

The entire room went silent with the knowledge of the deadly drama unfolding in real life, in real time, in front of each and every person there.

For a moment, time was suspended for everyone—

—not just Nell Fontanne.

And everyone saw and heard the explosion from the .22 as the Driver squeezed the trigger.

And everyone saw Nell Fontanne's mouth open ever so slightly, the curiosity of a question, *Why?,* framing on her lips—

—before she sank to the floor in slow motion.

Screams emanating from the audience and—

—the Driver studied his weapon—

—before the next gunshot echoed throughout the ballroom.

Maybe if I hadn't traded cops and robbers for politics, my reflexes wouldn't have worked faster than my mind, but they did. The instant I saw that bastard, my hand went for the .45 service revolver I holster in the small of the back, the way I did while serving and protecting as part of L.A.'s finest.

Thinking only he was about to murder Nell Fontanne, I pulled into the stance, found a clearing in the crowd, and got off a shot. Not fast enough to drop the bastard before he did her.

He turned to look at everyone as that eerie silence that precedes panic hovered over the ballroom and a circle of blood grew and melted into a stain on his jacket, spread onto his white shirt. His hand purchased his body, like he was about to recite the pledge of allegiance.

I thought I heard him say Nell's name as he stepped blindly forward and tumbled head first from the stage into a front row table, setting off screams and the first panicked dashes from the ballroom.

Those quickest to escape missed the most startling sight of all.

It wasn't seeing the orchestra and the dais celebrities charging into the wings, bumping over instruments and music stands and chicken dinners as an overture to the pandemonium on the main floor.

It wasn't seeing the cadre of security cops rushing to disarm me, yanking at my arms and wrestling me for the .45.

It wasn't seeing Fuzz Todd, who was suddenly there from somewhere, moving Anny out of harm's way and shouting, "Lay off of him you goddam sons of bitches; lay off him! That's a cop, goddam it!"

It was seeing Nell Fontanne rise majestically from the floor of the stage and instantly command the world with her scream.

Chapter 3

I was a hero when I woke up to a bright, cloudless cerulean-blue sky and weather expected to climb into the nineties, but it didn't last.

Media acclaim for the L.A. county supervisor whose fast thinking had saved the legendary Nell Fontanne and possibly others from a crazed gunman was being qualified by the time I had moved from page one of the *Times* over breakfast to the all-news radio stations on the tortuous freeway drag downtown.

Every bumper-to-bumper mile brought a fresh criticism from somebody in the government about the vigilante perspective Supervisor Daniel Marion had carried over with him from the LAPD. They were mainly people who had never had a kind word for me, but their taped comments and call-ins were coming too fast for coincidence.

I got the idea quickly that the negative opinion blitz was being orchestrated.

By whom became clearer when Police Chief Paul Crescent, in interviews with one news station after the next, talked animatedly about the need to discourage citizens from ever usurping police authority or responsibility.

"This even includes our supervisors, who would be up in arms if a chief of police such as myself so much as assumed to make their decisions for them," Crescent told one broadcaster. He told another one, "Our one-time vigilante chief still carries a badge and a deadly weapon. The former as a courtesy acknowledging his years of service, the latter as an accommodation we gladly make to all elected officials, but it's definitely not supposed to be any encouragement for any of them to take a human life while playacting at the role of police officer."

Crescent had become bolder by the time I hit the Temple Street exit, introducing the concept that LAPD already this morning had received hundreds of phone complaints about "Marion the Barbarian," hinting darkly about wheels in motion to possibly censure the trigger-happy supervisor.

He might be justified in criticizing me, but outright condemnation was personal and out of line. I needed a face-to-face with that moron.

I hung a left into street traffic and dodge-balled the lanes past the Kenneth Hahn Hall of Administration, where all the county offices are located, east to Parker Center, the "Blue Heaven" that was my home base for nineteen years.

I parked by a meter on First Street, tipped a shopping cart pusher a five to guard it, and propelled by mounting anger half-ran to the main entrance, over a tightly-trimmed City Hall lawn where the birds outnumbered the homeless for a change.

I waved my way inside, sucking in the foul air of the Blue Heaven corridors like an amnesiac enjoying the miracle of a rediscovered memory, exchanging greetings with passing uniforms and suits, most of whom still treated me like I was running their show and all of whom had a salute or a few words about the good kill last night.

Curiously, I wasn't as sure as they were. I had slept badly, unable to reconcile my killing a killer with the fact Nell Fontanne was still alive, so—

—how much of a killer could the dead man be?

Certainly not as much as I had become again, only this time in civvies, doing a cop's job by rote.

Who was the John C. Doe?

Why was he gunning for Nell Fontanne?

How had she managed to survive his shot?

I had the probable cause, but needed answers to at least those questions before I could be comfortable with myself again.

My old secretaries, Pearl Bailey and Grelun Hendrickson, rose as I entered the chief's outer office, and I thought for a second that Pearlie Mae's grandiose bulk would beat her smile over the waist-high railing, but she stopped short and leaned forward for my hug and kiss.

Grelun also looked like he needed some loving, at the least some appreciation, but he settled for a handshake.

It was common knowledge Crescent didn't like them and would have moved them out to pasture by now, except for civil service and the simple fact Pearlie Mae and Grelun were the only ones still around with a thorough working knowledge of the job.

It was a case of him needing them more than they needed Crescent, a reality I had hammered away at in the weeks before and after I was sworn in as supervisor and one of the few times he listened to me, proving nobody can be stupid a hundred per cent of the time.

"Still miss me, kids?"

Hendrickson made a face at the interior office door.

"No offense, Chief, but all things considered I'd miss Godzilla."

Pearlie Mae asked, "How's Rita?" Rita was the secretary I did take with me, and Pearlie Mae pronounced her name like it was a capital offense.

"Traitor that she is," Hendrickson said, exaggerating a

sneer. "She owes us, owes us big, Chief, and we won't ever let her forget it."

"Why's that?" I said, knowing the answer, just not how the words would come out this time.

"For not wrapping you around her little finger the way only Rita can and making you take us with you, too."

I answered his pout with my own. "Rita had seniority."

"Much longer here and what we'll have, I and Pearlie Mae, is senility."

Grelun got the laugh out of me he was fishing for.

Pearlie Mae nodded, chuckled, then turned awkwardly serious. "Suppose you been listening to the radio, like usual? Been getting one after another call, and he just having a fine old time with it."

"Marion the Barbarian." Grelun made it an announcement. "I think he got that one from the suck-ups in PIO. Too many vowels for him to have come up with it himself."

"Should I announce you, Chief?"

I shook my head at Pearlie Mae's question.

"I think I'll just barge right in."

"He's got company."

"Now he'll have more company," I said, and turned the handle on the door whose stenciled gold letters now spelled out Paul Crescent's name where mine used to be.

"Notice the handyman's mistake, Chief?" Grelun said, turning his words into a soft hiss. "He stenciled Chief of Police instead of Creep of Police."

I wagged a naughty-naughty finger at Grelun and stepped inside the office.

Nothing remained to remind me of my three years there.

Crescent had redecorated the room in self-adoration.

Framed photographs, certificates, letters of commendation, and an assortment of plaques and trophies. Familiar sports and movie star faces sharing a handshake or an arm around Crescent's shoulders; meaningless, kiss-ass puke inscriptions that might buy them out of a jam or just a parking ticket one of these days.

The only photo I ever had on my wall was of Anny and our kids, John and Alicia, to remind me what the job of a cop was all about, keeping all the Annys and all the Johns and Alicias of the world safe from all the bad guys.

It's still the only photo I have on the office wall, a sad reminder of happier times, when my family was intact, when John was more than a memory, here where I can keep him framed in my sight, just as John will never be out of my mind, or Anny's, or Alicia's.

I like to think I'm still trying to keep the world safe from all the bad guys, only in this job as a county supervisor I'm dealing with a different kind of bad guy, one who is harder to spot, a white-collar criminal who doesn't have to carry a weapon to destroy.

Crescent hadn't heard me coming.

Neither had his company—

—Rupert Bachman.

They were engaged in heavy, conspiratorial conversation in a sitting area away from the desk, in easy chairs on opposite ends of a coffee table covered with the remains of coffees and Danish.

Just seeing Crescent was enough to remind me how much I disliked him.

It was a hangover from our years of competition on the force, more Crescent's doing than mine.

To him, I was always in the way.

To me, Paul Crescent belonged in the back of a post office trying to remember which one was the meter mark and which one was the stamp.

He looked like a chief, though, however much it was a mask. He was six-six and had been a starting short forward at UCLA, where he majored in All-America, but never got to the pros, something else he resented about me.

He was still in shape, ten or twelve pounds over his playing weight, wore his thick hair in a Marine cut and had never gotten around to losing the brush mustache he grew in his first year on the street, the usual trick of rookies who are trying to look older. I'd hated mine, because of an itch and because it made me look stupid as well as older, but I had to keep it as part of a deal I'd made with myself—not to shave the mustache off until I made detective and could also shuck the uniform.

That took three years.

And gave Crescent another reason to become increasingly jealous and outspoken about his contempt for me.

He didn't have his own version of the "Frog Town Boys" for another year, and that figured against him when it came time to pick a new chief.

All things being equal, I had the seniority.

Last time, picking someone to replace me, Fuzz Todd also owned a year on Paul. And brains. And the respect of everyone in the department, but Fuzz didn't look the part.

Anybody who ever tells you looks don't matter has looks that matter.

Believe it.

Bachman was selling Crescent smoothly, like maple syrup spilling from the tree, explaining, "I tell you, Paul, you will have your day. Guaranteed. We are together on this all the way. I am the authority on thorns, possibly the ranking authority."

Crescent wasn't entirely convinced.

"You trust Duke Marion, you ask for disaster," he said, spitting out my name. His voice rose like the Goodyear Blimp and did not quite match his body, wrath turning his natural baritone into a ludicrous falsetto. "People like that don't have know-how to do it any way but their way, and you—"

He stopped when I coughed.

"Hello, Paul," I called, waving like an old friend and throwing an indifferent smile at Bachman, whose brows rose as he shifted his eyes from me to the floor. "Thought for a change you might want to say something to my face instead of my back."

"How does 'Fuck you' sound?" Crescent said, rising and giving me a venomous look.

"Familiar," I said. "And, as usual, a compliment coming from you."

Bachman, still seated, reached for his glass of ice water and took a sip. "Duke, come on in. Good to see you again. I was just saying to the chief—"

"The supervisor is not my biggest fan," Crescent said, feeling some obligation to explain the obvious. The word *supervisor* also earned some of his spit.

"See there, Crescent, we always manage to find some point of agreement," I said, and gave Bachman a wink.

Crescent gritted his teeth. "What usually gets you into the most trouble, Marion, your gun or your mouth?"

"Taking care of business. You should try it sometime."

"Fuck you!"

I cupped a hand behind my ear and turned my face into a question mark. "Is there an echo in here?"

"Enough!" Bachman called out.

He got up and headed for Crescent's desk, holding the water glass in one hand, his ivory cigarette holder in the other.

He eased into the chief's high-backed chair and interpreted the two of us, his eyes darting back and forth in a way that reminded me of Richard Nixon.

"Gentlemen, gentleman," he said, demanding a truce by his tone. "Please. Please. Please. You must save your vendettas for another time. All right?" Turning to me he said, "Your assumption we were talking about you is correct, Duke. You and Bruno Guy."

"You know? Your revolutionary nut-fuck killer bastard buddy," Crescent said, in as derisive a tone as he could muster. "Guy the one who taught you how to kill in the first place?"

"Paul!" Bachman said sharply, riveting Crescent with the sound of his own name. He was clearly unhappy at being disobeyed.

Crescent play-acted shooting a gun with his fingers, aiming first at me, then at Bachman, then at his own temple.

I took a deep breath, swallowed hard.

Bachman said coldly, quietly, "Don't make me angrier than I've become, Paul. Please."

Crescent's mouth opened to say something and hung that way while his mind confirmed Bachman's request.

The moment showed who was in control of this situation, and I wondered what Rupert Bachman might have on Crescent or what he had held out to him as a reward for compliant behavior whenever the two of them first got together.

Crescent's shoulders sagged. He tossed me a dismissive gesture, added a look that had me anxious to give him a new face, and began stalking the carpet.

Bachman appeared to finish a ten count. Swallowed. Took another sip of water. Swallowed again. "Duke, Chief Crescent has been aware for some time of my situation with Bruno Guy," he said, "and, subsequently, your involvement. I have been relying on his full support and cooperation in the matter, as I have yours, and he has been splendid, as I expect you will be."

Crescent stopped suddenly and his head wrenched, like he was uncertain he had heard Bachman correctly.

"Yes, Paul, and I don't want you to think for a moment Washington is unaware of your contribution," Bachman said, adding a layer of butter. "It's the kind that never goes unnoticed and, in time, is rewarded accordingly."

Crescent couldn't conceal his delight. He'd bought into the flattery, but—

I wondered if it was really me Bachman wanted to convince.

"And that's why you're here, to applaud Mr. Wonderful?"

Crescent hit a fist inside his elbow and raised the other fist.

Bachman closed his eyes to my sarcasm.

"I wasted no time in ringing up Chief Crescent and imploring him to see me upon learning about his comments about you to the news media this morning. As you arrived I was urging him to stop with the name-calling, because we absolutely cannot afford to do anything that will alienate you or dissuade you from completing your mission, Duke."

"Marion the Barbarian helping a killer rat get amnesty, he means."

Bachman's eyes grew smaller as he sucked in his temper. He bit down hard on his cigarette holder, clenched tightly between his teeth in a corner of his mouth, and it angled upward. He went from reminding me of Nixon to reminding me of FDR.

"Paul, I repeat—We need him. Both of them. We need Duke to help us bring in Bruno Guy. That's the deal. If it were otherwise, if I had my own way, trust me, Bruno Guy would be a dead man ten times over by now."

Crescent mumbled something under his breath. "Okay," he announced to the room, "but I'm telling you again,

Rupert—I absolutely can't do anything to stop the ME from calling a coroner's jury once his post is done."

"Coroner's jury?"

Crescent gave me a triumphant look and said smugly, "I caught the ME over pancakes first thing."

"Before I was aware," Bachman said, apologetically.

"They're asshole buddies," I explained.

Crescent ignored me. "The ME also has this thing about vigilante justice, Rupert. About all civilians, even county supervisors, who shoot people indiscriminately? There's laws against that and like me he thinks they should be punished."

"Couldn't get to the DA, Crescent?"

"The DA sleeps late, Marion. But I imagine it'll reach him right after the coroner's jury comes in with just cause for moving a murder two on to the Grand Jury."

"And you'll be testifying, of course?"

"Of course, supervisor. An act of conscience. The ME will call me and it'll be my duty as L.A.'s chief of police, not to mention as a law-abiding citizen, to give my opinion."

"Law-abiding? So you're saying the rumors I hear about you aren't true?"

Crescent waved off the implication, but not before I saw apprehension fly by his eyes. He checked for Bachman's reaction and, seeing none, croaked a laugh and said, "I got a dead body on a stage. What's your proof?"

"You silly shit!"

"And proud of it, Supervisor, proud of it!"

Bachman slammed his fist on the desk. He rose to his feet, clamped his palms on the surface, and leaned forward, waiting until he was certain he had our attention.

"I. Want. Bruno. Guy," he said. "Paul, I'll deal with you later, but hear what I'm about to say to Duke . . ." A look passed between them that I did not like. "You help me bring in Bruno and you'll have nothing to worry about, Duke. From the chief. From a coroner's jury. A Grand Jury. The district attorney. Can I be any clearer than that?"

My gut told me he was playacting.

I wanted to say, *Yeah, but what about you, Bachman? What is it that makes me worry about you?*

Instead, I said, "There was no message, no contact, last night. What now?"

"The usual," Bachman said philosophically. "We wait until we hear from him. And should Bruno Guy contact you direct rather than going through us, you'll let me know immediately, of course."

"Of course," I said, not so certain I meant it. "And if the bombs go off first?"

Bachman gave me an unhappy look. "Then it would be evident to all parties that Bruno Guy had changed his mind about amnesty and, of course, I would have no reason to keep the chief from his act of conscience."

"Mr. Bachman, why does that sound to me a little like blackmail?"

He scoffed at the idea.

"Blackmail? To me it sounds like the truth, Duke."

Crescent chimed in, "You give only as good as you get, Marion."

I said, "You ought to know, chief, and maybe you, too, Mr. Bachman," and, deaf to Crescent's invective, sailed from the office, almost banging into Grelun, who had been standing outside the door, eavesdropping.

He showered me with silent applause.

At about the same time, in an underground parking level of the Century City mall, Gustav Van Zandt, hanging against a pillar about fifty feet away, watched the VW van screw up negotiating the space between the white Mercedes and a green Honda that had parked over the painted divider line. The van banged into the right edge of the Mercedes' rear bumper and backed off to try again.

The driver made it this time, but then almost couldn't manage the door open wide enough to get out.

He was successful after a minute or two of grunting contortions and, in a major pique, kicked the rear fender of the Mercedes. Before marching off, he uttered something ugly that sounded Korean or Nam to Van Zandt.

"Fucking gooks," Van Zandt announced under his breath, pushing himself more into the shadows as the man closed in on his way to the exit escalator. He gave the man's back the finger, as if the kicking incident were a personal insult.

Van Zandt was a small man, dressed in jeans, T-shirt and a Windbreaker, a Dodger cap angled over a face full of nervous tics, companions to the twitches that kept his body in constant motion.

Checking as if enemies lurked around every corner, he took the escalator two steps at a time and, when he reached the plaza level, decided against several pay phones until he found one away from foot traffic that satisfied his desire for privacy.

He pecked in a number and tapped his foot impatiently while the system noisily clacked his call forward to another number and on to a third.

"Gus," he said, like it was a state secret. "Buggy's still there. Yeah, I know where the place is."

He finished his conversation, fished for more change, tapped out a new number and, when the mechanical operator directed, fumbled the coins into the slot.

"Van Zandt," he said in the same furtive tone. "We still on for later? Because I got somewhere to be after."

This conversation took a minute or two longer than the first. Van Zandt checked the coin return slot and cursed its emptiness. *A lot like my fucking life,* he thought.

Chapter 4

I slipped into my office through the private door off a corridor available only to supervisors. It's the best and easiest way to avoid the usual dozen or so people who are waiting for me in the reception room on the other side of the connecting door. Usually I'm pretty good about keeping my appointments on time and even working in those who show up unannounced. Now, however, I was verging on two hours behind on the day.

Charging to my desk across a room the size of a tennis court, I saluted Rita. She disconnected a caller with a few terse words and, rising from the desk I'd ordered for her immediately after we moved here, her steno pad in hand, she prepared to restore order to my day.

This is how Rita Gossage and I have always worked when we've had business requiring immediate give and take: elbow to elbow.

Other times, her command post is a desk outside in reception, where nobody can get to me who can't get past her first.

Out there now was her latest assistant, Layla, a sweet but timid moth of a girl who looked like she was fresh from a road company of *The Sound of Music*, not the University of Southern California School of Political Science, a 4.0 average and a summa cum laude—her ticket to what those in the know would not rank as a tremendous career opportunity—trying to survive Rita Gossage.

Before I could say anything, Rita was speaking in her flat, no-nonsense monotone that sometimes I swore she had stolen from Eve Arden, *Our Miss Brooks* and before that the wisecracking friend of anybody who ever starred in a Warner Bros. movie, even Nell Fontanne. It was *Lonesome Highway*, a trifle beneath Nell's talent, but Nell had wanted to work with Bogart, or so it was written by all but one of her dozens of biographers, whose surreal prose suggested it was under Bogart where she wanted to be.

"That was Fuzz just now," Rita said. "He wants to know what you just now did to Crescent, who's in the middle of a psychotic rampage . . . so do I."

I made the gesture she knew meant gossip later.

She looked at me like I was paint peeling on the wall.

Like Fuzz, Rita loved her gossip.

She said, "There's no ID yet on your John C. for Corpse Doe. The coroner is not cooperating. Our criminalists have asked the Feds to help out with prints and teeth. Fuzz says to tell you he'll scream as soon as he has better, Chief . . ."

I held out a hand with my palm turned upward, wiggled my fingers inward signaling for more.

"Anny called. She's off running some errands. She asks that Marion the Barbarian phone her when he can."

"Slot it after the board meeting or between my wanton killings, whichever comes first."

Rita's encyclopedic eyes briefly roamed the steno pad. She turned the page and said, "You have the Boy Scouts at three and a proclamation to give Luis Miguel at four. The orphanage comes kissing for the TV cameras an hour later, and—" She checked her watch. "By my reckoning you are an hour fifteen late for the board meeting, a new record even by your high standards."

I took a bow.

"And, of course, Chief Temple called to confirm the golf date."

"I was hoping the old man would forget."

Charlie Temple, my predecessor as police chief, was a great cop from his first day to the day he retired. He was pushed out of the job, actually, too honest for his own good and, in some circles, the good of the community.

Rita kept going, as if she hadn't heard me. "Chief Temple said don't count on him to forget. Just be there and bring Dickson along."

No surprise that, either.

Pearce Dickson had been the only member of the Board of Supervisors Charlie ever got along with in the days politics mattered to him and the only golfer Charlie was certain of beating, even on his worst day. Pearce was a champion when it came to serving the city, currently serving a second tour as board chairman, but a first class clunk on the course.

"And you got a call from Nell Fontanne, to come up and see her sometime," said Rita with a Groucho-like lift of her unplucked eyebrows.

The pronouncement stopped me halfway between my tracks and my chair.

"Me?"

Rita gave me one of those looks reserved for a dog that's failed a fetch.

"You were mentioned by name, Chief. Cocktails. Her place. Bring Anny at your own risk."

"Nell Fontanne said that?"

"No, I volunteer it at no extra cost to the taxpayers."

"Get her for me now. Anny."

"Already did. She's delighted to accept and wrote down the details, for when you can't locate the memo sitting on top of your desk—or later."

Anny wouldn't have been that delighted, me, neither, if we knew what awaited us.

About a mile away, Rupert Bachman emerged through the glass doors of Clifton's Cafeteria, one of the downtown area's last surviving links with its past, there long before the suburbs killed off the city, where a customer who can't afford the price of a meal still can get in line and buy the meal for a price he can afford. Gus Van Zandt was with him.

They shuttled a path to the busy street, just two more people lost in the maze of pedestrians minding their own business, and Bachman said a few words before handing off a small packet.

Van Zandt added jitters to the nervousness constricting his face.

He looked around with more hurry than care as he stashed the packet and hurried down the street, picking up his pace after a shoulder glance confirmed that Bachman was studying him.

A small man in a Brooks Brothers suit and dark glasses, his jaw working a wad of either gum or tobacco, emerged from Clifton's cafeteria, exchanged a barely visible nod with Bachman, and started in the direction Van Zandt had taken.

A tired Honda Civic with Nevada plates had been parked illegally in a red zone across the street. It pulled out and also headed in Van Zandt's direction.

A Honda that could have been its twin eased from the curb outside Clifton's and headed away from Van Zandt, in the same direction as Bachman.

Van Zandt was too immersed in thought to notice any of this.

He was replaying in his mind the Board of Supervisors layout and how he was going to slip the word to Bruno's buddy.

Chapter 5

The Board of Supervisors meeting chamber is the centerpiece of a municipal building, constructed in a time when public edifices were intended to be inspirationally immense and awesomely overpowering to the citizens whose taxes and revenue bonds paid for these and other government excesses, like a set from a Cecil B. De Mille epic, except here, the extras wear suits and ties, not togas, and imported marbles and burnished wood veneers come together under a graceful arched ceiling that bounces echoes around the chamber whenever members are shouting into the sound system, which is usually the case.

It was noisy now, as I slid through a door that gave me direct access to my seat at a curved table custom designed to provide each of the supervisors equal space in front of ten rows of church-style benches divided by a center aisle and meant for county residents who had the curiosity or need to see their elected officials battling for or against progress as often as they fought one another.

However, my brethren were not the source of the verbal fisticuffs currently in progress. Most of them were reading newspapers, position briefs, or hastily-scribbled notes they were passing among themselves while the Board chairman, Pearce Dickson, calmly reasoned with one of the two disparate sides in another silly dispute we had been unable to resolve in committee. My aide, Lewis Tully, holding his glasses in place with the tip of a finger, leaned forward anxiously to brief me. I held him at bay with a palm. This wasn't one of the tougher interpretations.

Pearce Dickson was saying, "I reassure you one more time, Señor De Cordoba . . . my colleagues and I do not propose ignoring this most serious matter. A heritage of singular import is at issue here. History. Tradition."

The group of Hispanics massed on one side of the center aisle promptly muttered approvals in Spanish and waved their handled signboards:

Olvera Street is Ours.

Tacos Not Tokios.

Chicano Power Forever.

No More Raw Fish, No More Raw Deal.

Their leader, Alfonso De Cordoba, the gent Pearce was addressing with his usual masterful blend of sincere concern and insincere politics, stood at the visitor's mike in the middle ground between the elected and the electorate, decked out in a Caballero's outfit straight off the rack at Zorros 'R' Us.

De Cordoba was visibly indignant, not so, the gent with whom he shared the space, Moki Nakamura, who wore a discreet blue pinstripe and a solemn expression. Nakamura was leader of the parties of the second part, who sat with a quiet dignity on their side of the center aisle.

"Olvera Street is at the very root of Mexican culture that pervades the history, tradition and essence of Los Angeles," Pearce continued. *"La Ciudad de la Reina de Los Angeles,"* he said, pausing briefly, and I knew by the look that he was wondering if he'd gotten the original name right for a change. "Los Angeles. Our city's history begins right there, at Olvera Street."

More muttering from De Cordoba's people.

Pearce refilled his water glass and signaled them to quiet with a hand.

"But please try to understand, Señor De Cordoba . . . this body in its deliberating wisdom must also be fair to Mr. Nakamura and the fine members of our Japanese-American community."

This time De Cordoba motioned for the muttering to stop.

He narrowed his eyes and aimed them at Pearce.

"Your words are beautiful like always, Señor Supervisor Dickson, but do not you think some action would be better?"

Pearce feigned surprise and suppressed indignation as De Cordoba's people cluttered the air-conditioned streams of cool air with their approval.

Nakamura eased the microphone away from De Cordoba and wondered, "If I may have a word now?"

Pearce said, "Certainly, Mr. Nakamura. After all, freedom is fairness."

Nakamura nodded, as if he understood what Pearce meant.

I didn't, although I could take both *freedom* and *fairness* unto themselves.

Pearce did that to the language often, but would never own up to it being a trick meant to help keep the edge for himself.

"You invited us here today so we can listen," Nakamura said. "We listened. Your deliberations, however well meant, are meaningless." He held up a sheaf of papers. "It is these documents that matter, not any deliberations."

A zoo growl rose from the De Cordoba side of the aisle.

The Nakamura side continued to hug its composure.

Nakamura declared, "Our associate Mr. Higa's sushi bar shall occupy new quarters on Olvera Street no matter what is said here today!"

De Cordoba exploded. He grabbed the mike from Nakamura. *"¡No es possiblé!"* he ranted. That's not possible! *"No! No!"*

His guys were getting more unruly.

Signs were pumping.

Lewis Tully tapped my shoulder for attention.

He handed over an envelope, indicating he had just received it from the bailiff standing alongside him.

De Cordoba declared passionately, "Mr. Gonzales will not move from the quarters where he has blessed visitors with the finest and most authentic of Mexican dinners for more than a quarter of a century. I defy your documents, *señor!* Padre Serra needed no lease when he walked through these very streets of old Olvera!"

Nakamura yanked the mike away from De Cordoba. For a second it appeared a wrestling match would be next on the agenda.

"Padre Serra?" Nakamura said, waving his papers. "You cannot confuse his deed with this deed."

I had the envelope open by now.

I withdrew a photograph mounted on gray board. Small. Browned. Fading. Two young men staring at the lens, their expressions challenging destiny. Each toasts with a can of beer, their arms locked around one another. There was a fresh inscription at the base, written in black ink:

Duke—Shazam! Bruno.

The fury had mounted, clearly uglier and spreading across the aisle as I leaned across Lewis to ask the long-faced bailiff in a voice loud enough to be heard, "Ernest, who gave you this?"

Ernest glanced outward and used his chin to direct me to a back corner of the chamber. For a fraction of a second I caught someone staring nervously back, unable to get his head turned away fast enough before he was lost behind a wall of bodies that had catapulted from the benches.

Pearce was banging his gavel, imploring, "Gentlemen, gentlemen. This is a call to order! A call to order! Please! Gentlemen, please!"

The bodies shifted. I once more caught sight of this goosey little guy, a squirrel in a Dodger cap, face ticking like a time bomb. He had risen onto his feet and was nervously dancing side to side, clearly looking for the fastest way to get away.

I started after him, moving along the rim of the room in order to avoid the crowd, which had broken into a circus of flying fists.

"I say this is a call to order, a call to order!" Pearce Dickson was bellowing into the mike, uselessly banging his gavel.

Some of the supervisors also were shouting for order, some of them louder than Dickson, and one—it sounded like Harry Michener—was urging everybody, somewhat improbably, "Remember the Olympic spirit!"

I lost sight of the squirrel for a few seconds.

Then, there he was again, looking petrified.

Then, buried again behind the battlers.

A fist came out of nowhere, attached to a giant-sized Hispanic who appeared intent on reshaping my face. I edged to one side and felt the breeze cut past me as I swung on my heel and in the same motion struck enough balance to lay on a right uppercut to the jaw.

His head snapped backward before he staggered backward into the crowd.

The next guy after a piece of me was my size, but had at least fifty pounds on me. I ducked. His roundhouse sailed harmlessly overhead. I let him have one in the balls. He grabbed for them with his hands and an open-mouthed, silent scream.

I belly-elbowed another Hispanic and sidestepped a pair of Nisei, only to be confronted by two others bent on using me for karate practice. A pair of sluggers came between us and, as I adjusted my path, got a glimpse of their faces taking heavy-heeled foot massages.

The squirrel was closing in on an exit door as I closed in on him, momentarily delayed by someone coming at me with a thick slat board. I wrestled it away from him and, using it like a sword, kept opening the path.

The squirrel ducked through the exit as somebody's imitation of a sumo wrestler blocked my way.

He reared back to disenfranchise my head. Before he could deliver, I extended my arms, inviting him to take the slat board. He did, on reflex. I did a slick pirouette around him and, a few seconds later, was bursting through the door I'd seen the squirrel use.

The squirrel was soaring down the corridor, aiming toward the central staircase, one of those grand, multi-tiered extravaganzas that in its day was all that money could buy.

"Hey!" I shouted.

He stole a look and, when he saw it was me, put on another hundred miles an hour.

I gave chase.

People in the corridor jumped aside to get out of our way.

Avoiding the body block of a burly six-footer who had not stepped back far enough, I banged into the woman with him, a leggy brunette with movie star looks, grabbing onto her before her legs buckled.

She gave me a toothy smile that sank in as I handed her back to her companion. It was full of insinuation, the kind of smile a man remembers if his hormones are working.

The squirrel had reached the grand staircase, but—
—he seemed to be dragging.

"Hey, wait!" I called out. "Hold on!"

He stopped.

Gripped the staircase railing with a hand.

About twenty-five or thirty feet separated us.

I paused long enough to gulp some of the air—I had forgotten to breathe in the last minute or two—and speeded toward him.

The squirrel turned to face me.

He was wearing a disengaged look.

The hand not clutching the railing had a grip on the long, slim handle of a knife jutting from his belly.

He tried pulling it out and failed.

The next time, using two hands, he managed to yank it free and elevate it above his head.

The force of the action sent him hurtling backward.

He twisted.

Fell forward.

Slid head first down the full length of the massive staircase.

When I reached him, the squirrel could not have been deader.

Chapter 6

The police came and went, along with the coroner's crew and the last of the news crews that had badgered me with their shouted questions, cameras and mikes shooting at my face. Meanwhile Lewis Tully ran interference, repeating, "At this time, Supervisor Marion has no further comment beyond his statement to police officers," as I jogged the echoing corridors to Pearce Dickson's office.

Pearce was behind his desk, working the phones, trading off instruments with his press secretary, a nicotine-eating, eye-shifting *Times* retread named Manny Sutton. He didn't trust Manny a hundred per cent. Maybe in the sixty-to-eighty percent range. The same way Manny had his spies in the other crevices and crawl holes of government, he sometimes wondered if Manny's eyes were on long term lease to someone who might have it in for him.

"If you feel that way, get rid of him," I would urge Pearce.

Pearce would shake his head furiously. "And definitely put him against me?"

"What difference does it make if you have nothing to hide?"

"Duke-o, at some time or other in his life, *everyone* has something to hide," he said, using the *take no prisoners* tone he applied now over the phone.

His words grew louder. They were a passion play meant for me to overhear and understand who was on the other end of the line, taking the brunt of his fury.

"I said I don't give a fuck, Crescent," he said, seething, every word dripping past his lips like lava. "That's *fuck*, Crescent—as in *you*."

He waved me inside without missing a beat, managed a smile pointing to a visitor's chair and mumbled a few final series of four-letter recommendations before replacing the receiver, settling back in his high-backed executive chair and propping his size twelves on the desk, a battered antique distinctively out of place in an office more casual than traditional. The personally inscribed status photos and formula citations were almost lost among sports posters, banners, megaphones, autographed footballs, basketballs, and baseballs, a piece of a goal post, and other souvenir trappings of the professional fan.

The new call was pitched a hundred decibels lower.

"Uh huh, uh huh, yeah . . . . Minute." Pearce covered the mouthpiece and turning to me said, "Jeannie thinks this must be a tough day for you and Anny. She wants the two of you over for dinner tonight."

Even before I started to shake my head, he was announcing, "Duke says you're a love, love, and you are, but he and Anny have plans . . . I'm not sure . . . no. Something about a mutual suicide pact. How the hell should I know . . . ? Later, love, okay? Okay? Okay!"

Pearce hung up, contorted his face and shrugged. "You ever notice how every situation reduces itself to a meal with Jeannie?"

"But she is a love, and what if Anny and I do feel like joining the two of you for dinner?"

"Then I'd have to tough shit you again. Besides, I know already about yours and Anny's date with Nell Fontanne."

"Rita told you?"

"Rita told everybody."

I smiled. Nell Fontanne was the sort of gossip my secretary would have a need to share, especially with the secretaries of the other supervisors. One-upmanship is a game played at all levels, although Rita had proven over the years she could be counted on never to traffic with the important stuff.

"Besides, Duke-o," Pearce said, "Even if there was no Nell Fontanne in your future, I have my own plans for dinner with Jeannie tonight and they definitely do not include you and yours. Dessert, if you catch my drift?" He cocked an eyebrow.

I held him off with a palm and asked, "What was that business with Crescent?"

"What you'd expect, the usual anti-Duke Marion crap. You didn't by chance show up here today carrying a Bowie knife, did you, intent upon wiping out a voter who cast his lot with your opponent in the last election? That sure would make Crescent a happy man."

"Some days there's something about your sense of humor, Supervisor, but I don't know if this is one of those days."

"Not to mention your proclivity for dead bodies," he said, ignoring my comment. "I told Crescent it had to be someone else done in our mystery victim. I said most I ever saw on you was a Boy Scout knife, but it might have been a Swiss Army knife, so I'd be sure to ask when I saw you . . ."

Manny Sutton interrupted. "Channel Eight on the horn, Pearce."

"You suppose they're calling to see if the presentation to that singer Miguel Whoever is still on for four?"

"Luis Miguel."

"Him." Pearce took the receiver. "Yeah, Harry, how are you?" He listened more than he talked, interjecting a few *No, Harry*s, before his voice rose to Crescent level and he instructed, "Shove it up your ass, Harry, and quote me on that!" before slamming down the receiver. "Damn it, Manny. Deep six any more calls for now, okay? Okay? Okay!"

Manny arm-signaled surrender. He retreated from the office, backward, as Pearce advised me, "Harry was asking me about rumors that the Board might be getting ready to censure you for letting a killing occur in our hallowed halls—like you went out of your way to help find a proper body part for the Bowie."

"I feel Crescent's hand in that one . . . calling Harry and fueling the rumor."

"You know what I think? I think the fucking security guard who fucked up should be axed, letting some knife-wielding mook get past his body check."

"The guard did nothing wrong."

"Except the fucking press asked him a question. The dumb shit answered it and now it's all over the goddam tube and worse and you ain't looking so hundred per cent. Better we should fuel the flames of civic outrage with a low-end civil servant and again save your ass for bigger and better days."

"Not the first time a blade slipped by a detector."

"First time it caused a corpse. You been any closer when the goddam knife cut and the media'd also be out scouting ways to accuse you of doing the deed."

"It'll pass."

"Yeah, and so will my kidney stone, but the truth is, Duke-o, these aren't farts we're dealing with here, especially coming off the old geezer you popped in a ballroom full of VIPs. Gun-toting Supervisor Daniel F. for Fanatic Marion rides again as—" He made a blowing bugle sound "—The Vigilante! Marion the Barbarian, for Christ's own sweet sake."

Before I could answer, there was knocking on the door to the outer office and Pearce called, "Friend or foe?"

The door swung open and in marched Alfonso De Cordoba.

Moki Nakamura trailed him by half a step.

Neither looked happy.

Moki started to say, "Pearce, you gotta—" before he realized I was sitting there. He stopped short and made a concerned face. "Duke, so help me, Buddha! Neither Al nor me knew that dead bum from nowhere. He wasn't one of neither of ours."

Fonzy De Cordoba's head was bobbing furiously. "The truth, Duke, on my dear dead *mamacita*'s grave." He crossed himself to assuage any doubts I might have.

"Well, your goddam theatrical battle inspired someone to play for keeps," Pearce decreed. He moved to an upright position, propped his elbows on the desk, and formed a pyramid with his fingers. "C'mon, fellas, tell Uncle Pearce the awful truth. Whose good little soldier boy got carried away with the Bowie knife? A little *banzai* practice, Moki? Or was it the mark of Zorro the Taco King, Fonzy? Let us do what we can to get Duke here off the hook, okay?"

Fonzy showed his pique. "Lay off it, Pearce. We only played the game like always. I almost shit bricks when I heard and seen what happened."

"The absolute, Pearce," said an equally bothered Moki. "Fonzy and I were getting ready to turn off the fireworks just before it went down."

"What some people won't do to stay leaders," Pearce said, philosophically.

Moki made a face. "Is that any way to talk about your friends, Pearce?"

Pearce said, "I'm talking about myself, dick-brain."

"Besides," said Fonzy, "why do we gotta do anything

67

more than we done, putting on that little show, considering what we all know's—"

He stopped suddenly and shot me a glance.

The room got quieter than sign language.

Looks passed among the three of them before Pearce got up to come around the desk, take me by the elbow, and start me to the escape door to a private corridor that served only supervisors and their staffers.

"Hold that thought, Fonzy. Duke's got to take off now and I need him for a long minute."

"I'm in no hurry," I said, my curiosity rising, fed by what the cops call guilt by asphyxiation, when the air's so thick you can't breathe.

"Just the usual peace pipe stuff," Pearce said, tossing off the explanation like a used handkerchief.

The three of them laughed too heartily as Pearce and I slipped into the corridor and he pulled the door shut behind us. He stepped in close enough for me to smell his mouth-wash and said, "This matters, what I'm about to say to you, Duke-o . . . You know who Clement McAllister is?"

"The man who invented money, that Clement McAllister?"

McAllister was one of those billionaires whose cash flow falls somewhere south of Bill Gates III but far, far ahead of Eli Broad, David Geffen, and other Angelenos whose names decorate public buildings and fund-raising campaigns the same way billboards line the boulevards.

Nobody knew for certain the source of his wealth, so the media usually referred to him as an "entrepreneurial wizard" or an "investment genius."

"The man who invented—Good one, but maybe you should make sure the vibes are right before you try one-on-one-ing it with him."

"One-on-one-ing?"

"Clem wants to meet with you," Pearce said, dropping his voice a couple notches. "He called me earlier and asked me to arrange it."

"What about?"

He shrugged. "Clem didn't offer, I didn't ask. Only that he'd consider it a personal favor if I saw to your visit. Believe me when I tell you, Clem's one guy who never fails to make good on a marker. You will probably leave with one of your own from him."

"You have a lot of them, Clem's markers?"

He understood the question and thought through his answer. "A few. Saving them for a rainy day."

"It hardly ever rains in Southern California."

"Only in the song, you mean."

"What did you have to do for the other markers?"

"Nothing illegal, immoral, or fattening, I assure you," he said, shaking his head. He took a step back and grinning too good to be true said, "There's not a breath of scandal on the guy, Duke-o, never has been, so what the hell? You'll meet with him?"

Pearce had a point.

For all of the corruption that passes for Business as Usual in L.A., in my memory the tar brush has never gotten any closer to McAllister than friends of friends of friends, the kinds of bankers and business speculators that the media loves to label "capitalists" and "con men," the Milkens and Keatings of the world who oops in and out of the Club Feds not listed on the menu for the cloutless, clueless run-of-the-mill crooks pleaded out by court-appointed dollar-an-hour lawyers.

Maybe that's why I had my doubts about Clem McAllister.

Too good to be true is usually that.

"I'll do it, Pearce, but for you, not for any marker."

"My man!" he said enthusiastically, popping me a good one on the arm.

"Anytime tomorrow that works for him. Just let Rita know the time he'll be here and she'll ink it in."

Pearce shook his head furiously.

"Clem wants it today, my man. At his place in Malibu."

Now it was my turn to shake.

"No can do. We have the Luis Miguel thing coming up at four and then—"

"Fuck Luis Miguel. Luis Miguel is one beaner where Clem McAllister is the whole goddam cannery. I can handle Luis Miguel solo. You've already had enough photo ops this week anyway and the last thing you want is letting the news nuts have another go at you."

His face was tense, his eyes flitting for someplace to land.

I checked my watch.

"Pearce, this time of day, the hour drive there is two hours and at least that back. It would cost the thing with Nell Fontanne and that's a big no sir, not for McAllister or anyone."

"Including me?" He said it like the shock would kill him. His eyes held mine in a death grip. He rolled his hand over his face, wiping away imaginary sweat. "You're putting me in a two-balls squeeze, Duke-o. I sort of told him you'd drop everything for me."

"Everything but my tail between my legs, Pearce, and that's what it would feel like to me if I went charging out to the beach on no minute's notice for someone who thinks he owns the city—"

"And probably does."

"And maybe does. But not me, Pearce. He doesn't own me."

Pearce didn't like the question cooking in my stare.

"Me, neither," he decided, with about as much bravado as Bruce Dern showed shooting John Wayne in the back. "I'll call him and let the schmuck know."

"Tomorrow," I repeated. "Tell Mr. McAllister he can set the time, any time tomorrow that's convenient, and I'll be there."

"And fuck him if he can't take a joke," Pearce said, but now the sweat beads on his forehead were real.

Maybe I would have been sweating, too, if I knew what Clem McAllister had in mind.

Chapter 7

The balance of the day was full of the grunge work that defines a supervisor's day, including pissants on the phone about potholes in the streets. I found myself wondering all over again how someone like dear departed Kenny Hahn, in whose honor this building had been renamed, was able to pull it off year after year after year.

Kenny had put in forty-five of them as the "people's politician," serving L.A. first as a councilman and then, for forty years, as a supervisor, before retiring because of a massive stroke that trapped him in a wheelchair the last five of those years.

Along the way, he'd helped steal the Dodgers away from Brooklyn, pushed through his idea for emergency call boxes on the freeway and elsewhere, engineered development of the county's paramedic program, created the tax measure that got us a mass transit system, made the Music Center possible, so much more, while never failing to walk his district and talk to the people he represented on a regular basis, to ask what they might want or need from him.

I had grown up remembering him for something else, how in '61 he was the only elected official to greet Martin Luther King when King visited Los Angeles, and I told him this when I paid a courtesy visit after my election to the modest home on 76th Street he had lived in most of his life, about three miles from the house where he'd been born.

We settled on the front porch over iced lemonade and cookies, where he could enjoy the afternoon breeze and the noisy congregations of birds, wave back at the neighbors, and sometimes excuse himself while he greeted someone who wandered up the walk with a question or, more often, a joke for Kenny.

His eyes were alert, attentive and inquisitive behind the thin-framed lenses that magnified his interest in what I had to say. His laugh was as engaging as the full-faced grin that once seemed a fixture in stills and video clips and was also a part of his legacy, and I heard it when I mentioned Martin Luther King.

Kenny's body was a problem, but not his memory, and once he reminded me that I'd told him the same thing when we met for the first time, after I'd been appointed chief of police.

"It's possible to achieve strength walking in a great man's shadow," he said now, feeling his way slowly through each word. Anyone who didn't know Kenny might have thought he meant his shadow, not Dr. King's. In fact, people who knew Kenny might have thought so, too. "I did what I did because it was the right thing to do, and it only made me stronger. You play your politics the same way, Duke, and there's no telling what kind of muscles you'll build, what kind of results you can achieve for the good of the city."

So far I had not done much, I considered, as the day dragged on. Tree plantings here and there. Some traffic signals at intersections where there had been accidents and fatalities that might not have happened otherwise. Support for county measures meant to improve the quality of education in our schools.

Certainly, I was no Kenny Hahn. I'd been in office long enough to suspect I never would be. It was the kind of thinking I was doing too often, as routinely as Kenny walked his district, and it frequently made me wonder if I'd have been better off sticking with the cops.

I regaled myself with solitary laughter at the thought that this could have saved the city from Paul Crescent as chief of police, possibly a greater accomplishment than anything I might achieve as a supervisor.

Finally, I pushed my last piece of paper.

Checked some end of the day details with Rita.

Made a clean getaway in time to trap myself inside the early wave of commuters escaping downtown for the valley.

The old Pasadena was bumper-to-bumper. The 5 wasn't much better.

The Ventura was worse, but not as bad as the Hollywood, where an eight-car pileup closed off three of the five lanes and married bumpers while, according to the news vultures circling overhead in choppers, ambulances and the CHiP jaws of life negotiated shoulders and lane crannies trying to reach two people trapped inside the overturned van caught in the middle of the automotive accordion.

I got home too late for dinner with my Alicia, before she ran off to be a teenager among teenagers, and heaven forbid her parents should have a clue besides a name and an 818 number to where "where" was. I gobbled the turkey dinner Anny had to reheat in the microwave, hers and mine, because she never ate without me if there was the slightest possibility I'd be arriving at anything remotely resembling a dinner hour.

I changed into my best off-the-rack dark suit and Anny was looking sensational in an ankle-length wraparound skirt and clinging black silk blouse accented with the simple strand of purebred black and white pearls I had surprised her with a few birthdays ago by the time we climbed into the Porsche.

I made good time taking the route over Benedict Canyon

and got us to the drive-up entrance of the Beverly Hills Hotel with ten minutes to spare.

"You're speeding," Anny cautioned as we navigated the curve past Rolls Royces and a fleet of stretch limos parked in all the safe and showy status spots.

"That's my heart, you hear. Nell Fontanne, you know?"

"And you're certain the invitation included me."

"Swear it."

"That usually means you're not certain."

"Would I have had Rita call and alert you otherwise?"

"When she phoned she said you weren't in yet, so you didn't know. She didn't want to chance you forgetting."

"That is also true," I said. "I have included you, and that's good enough."

"I could have stayed home. You would have been alone with Nell Fontanne."

"Then I would have stayed home, too. I'd still rather be alone with you."

"Flattery will get you everywhere, Sailor."

"You think I don't know that?"

A parking attendant helped her from the car while I asked the one who'd opened my door if he'd mind if I parked myself in the empty spot—

—over there.

He said he'd mind.

I tried a ploy that's worked before when I've felt my Porsche's sanctity was jeopardized. I identified myself.

The attendant went from minding to not caring.

Singularly unimpressed.

I can't say that I blamed him.

He already was shooting sideways glances and being impressed by Al Pacino, who had hopped from the limo behind us.

Me, too, impressed, but I tried not to stare.

I accepted my defeat and a parking ticket and came around the car and locked my arm inside Anny's elbow. She slowed us to a crawl, determined to let her eyes feast on Al while he walked briskly under the canopy and took the steps into the hotel two at a time.

"I bet they would have let him park his own car," I said.

"Me, too," Anny said.

I got directions from the concierge and headed us up the north corridor to a small elevator that took us to the third floor. A minute or two later, was checking suite numbers along the pink corridors.

The Beverly Hills Hotel had been bought several years ago by an Arab sheik, who poured millions and millions more into rehabbing the landmark, giving it a contemporary feeling while bowing to tradition and keeping the basic pink color scheme inside and out.

I pressed the chimes button at the double doors to the suite. After a minute with no response, I pressed again.

"You're sure it's for tonight?" Anny mumbled while she finger-painted curlicues on my sleeve.

"It is now," I said, and pressed the buzzer a third time.

The door on my side opened.

We found ourselves being analyzed and explored by a tall, courtly man dressed for a diplomatic reception. His penetrating coal-black eyes shifted between us as if we were two of those squiggly things under a microscope. His high forehead narrowed into high cheekbones and a small chin. A pencil-thin black mustache looked like a draftsman's mistake on the vanilla mask he called a face.

"I'm Dan Marion and this is—"

"Of course you are," he said, his deep, accent-tinged voice to the manor born, and he directed us inside with a sweeping gesture, swiping a glance at Anny as she passed by him.

The suite's posh entry spilled into a sitting room with a luxury level high enough for oxygen masks and a Saint Bernard. A splendor worthy of a, well, a sheik with more oil than sand dunes, created in a hundred tones of white and extended to the baby grand artfully placed in a faraway corner.

We stood awkwardly until this Conrad Veidt sort of guy gestured us to a sofa that worked as the room's centerpiece and said in a voice as flat as his eyes, "The princess will join you shortly."

He turned in military fashion and marched beyond a set of connecting doors. He opened and shut with precision and made me think now not of Veidt in *Casablanca*, but Alec Guinness in *The Bridge on the River Kwai*.

"Shortly" turned into ten minutes, then fifteen.

We sat dumbly in the center of the sofa, Anny with her hands in her lap, humming tunes under her breath from one of Nell's musicals, me with mine locked across my chest, my wandering gaze memorizing the room.

At almost a half hour, the beeper in my pants pocket gave me a silent buzz in the crotch.

The readout said Fuzz.

Calling from home.

Anxious for a fast callback.

I showed it to Anny, then crossed the room to the pink wall extension alongside the bar and had the operator place the call.

"You there yet, Supe?"

"Yes, but in a holding pattern."

"Talk or listen?"

Alec Guinness momentarily returned from behind the

door to signal it would be another moment. He squandered a curious look at me.

I turned away, for privacy. "Both for the moment, Fuzz."

"Something you would want to hear on the speed track, I thought. Word just down about our John C. Doe, and you will never guess who."

"I'm listening."

"Name Powell ring a ding? Edwin O. Powell?"

I actually had to pause and think, holding the receiver at arm's length, before the name sank in.

"Edwin O. Powell?"

"Didn't I just hear that somewhere?"

"Nell Fontanne's co-star?" My mind couldn't stop whirling at the news.

"Didn't you say they also went at it off of the screen, too, Nell Fontanne and this Powell . . . ? Forensics made the ID from his dental records. Right after, his prints turned up in old Army Air Force files . . ."

"Jesus!"

"And another sixty-four dollar answer—the .22 couldn't kill a fly, unless Powell intended to hold it by the barrel and hammer the fly to death. Loaded with blanks, Supe."

Dumbfounded, I turned to look at Anny.

"Duke, you still there?"

"Yeah, Fuzz. Go on."

Anny could see something was wrong.

Fielding her own puzzled expression, she started to get up—

—as Nell Fontanne's lyrical voice carried across the room, as if she were playing to the second balcony at the Doolittle Theater.

"My hero!" she called to me. "My savior!"

Hero. Savior.

Would she say that if she knew it was her old lover I had killed, or—

—did she know?

Chapter 8

Something was wrong, but I didn't have time to think about it. Nell Fontanne had entered the room by the same connecting doors Alec Guinness had passed through thirty minutes ago and now stood framed within the arch in a pose of supreme graciousness, in an exquisite full-length evening dress, a regal velvet in royal purple; matching arm-length gloves.

"Later, Fuzz," I said and hung up on something he had started to say about Paul Crescent.

I reached Anny's side an instant before Nell got there and swallowed us up in her presence.

"Daniel F. Marion," she said to me and to the second balcony, as if my presence were the denouement to her life's dream.

Curiously, Nell had shrunk the closer she came, and I realized how petite she really was, where her carriage and bearing on stage and screen had made her a giant.

I also saw how poorly her fabled beauty stood close-range inspection. Decades of erosion lined and creased her face, however faint underneath the thick theatrical makeup that, in natural light, gave her skin a clownish cast.

Her chin strained upward to bring her eyes into line with mine. She was oblivious to Anny's presence, something Anny also noticed. She stepped away to leave us alone.

Alec Guinness had quietly entered the room and taken a

post near the piano, and I thought I saw something different in his dark, probing stare—

—a protective concern for Nell.

"Princess Nell, I'm honored," I said, taking the hand she extended and kissing it in true European fashion, lips not quite touching the velvet surface.

"My Lancelot," she said, making every syllable a love note. "But this is America, where I'm always Nell, so won't you?"

"Thank you . . . Nell."

"Colonel Soulé, you didn't tell me how handsome my prince was."

The colonel said something undecipherable and forced a slash of a smile. I caught Anny from the corner of my eyes, rolling hers.

Nell wondered, "Are you always so brave, Sir Lancelot?"

"I'm happy I was able to do something when I saw you were threatened," I said.

"So brave. Colonel Soulé, he's so brave."

"Yes, ma'am," Alec Guinness said, reluctantly, when he saw only a confirmation would satisfy her. "Brave."

"You are right, Colonel Soulé. He is brave. And handsome . . . did I mention how handsome?"

"Yes, ma'am."

"You know who you remind me of? You know who he reminds me of, Colonel Soulé?"

"No, ma'am."

"He—you remind me of an old flame of mine. An old flame, Colonel Soulé. You're probably too young to remember him, Sir Lancelot . . . Edwin O. Powell." A beatific smile on top of a questioning look.

I'd been wondering how to broach the subject of Powell.

She had just given me the opportunity. "My wife and I have seen all your movies, Nell, so of course we know who Mr. Powell was," I said, easing onto the subject.

"Was?" She made a face, trying to understand the word. Shook her head.

I said gently, "It was Mr. Powell I shot and killed."

Nell's cheeks pushed her eyes into slits, deepening the furrows and laugh lines on a face struggling to see the joke of my statement. "Is this some cruel jest, Sir Lancelot? I would not have thought you capable of such a deed."

Softly, "He was the man who tried to shoot you."

I turned to see if Anny had been listening. She put a finger phone to her ear, silently questioning if that was why Fuzz had paged me. I nodded. Her brows lifted in wide-eyed surprise.

"I'm sorry to be the one who—"

Nell thrust her palms at me.

Her head quavered like Katharine Hepburn's.

She put a hand to her chest.

The fingers of her other hand found a perch by her nose and lips.

She stagger-stepped a few feet in order to use a table top for support.

"But we spoke, he and I. He—we were to see one another before I returned home. Colonel?" Her voice shattering the way her face already had. "Colonel? How can that be? Mr. Powell and I are scheduled to take lunch. Tomorrow isn't it? Or the day after?"

"Tomorrow, Princess. Please, Supervisor Marion. You're upsetting the princess."

The colonel started forward.

Nell held him back with a gesture. "The Polo Lounge. Such a lovely lunch. Like the olden days, when . . ." She stopped, like it was something not to be shared and appealed to the ceiling with her eyes. Mixed a crying sound with his name. "Eddie, Eddie, Eddie . . ."

"The police will want to visit with you in the morning, Nell." I nodded at Alec Guinness. "They're going to be asking you some of the same questions I have."

She stared blankly at me.

Anny shook her head and shot me one of her *once a cop always a cop* looks.

"Why would Edwin O. Powell want to kill you, especially since you say you had spoken and were planning to have lunch? Why, if Mr. Powell wanted to kill you, would he load his gun with blanks? Why that night, in so public a place and in so public a way? I didn't recognize Mr. Powell behind the white beard, but you—"

"That's quite enough, Supervisor Marion!" Alec Guinness demanded.

He moved on us again, a few steps before Nell once more stopped him.

She stepped back to me, close enough for me to see the lake of tears floating in her mesmeric eyes, skiing down her cheeks.

She began to recite:

When, in disgrace with fortune and men's eyes,
I all alone beweep my outcast state,
and trouble deaf heaven with my bootless cries,
and look upon myself, and curse my fate,
wishing me like to one more rich in hope,
featured like him, like him with friends possess'd,
desiring this man's art and that man's scope,
with what I most enjoy contented least;
Yet in these thoughts myself almost despising,

haply I think on thee, and then my state,
like to the lark at break of day arising from sullen earth,
sings hymns at heaven's gate;
For thy sweet love remember'd such wealth brings
that then I scorn to change my state with kings.

She reached up and, placing a hand softly on the back of my neck, drew my head down to hers and placed a gentle kiss on my lips.

I was frozen by the moment.

Bedeviled by a woman almost twice my age, who years ago had helped me to see, appreciate, and understand what beauty, charm, grace, intelligence, and wit were all about.

The snap of a lock brought me back.

The connecting doors had closed, and—

Nell Fontanne was gone from the room.

Anny reached me in a tie with Alec Guinness, who said, "Thank you for visiting with us, Supervisor Marion."

I wasn't ready to leave.

I said, "It wouldn't hurt her to discuss some of this with me."

His mouth answered with one of those flicked smiles that's barely there before it's gone. "I'm sure you mean well, but the news you have already shared, by its very nature, makes this neither the time nor the place."

"Perhaps you and I could talk about it then, for a few minutes?"

"Is a supervisor part of the police force?"

"No, but—"

"Then I have a princess to attend to," Alec Guinness said, curtly. "I'll see you to the door."

Anny pressed her mouth to my ear. "Time to say good night, Sir Lancelot."

★ ★ ★ ★ ★

Less than ten minutes later, working my way around the Porsche, checking for damage and ignoring the irritated look on the freckled face of the parking kid, I glanced up at Anny on the hotel portico and—

—saw Alec Guinness again.

He had stepped up behind her and was tapping Anny's shoulder for attention.

They traded a few words before she signaled me with a series of hand gestures that said *Let them park the car again,* and—

—five minutes after that the three of us were seated in a front booth of the Polo Lounge, Anny in the middle.

The smell of fresh leather was as strong in the room as the undecipherable sound of converging conversations from an assortment of deal makers, expense account tourists, and attractive women at the bar waiting to be discovered, or available for a price, or both. The hotel's legendary bar may have had its face lifted, but the world's oldest profession always looked the same.

"I am pleased I was able to catch you in time to invite you back for a cocktail," Alec Guinness told Anny after the waiter took our orders.

"For a second I thought you had some Shakespeare of your own for me, then—poof!—you'd disappear like Miss Fontanne," she said, cheerfully.

"I most certainly did not come after you to apologize for the princess," he said, not amused, his eyes shifting from Anny to me before they settled on her again.

"Sorry, that was rude of me."

"It was, yes," Alec Guinness agreed.

Anny faked a smile.

"Why did you?" I asked, calmly, but only because Anny

was squeezing my hand under the table, a signal not to lose my temper on her behalf. It probably was the way I noisily swallowed the room that gave me away this time. How well she knew the signs. It's what almost twenty years of marriage can do.

The waiter returned with our drinks.

"Cheers!" Alec Guinness said, raising his glass of sherry.

We cheered him back, Anny with her usual vodka martini, me with a tall Chivas rocks.

I repeated my question. "Why then, Mr.—"

"Soulé," he said. "Karl Soulé . . . and it is Colonel." He expressed it with the military certainty that a colonel outranks a member of the Board of Supervisors and no suggestion he might like to be addressed as Karl. "Circumstances made it impossible for the princess to afford you her usual hospitality, so I elected to try making up for it, lest you think ill of her . . . ?"

I shook my head. "Not a chance, believe me."

"The princess never allows alcohol in her presence, unless she herself is inclined to a cocktail," he said, making small talk.

"I had the feeling she started without us," Anny said.

Soulé gave her an unkind look and took another sip. Ran his tongue around his flat line lips.

Anny suppressed a smile and began studying her stuffed olive.

This time I squeezed her hand. I didn't want either of us blowing him away until I'd put to him the questions Nell ran from.

"A fine sherry this, what one would expect and no less at the world famous Polo Lounge," Soulé said. His eyes clicked on a tawny brunette half-sitting on a bar stool and displaying mounds of flesh like hills of hamburger in a butcher's showcase.

A connection between them, briefer than a blink.

He ran his tongue around his lips again and eased his attention back to us.

I said, "Anny and I did a lot of hand holding at Nell Fontanne movies, so tonight was quite a thrill for us, Colonel, even for those few minutes."

"I have never experienced any of her moving pictures, Supervisor Marion. I know her only as the beauty who came to us as our beloved princess."

Anny said, "*London Days, Paris Nights*," and Soulé looked at her curiously. "The title of one of the movies, Colonel Soulé. Duke proposed to me during the London days and slipped the ring on my finger after the Paris nights."

His almost-smile flickered again.

"The princess once mentioned a dancer, a—" He searched the ceiling. "Fred Astaire?"

"Nell came gliding down the royal staircase and straight into Fred Astaire's arms," Anny said, closing her eyes to the memory. "That's why we had to get a two-story house when we finally could afford to get a house. Duke here wanted his stairway."

"I sure did. I already had my princess."

Anny blushed softly. "Duke," she said, and leaned over to peck my cheek.

Soulé looked forgivingly at Anny and let a real smile ease across his tight face, as if the moment had melted the iceberg he used for body armor.

His mind seemed to turn on some happy memory.

"Supervisor Marion, you are quite the romantic," Soulé said, "a quality, frankly, I would not have imagined before our meeting." Turning to Anny, "With a princess of his own, to be sure, Madame."

Anny reached over and touched his hand.

Soulé acknowledged her with another smile before easing his hand away and slipping it under the table.

He said, "I want you to hear, to know, both of you, why the princess chose to accept the invitation to return here and be honored, see old friends from a life she left so long ago, after years of declining similar invitations to . . ."

I had a sense we wouldn't like what was coming.

The colonel lowered his voice and said, "My princess, your Nell Fontanne, is dying."

Anny gasped audibly and gripped my hand.

When she turned to me I saw tears clouding her wondrously blue eyes.

I bit down on my back molars and swallowed hard.

Soulé let his revelation sink in for a few more moments before explaining, "In what time remains, the princess wanted to say goodbye to as many cherished memories as possible."

"We didn't know," Anny said, unnecessarily, dabbing at her eyes with a cocktail napkin.

I hid my own sudden grief inside my Chivas.

"It was nothing to broadcast, Mrs. Marion. Where I come from—unlike here in this country—we are quite practiced at buying and keeping secrets. I share this one with you only because of your clear affection for the princess."

I had my opening and took it. "Even from Edwin O. Powell?"

"Begging your pardon, Supervisor?"

"Was your princess keeping the secret from him? Edwin O. Powell?"

A curtain began to descend over Soulé's face.

"Her killer, you said."

"Her co-star in five of her movies?"

"I've already told you I never saw—"

"The heavenly messenger in *Dancing Clouds*, that was Edwin O. Powell," Anny said. "Also, Sweet Benjie in *The Tap Dance Kid*."

I said, "Her one-time lover, off the screen as well as on the screen, Colonel Soulé."

"I know nothing about that, Supervisor."

"Nothing? I'd have thought a man in your position would make it a point to know *everything* about your princess."

"Everything worth knowing," he said archly, playing the *New York Times* to my *National Enquirer*.

"An old boyfriend tries to kill your princess. Seems to me that's worth knowing about."

"You're certain about this?"

"The call came while I was in the suite. A friend on the police force. There was a match on Powell's fingerprints and his dental records."

"Everyone can do with a friend or two," he said, buying a moment. "If he intended to kill her, why would he put blank bullets in his weapon?"

"Maybe he didn't intend to kill her?"

"Maybe now we'll never know?"

"The phone call. Did Nell call him or did he call her?"

"Don't be melodramatic, Supervisor. If you think it through, the princess would have had no business with Mr. Powell's telephone number after so many years, but Mr. Powell would know of her presence from newspaper accounts or television."

"He called her."

"He called the hotel. The operator inquired of me if the princess wished to speak with him."

"Because you make those decisions?"

"Because I screen all her calls."

"She chose to speak with him."

"Yes."

"For how long?"

"As long as it took for her to set a luncheon date, whereupon she handed over the telephone to me, so I could conclude the arrangement with Mr. Powell."

"Without knowing who he was."

"Correct. Without knowing. Supervisor, it is not my business to know the people the princess knows, only to accommodate her wishes in accordance with my instructions from her husband, the prince."

"After they spoke, Nell and Mr. Powell, did she seem pleased?"

"I doubt any displeasure would have resulted in a luncheon date, don't you?"

He looked for accordance from Anny.

Anny smiled pleasantly and bit the last olive off her martini pick. She always requests three and, sometimes, an onion, as well.

I asked, "Was anything said about Mr. Powell attending the dinner?"

"Not to me."

"To Nell?"

"Not that she told me."

"And she would have told you."

"It would have been left to me to arrange his seating, and if he were so important in her life I suspect he would have been invited to be on the dais."

"But he wasn't."

"Did you see any empty seats on the dais?"

Anny said, "Except when Dustin Hoffman sneaked off, probably for a quick pee."

The colonel glanced at her whimsically and *humphed* inside a half smile.

I said, "What I saw was a man marching out with a gun to fire a blank at the guest of honor."

"A cry for attention, perhaps. At being ignored by the sponsors?"

"Now who's being melodramatic, Colonel Soulé?" I saw he was beginning to retreat back inside himself. "And, where were you when this occurred?"

"Perhaps taking my own pee, Supervisor?" His face told me nothing. "So, then—I'm pleased we had this opportunity to get acquainted. Regrettably, I assured the princess I would not be gone long."

Soulé inched his way out of the booth and onto his feet.

"Finish your cocktails, please. Have another, should you and your charming wife care to linger. My compliments. I arranged for the bill earlier."

As Soulé turned, I stopped him with his name.

"You never told us what the princess was dying from?" I said.

"Nothing pleasant, I assure you." His last word on the subject.

"The police'll want you to be more specific. About that and a lot more, Colonel."

The corners of his mouth flicked a smile.

"Oh, yes, the police. Not before one o'clock, I trust. The princess rarely if ever rises before one o'clock."

Soulé half-bowed, turned and sauntered off, pausing to say something to the maitre d' before he marched out of the Polo Lounge.

The maitre d' glanced in our direction, then waited a few minutes before stepping over to the bar and whispering something to the overbuilt brunette Soulé had eyed earlier, about the time I had finished recapping my conversation with Fuzz. The brunette nodded confirmation at him and slid off her perch, heading for the same exit Soulé had passed through.

Anny watched her go, then turned back to me and said, "So the good news is—everyone will understand you couldn't have possibly known that before you drew and fired to protect Nell Fontanne."

"And the bad news is Edwin O. Powell is still dead, and we have a vindictive chief of police, whose grudge against me leaves no room for reality, and a handful of hack politicians only too happy to go along with the gag."

"They'll all try to use what happened today against you, won't they?" Anny asked, rhetorically.

"They'll try, although they won't be able to put the knife in my hand. Too many witnesses for Crescent to find anything more than some blood on my shirt."

"But Bachman put him on notice, you said. Would Crescent be stupid enough to try anyway?"

"As Fuzz'd say, If Crescent were any more stupid he'd have to be watered twice a week. Crescent is not going to ignore any opportunity to bust my caps."

"Not even for Bachman? Didn't you tell me he came down hard on Crescent?"

"I didn't tell you I think it was an act. Bachman wants to get Bruno and he'll do whatever it takes to keep me playing the game. Good guy, bad guy."

"Shit," Anny said, swallowing the last olive. "Shit, shit, shit."

It was not supposed to turn out like this.

Colonel Karl Soulé considered the problems, old and new, en route back to the suite, where he tapped lightly on the door to the princess's bedroom before inching it open. He crossed the room to her bed and verified she was asleep, an easy rhythm to her breathing, her breasts rising and falling methodically under the covers, a dreamer's enchanted smile on her enchanting face, in the soft glow of a bedside lamp shadowed and bereft of all the lines and crevices that had struck harshly with time.

He gathered the covers around her, under her chin and just so over her shoulders, and leaned forward to kiss her on the forehead, but thought better of it, whispered another good night, and returned to the sitting room. He picked up the phone and asked the hotel switchboard operator to connect him to the number he had committed to memory.

The familiar voice answered, as usual, after the first ring; as usual, with his name:

"Rupert Bachman."

"Colonel Soulé here. You're sure I'm not disturbing you, sir, ringing you up at this unusual hour?"

"You're not disturbing me at all," Bachman said, quietly. "As I have made plain before, I always make time for friends of the agency, Karl, and you most certainly are in that select category."

"Thank you," the colonel said, and proceeded to tell him about Supervisor Daniel Marion's visit.

When he'd finished, Bachman held a long pause, then replied, "Interesting, very interesting, Karl," as if he were hearing second-hand information he already knew. "But nothing about Bruno Guy?"

"The name never came up."

"Stella Ivers?"

"No."

"Some other name, perhaps?"

"Edwin O. Powell. We talked about him and we talked about the princess. That was all."

An audible sigh. "I had hoped for more."

"Mr. Bachman, I am quite bothered about the police speaking with the princess tomorrow."

"Understood," Bachman said, "and let me put that fear to rest at once. Nothing the princess says will make news, Karl, trust me on that score."

"Nothing?"

"Nothing. The good thing about having friends in high places is that they, too, have friends in high places. Be assured that the police are in good hands, Colonel. My hands. Personally."

"Thank you."

"One other thing, Karl?"

"Yes, Mr. Bachman?"

"Stella Ivers. If she should in any way look to contact you or the princess again, advise me immediately."

"Of course."

"I remain in your debt, Karl. Good night."

Bachman clicked off and, before he could settle the receiver, the colonel thought he heard a second click.

Someone else on the line?

He crossed back to the princess' bedroom and quietly opened the door just enough to verify she was still asleep.

One of the hotel switchboard operators, then?

They were notorious for tricks like that, at every hotel in the world, especially on slow nights, picking up gossip they could sell to a scandal-mongering tabloid for a few hundred dollars, those that weren't already on an annual stipend.

The door chimes startled him.

He crossed the room quickly, before they could sound again and possibly disturb the princess, opened the door without first checking through the spy hole.

The brunette from the Polo Lounge.

Her heavily painted eyes brimming with erotic promise.

She smiled back at him and inquired in a withering whisper, "Mr. Brown?"

Cautioning her to be quiet, he opened the door only wide enough to let her pass. Quickly closed and locked it. Led her from the hallway to his bedroom on the side of the sitting room opposite the princess' bedroom.

Chapter 9

We live in a typical middle-class neighborhood in the San Fernando Valley, North Hollywood, a convenient freeway hop to almost anywhere, except when there are other cars on the freeways, which is most of the time. The streets are wide and many of them tree-lined, including ours, and the homes date back to before the end of World War II, when tract builders bought up and plowed under the citrus groves and replaced rows of orange and lemon trees with rows of replicated homes that, thankfully, over decades of remodeling took on individual characteristics.

With the passing years, they also took on more and more safety features.

High fences.

Gates.

Bars on all the windows and more bars enclosing vulnerable front porches.

Lawn signs announcing security patrols on constant alert and ready to charge with weapons drawn.

Any difference at our two-story Spanish hacienda, purchased on a cop's modest salary and destined to be fully paid for in about two hundred more years?

Nope.

The Marions are also society's prisoners at the happy homestead.

North Hollywood ranks first among all valley areas in incidence of crime, every type and level of criminal activity, with no discount on the violence for former cops or sitting supervisors trying to better the odds against innocent pedestrians being shot by drive-by snipers, who usually belong to one of the gangs that also call the neighborhood home turf, or the two or three other gangs who have their own ideas.

So, better safe than six feet under, and why I trained my kids when they were growing up and at their most curious to understand and respect how firearms work.

Finally, how to use them, the same way I had turned Anny into a sharpshooter early in our marriage.

Back from the Beverly Hills Hotel, I had just stashed my piece and was checking for messages when Anny waltzed back into the kitchen wearing my favorite brief bikini nightie and a smile.

Like a traffic cop, I motioned her to stop, then to turn around pirouette-fashion.

She obliged.

"Okay," I said. "Just wanted to be certain it was you."

"Is it?"

"Probably."

"Probably?"

"Good chance. Odds on it are fifty-fifty."

"Bastard—and the odds on *that* are eighty-twenty."

She stuck out her tongue as she sashayed past me on her way to the fridge. She pulled out a beer for me and one for herself and cuddled against me while we popped our tops.

"You disappointed in the way I look, Sailor?" she said, in what was her Moana of the Seven Seas accent.

"Never."

"I bet you say that to all your wives."

"I do, yes. Except for Number Nine."

"Why?"

"I'm disappointed in the way she looks, so to her I say *Nein*."

Anny nuzzled her head under my chin and played with my tie. "So maybe you won't say *Nein* to me—if I ask what else is bothering you?"

"What do you mean?"

"All the signs were there driving home. Nell Fontanne? Edwin O. Powell and his load of blanks? Crescent's crock of dirty tricks? Something specific or just the world in general?"

"Everything specific. Too many questions. Not enough answers . . . Crescent . . . Nell Fontanne . . . the way I can't make a fit out of Nell and Powell."

"You can't stop being a cop, can you, Duke? Will you ever really start being a supervisor?"

I thought about it. Shrugged. "I am what I am, Anny."

Another moment and she kissed my cheek. "I love it when you talk dirty," she said, sliding a hand inside my shirt.

She understood I was talked out on the subject.

I touched her cheek and found a spot to kiss, a small freckle that always embodied her essence for me.

And nothing else mattered now but Anny and me.

We kissed and fondled our way upstairs to the bedroom, where she struck a half-standing, half-sitting pose by the dresser while I climbed out of my clothes. She sucked on her beer can and, reining in a distant look, wondered, "Remember them in *Take My Romance*?"

"How many times have you asked and when was the last time I forgot?"

She blew a kiss at me and began reciting lines we knew so well. It was one of the earliest Nell Fontanne-Edwin O. Powell scripts we committed to memory all those years ago, in our youthful, exuberant lust and need to share.

"I cannot see you anymore, dearest Derek. Father will not

allow it. But I will eternally remember you in my mind and feel you in my throbbing fingers and recognize you in my endangered heart."

Easing to the bed, she deposited her beer can on the night stand, stepped out of the puddle her nightie made on the floor, and slid sensuously onto the mattress without bothering to toss back the covers, all the while directing me aloud:

"Derek moves closer and takes Constance in his arms."

I stashed my beer on my nightstand and joined Anny on the bed. Took her in my arms and held her so tightly I could hear her heart racing to catch up with mine.

She struggled to explain, "Constance's sightless eyes strain for some image as her fingers caress his face."

"Their lips meet," I said, and we joined in a lingering kiss.

"Oh, Derek," she sighed, "I see you, Derek. I see you, beloved of mine."

And we played out the scene in a way that in the time of Nell Fontanne and Edwin O. Powell could never have gotten past the censors.

I stopped being a cop and became a supervisor.

But later, while Anny slept soundly with her body cradled beside mine, I stared blindly through my closed eyes, unable to sleep, my mind churning through the confusion created by puzzle pieces that refused to fit.

And Bruno.

When would I hear from him again?

Would I hear from him again?

How many people would be blown to heaven if we didn't make the connection?

Chapter 10

Clem McAllister lived in a castle of brick and glass on a bluff overlooking the Malibu Colony and the Pacific Ocean, reached by a gated, guarded two-lane road off Malibu Canyon Road and Grande Vista.

The armed security cop asked for some photo ID before he checked off my name on his clipboard and buttoned open the elevator gate after jotting down the plate number on the Porsche and complimenting, "Nice set of wheels you got there. A '62 or '63?"

" '62."

"Did a nice job matching the original paint. That's a red you never find nowheres else, like what's-her-name's slippers in *The Wizard of Oz*. Dorothy."

"Thanks. We worked hard on that. All original parts under the hood, though. My mechanic tours the scrap yards better than anyone."

He weighed my answer for a moment. "Tobias Buck, huh?"

"You know Tobi?"

"Never to say hello to, but seen enough about him and his toys in *Road & Track* to know his work. Grew up wanting to be like him and do a victory lap in the formulas, but I never got past the dirt tracks and demolition derbies."

He closed his eyes to the memory and pushed his shirt inside his gun belt, over a jutting beer belly that would have blocked his view of the windshield inside a formula.

"Farther than I ever got," I said, "so I envy you. I never got out of the bleachers."

"Yeah, ain't I the one," he said, melancholy dressing the smile my comment had evoked as he stepped aside and wished me a good day.

A winding mile later, marveling alternately at views of white-capped waves running up to nip at joggers, dog-walkers, and strollers on their morning constitutional and the silent majesty of mountain slopes dressed in either lush greens or, where the last brush fires had struck, crippled bush browns, I reached the landscaped circular driveway fronting the castle and pulled into a parking spot between two powder blue Rolls Royces, identical except for their personalized plates. One read CLEM WON and the other CLEM TOO.

I tried guessing where the security cameras and lasers were as I sauntered across the foot bridge over the moat and toward the castle steps, repeatedly distracted by the sculpture, immense and overpowering works by Smith, Moore, Brancusi, Caro, Rickey, Barlach, and Maillol; a DiSuvero earthwork; a Rodin bronze, whose twin was at the L.A. County. I felt as if I had stumbled into the secret annex of the UCLA sculpture garden.

I found more art treasures inside after a moon-faced heavyweight with a fresh five o'clock shadow at nine in the morning and a noticeable bulge under his silk Armani jacket, where a shoulder holster would be, greeted me by name at the front door. He led me to a room that could give Donald Trump an envy rash and before disappearing urged me in a pleasant baritone to, please, make myself at home until the boss came down.

That was about five minutes later, as I moved from one of Nevelson's black sky cathedrals dominating a wall across from the Van Gogh postman over the fireplace, past the Segal sculpture of two mummified old-timers eternally waiting on a bus bench, to a petite, sublime Picasso cubist portrait of his mistress, Marie-Therese Walter, sitting as lost as any Picasso could be on a shelf of a library case otherwise full of gold-embossed, leather-bound classics.

"Find anything you like?"

I turned as McAllister stepped from an elevator built for two or three, four max, with ceramic door facings that looked like Giacomo Manzu's work.

"Bought them off the wall of a church in Venice," he said proudly, complimenting me on my guess. "For whatever it took to restore the building, maybe two, three hundred years old. Ravages of time. Rain damage not to be believed. Holes in the roof the size of port holes."

McAllister paused for a second under an enormous Calder mobile, playful angels in primary colors mocking the clouds, that hung from the center point on a ceiling two stories high and braced with natural redwood beams, then moved behind the full bar.

"To be honest with you, I'd've underwritten the repairs even if we hadn't come to an agreement, rather than see that beautiful joint continue to rot away. . . . You up for a wee shot of courage this time of morning?" I shook my head. "Little hair of the mongrel for me," McAllister said, holding a bottle of Jack Daniel's like a trophy. "Long night for me and I don't party as well as I used to. Comes with age, I suppose. You know?" I nodded. "Well, all of us get old sooner or later. I was hoping for later, but—" He shrugged. "It's something what's not my call, if you know what I mean?"

He came out from around the bar carrying the fifth and strolled across the room with the jaunty indifference of a traffic cop. I had settled on a twelve-foot divan covered in a salmon-colored silk brocade and he eased into the matching stuffed chair across from me. After taking a swipe from the bottle, he leaned over and planted it in front of him on the etched glass surface of the huge square table separating us.

Gave me a healthy grin.

Said, "Glad you could make it on so last minute a call. I hate to drink alone."

"I said 'no.'"

"But you're here, so I'm not alone," he said, marking the air with an index finger. "The hired help don't count."

McAllister appeared to be in his late thirties.

He was of medium build and medium height, as ordinary-looking as everybody's next door neighbor except for his hair, which was bushy and prematurely gray, as if he had spent most of his life worrying about the rest of his life, and it made something special of his enviable tan.

McAllister wore a dark, hand-stitched suit of imported gabardine. The traditional, conservative English cut draped exquisitely and added esteem to the casual elegance of the man. His imported silk tie was perfectly knotted and paired with the silk handkerchief in the jacket pocket. His wing-tip shoes were also expensive and polished to a high gloss.

He slipped the shoes off and continued with what was almost a monologue, in an ingratiating voice that aspired to culture but frequently slipped to another time and place, an accent I couldn't pin down and twists of grammar that would never have gotten past an English teacher.

It added to the enigma that was Clem McAllister.

"Pearce Dickson caught me over my oatmeal," I said.

"I didn't give him so much notice, neither. Yesterday would of been better, but the sun came up this morning and here we are, you and me." He held out a palm, "*da-da-dah*-ed" the opening notes of *Annie*.

"Because?"

"Pearce didn't tell you?"

"Pearce said he didn't know why you wanted to see me."

"He got that part right," McAllister said with a wink. "Pearce is a good boy. Does good by the city and not so bad by me." He took another swallow of Jack Daniel's and used it to rinse his mouth. "Sinatra always said Crest only fought the cavities and Jack Daniel's destroyed them for good. He never told that to my dentist, or why do I have two rows of piano keys that cost me as much as a Bel Air knockdown?"

I gave him the smile he wanted.

His teeth were pretty and, looking again, I saw hints of surgery around his eyes, possibly a little tug to pull in his chin and subtract five years from his age.

He put down the bottle and, screwing his own smile onto his face, said, "Tell me about yourself first."

"Why do I think you already know, Mr. McAllister."

"Clem to my friends and Clem to you. Obviously, because I do and also because you are wise enough to understand that coming in." He folded his hands in his lap and I noticed how his nails glistened with polish, but they had been picked to the quick. "We got a common interest in the fine arts, I believe, and you even got a museum dedication coming up on your busy, busy sched-ulowe?"

"A Rodin for the sculpture garden, not nearly as fine as yours."

"You mean the Rodin or the sculpture garden?"

"Both."

"Ain't that the truth though?" He laughed heartily. "Micah Delacroix trying to buy respectability before the DA gets enough goods to shut him down for keeps. Thinks it'll help him in front of the jury."

McAllister second-guessed himself and shut down that line of conversation.

104

He said, "Besides art, there's also music, although I lean more to the show tunes and you got a thing for jazz. You plug into that new station yet, the one that only plays Broadway and movie soundtracks?" I nodded. "How's that for a gas . . . while it lasts?" He "*dah-dah-dah*-ed" something by Richard Rodgers and that somehow led to mention of my high school and college football careers, the brief go at the pros, the war, Anny and our kids.

He stopped short of my son, John, but I could tell he knew, by the way his eyes and his smile briefly went limp and I felt more than empathy from McAllister.

I wasn't about to ask why.

Johnny was not a subject for friends, who knew better than to raise it with Anny or me, so how could it be one for strangers, even a stranger like McAllister, who seemed to know too much?

I said, "What's my shirt size?"

"Eighteen collar, thirty-six sleeve, although it looks like you might want to think about dropping five?"

I finger scored this point for him.

He made an *of course* shrug, then, "And, of course, the movies! My passion, too, like you and the missus, and why I was at the NMPAA's do for Nell Fontanne. I go every year and get the same two tables for twelve way on down front. Should be up on the stage considering the chunk of change they know to always expect from me, year-in and year-out, reliable as Big Ben."

He saw I was getting restless and used the next moment to cut into the Jack Daniel's again. Wiped his mouth with the back of his hand. Finger swept the corners. Said, "You did a gutsy thing that night, Duke."

"No choice."

"Sure you did. You could've ducked under the table the

way some of my people did and, to call it straight, me, too, almost. There was a panic second I thought the shooter was going to turn his barrel in my direction, before two of my human shields sandwiched me out of there. Edwin O. Powell must've flipped big time to try a stunt like that, like he was out begging to get himself whacked by someone."

"Cops are working it."

"Yeah, and the chief, Paul Crescent, working you pretty good the same time." He looked me hard in the eyes. "It's personal, huh?"

"Something you don't know, Mr. McAllister?"

He reached for the Jack Daniel's, changed his mind.

"I got his version. Thought I might audition yours."

"Takes too much breath."

"If you like, I'd be happy to put in a word with him."

"It would have to be a short one for Crescent to get it, but no. Thanks, but no."

"Stop it before it gets any uglier? Your plate is full enough with the government, the Bug Man, and that Bruno Guy business, not to mention the old job-ola. It's not enough to earn public trust, you got to shine 'em on sometimes to keep it, especially when all the Crescent types are stacking the deck against you."

"Tell me about my shoes."

"Tens. Wide in the arch. Crescent knows me, Duke. An intro by a mutual friend before the City Council chose him to take over for you, if you get my drift?"

"It drifted, and now it's drifting back."

"With him like I could never connect with you when you was chief, and he owes me an echo, Paul."

"We didn't have a mutual friend?"

"Plenty of them, and every one of them told me not to waste my time, like they're still doing. The reason I needed to have this up close and personal. To see if maybe I could owe you an echo instead of you owing me."

"You'll do much better in the Alps, Mr. McAllister. You should have listened to our mutual friends."

I started to rise.

"How about you hear what I have to say before you tell me to go fuck myself? You might be surprised."

"I don't think so."

"Did I forget to say please? Listen, first, then answer. Didn't they teach you that in politician school?"

"I'm not a politician, Mr. McAllister."

He shot me a greedy grin.

"Not so's anyone would notice. What is it then? You like the aggravation?"

"More than I like owing anyone."

"So, look at it this way. Our friend Pearce is the politician. You're here because of him. Pretend you're listening for him, too. Sit." His grin disappeared on the last word, an order more than an invitation, compounded by his lip-puckering salesman's smirk.

He jabbed a finger in the direction of the chair.

It was easier to sit than argue.

McAllister leaned over and started rubbing his toes, addressing them instead of me. "The MacMurray?"

He meant the MacMurray Basin, eight hundred acres of undeveloped county-owned property near the border between Los Angeles and Ventura counties.

For months, the Board had been considering a controversial proposal that within three years would convert the MacMurray into the nation's largest sports and shopping complex.

The deal would bring millions of dollars to the county and create a new tax base that could result in a substantial tax offset for residents, in the process creating thousands of new job opportunities—

—*if* the proposal wasn't a scam off the paperwork we had to deal with, hundreds of pages of finitely detailed, self-serving documentation and financial data—

—"we" being the civic review committee Pearce had appointed, with me as the chairman, over my protest that I knew nothing about real estate and less about anything financial that started with a dollar sign.

"What about the MacMurray?"

"My source tells me your committee is close to a vote."

"Yesterday's *Times* could have told you the same thing."

"That was my source." He looked up grinning. There was no escaping his elfin charm. "I have important acquaintances who'd like to see the MacMurray leave your committee with a favorable recommendation, Duke."

"Why did I know that's where you were going with this?"

"It's closer than a trip to Disneyland?"

I named the developers.

McAllister shook his head.

"It doesn't matter. The deal is exactly as it reads on paper. My word on that. No curves anywhere. No boilerplate to beware of. A kind of deal every other state will be begging for if you let it get away from L.A."

"And you're asking me to influence the committee vote, assuming I can, is that it, Mr. McAllister?"

He put a shocked look on his face.

"Not in a million bucks, I mean, years," he said, a twinkle in his eyes, using his eyebrows for emphasis. "I just thought you'd tell me how you're leaning, so's I can tell my acquaintances and let them appreciate me more than they already do."

"And that's worth an echo to you?"

"You should only know the half of it."

"Even if I tell you I'm voting against the deal?"

"Yes."

"That I'm the tie-breaker right now and the MacMurray will go back to the Board with a negative recommendation?"

"Yes."

He stretched his eyebrows and nodded. "This is the information era, Duke. What happens once the information moves on does not involve me or you." An enigmatic smile this time. "Are you the tie-breaker?"

"I don't have a clue. It's a secret ballot when we take it and we haven't taken it yet, not even a straw."

"I have a clue . . . you are the tie-breaker."

I took a deep breath, another, pushed them out hard through my nose, to keep from losing my temper. I had been trying to make a point. McAllister had just turned it into reality.

"And you are the octopus."

"All compliments gratefully accepted."

"I can't help you."

"You already have, Duke, and I'm in your debt."

"What are you talking about?"

McAllister cupped a hand behind an ear. "Body language, baby, body language," he said, breaking into easy laughter while he snapped up the bottle of Jack Daniel's and toasted me.

Working my way down the mountain and back onto Malibu Canyon Road, I wondered if he really had figured out I was supporting the MacMurray proposal.

Chapter 11

I got to the Board meeting in time to make the morning recess vote unanimous and, from the moment he saw the look on my face, Pearce Dickson became extremely nervous, although he tried mightily to muster something that passed for a smile.

"Not now, Lewis," I told my bushy-tailed aide, Lewis Tully, who wanted to brief me on the status of the agenda. I gave his arm an appreciative squeeze and closed in on Pearce.

Pearce was shuffling papers and a five-inch stack of folders in rainbow-colored files. He muttered something about not wanting to be late for a lunch huddle with some Board of Education members.

"You need some educating yourself," I told him, and watched the blood drain out of his face. I could see he didn't need to be told what the lesson was about.

"It didn't go well with Clem McAllister?"

"It didn't go well with *me*, but you got your echo out of it."

He fumbled a look that was supposed to convince me he didn't understand the reference. "What the hell was it Clem wanted anyway?"

"You're still going to play like you didn't know?"

"If it's not asking too much, didn't know what?"

"You really want to do this here, Pearce?" I said, not sure how much longer I could control my temper. My heart was doing the rumba.

He pushed back his sleeve to check the time, had second

thoughts and abruptly, almost guiltily, stashed the hand in a pocket, making me wonder anew about the origin of the 18-karat gold and steel Cartier Tank he'd worn everyday for the last year, boasting it was inherited from a dead uncle.

"Whaddaya think, I could afford this little chatchka trinket on the salaries we pay ourselves?" he would challenge.

I was thinking now: *No, but your little chatchka trinket does cost the equivalent of parking meter money for people like Clem McAllister.*

He said, "You putting something ahead of our kids and our kids' kids, Duke-o? We'll be talking about boundaries and appropriations for six more magnet schools. Sit in. We can update on the way." Sounding as sincere as a junkie's promise to quit tomorrow.

The chamber was emptying slowly. Lobbyists working the room and some TV field reporters doing summary lead-ins or interviews with the guy flexing in a pink Elvis jump suit and cape, a Lone Ranger mask over his eyes, whom I knew could only be Item Three on the agenda, under New Business, The Lone Presley. Except, leaning against one of the pillars was a woman in a matching costume, equally muscular, hiding her face behind slender hands whenever a camera moved within five feet of her. Maybe the Lone Presley wasn't so alone?

"Got a lunch," I said, "so let me do this real fast and clear for now, Pearce. If you put value on our friendship, don't ever put me in a spot like that again."

"For Christ's sake, talk about friendship. I told you it was important for me."

"You should have told me more."

"I didn't know more."

"I think you did. I think you know he wanted to talk MacMurray."

Pearce shook his head dramatically. "He said he wanted to

111

talk getting you out from under that putz, Crescent. I didn't tell you because he wanted it to be his surprise. He likes surprises."

"You know I don't."

"One little surprise? You're talking about deep-sixing a friendship over a surprise that had a good deed attached?"

"The MacMurray, Pearce. He knows how tight the vote is. I only told you."

His press secretary, Manny Sutton, approached us and, after a moment, maybe smelling a stink, made a show of waving to some invisible contact and hurried away.

Pearce had been saying, "There're eight other people on that committee who last time I looked had the power of speech, Duke-o. Fucking kiss-and-tell's a cottage industry in real life."

He reached out for my shoulder.

I stepped back. "Not you, Pearce, that's what you're telling me?"

"On my stepbrother's life." He raised his right hand shot to the ceiling.

"You hate your stepbrother."

"Why do you think I chose him?"

I didn't answer his grin.

He shook his hands, trying to figure what to do with them. "Okay, so a little more. So Clem said he might want to talk MacMurray. So I told him to save his breath, because you don't talk outside of school. So he said he operates from a different classroom than most people. So, you know what?"

"Talk to me."

"I knew I could count on you to do the right thing. And you didn't spill to him, did you? C'mon, Duke-o, tell me you didn't before I lose more faith in honest public servants dealing out good government."

My friend the son-of-a-bitch had turned things completely around.

I don't know which of us started laughing first.

He checked his watch.

I said, "Where'd you get the Tank?"

"My dear dead grandfather," Pearce said. "It was in his will."

"I thought it was your late uncle."

"What I said was my uncle was always late, because he didn't have a watch."

At approximately the same time, Stella Ivers reveled in the knowledge she was turning heads as she crossed mid-block from the Coventry Arms Hotel to the Century City mall. She enjoyed being beautiful. She enjoyed getting off on the knowledge men found her drop-dead looks eye boggling.

She smiled at the lawyer type who narrowly missed bumping into the lamppost, so intent had he been on eye boffing her.

The connection startled him into a trot past her and, glancing over her shoulder, she caught him looking back at her.

Her wave spurred him to greater speed.

What made the moment a special treat for her was the way she was dressed: A green, plaid silk shantung shirt over olive moleskin pants, the shirt topped by a quilted olive moleskin jacket, picked up earlier today on sale at Saks. Not so provocative this afternoon, not enough to stand out in a crowd or be remembered.

Usually, Stella liked being remembered.

But not when she was working.

Not this afternoon.

So nothing visible beyond her model's form, not even her great set.

Clearly, the heads were turning because she had a great face, too.

It was out there for the world to admire, too, right now: her face. No makeup to hide the abundance of freckles contradicting the subtle knowing of her outsized, lustrous brown eyes. Her brown hair in ponytail, an olive bow floating down her back to her tight ass.

Looking younger than her thirty-two years, almost like a teenager.

And all of her for real.

No implants.

No lifts.

No liposuction.

She skipped up the steps to the plaza level, her long legs taking the steps two at a time, and shopped the windows as she headed for the escalators to the garage. A dress in a window attracted her attention—nice, silky, skimpy, sexy—and music blaring like a great orgasm from the Tower Records sound system stopped her long enough to check out the album displays, snapping her fingers to the beat of the rock video emanating from the TV monitor above the entrance.

That British band, those Beatles wannabes.

Fat chance.

Passable.

Over and out.

The end.

Stella reached the first parking level and headed for the ticket machines, one of the sets invisible from the cashier's booths. She waited while the black Cad heading in paused long enough for the driver to roll down his window and punch the button that spit out a yellow ticket good for three hours of free parking. She hesitated after the Cad shot by her, to be absolutely certain no one was watching, then stepped over to the machine. After checking again over both shoulders, she punched the button and quickly strolled away with her own free parking ticket.

Now all she needed was the car.

Three levels down, she found the vintage white Mercedes parked exactly where it was supposed to be. A minute or two later, Stella surrendered her yellow parking ticket to an eager young cashier with a buck-toothed smile that easily put her own modest overbite to shame.

He wished her a nice day with a look that said he would rather be offering her a nice boff right now.

Except that she was working, she might have taken him up on it.

As the car tooled out of Century City, Stella rummaged the cassette storage box on the passenger seat.

It was full of classical music.

She rolled her eyes, pushed the box away, and snapped on the radio.

Laundered the stations until she found one to her liking.

Rock and roll, baby!

Way to go!

Chapter 12

I met Fuzz Todd at The Place, the place downtown where we had met millions of times before, when I was still packing a badge. It was a seedy landmark, built in the days when it was cute to shape diners like anything but a building, in this case one of those old Red Line streetcars, a long and narrow counter on one side, a single row of faded booths on the other, their green-vinyl coverings full of rips, tears and poke holes exposing tufts of smoke-stained cotton and layers of accumulated grease and grime.

None of the customers minded. Almost all of them were regulars whose eating habits were etched in amino. The food was basic, good, plentiful, and cheap, perfect for any civil servant's salary, and the coffee in particular met official cop standards, strong and thick enough to pass for caffeine soup.

Fuzz was settled at his usual booth. It was the small one at the extreme far end, where he always sat feeding his neurosis, facing the entrance to protect his back, he said, against sneak attacks by bad guys nursing a personal grudge or a psyched-out post office worker no longer able to tell the difference between a post office and a piss hole.

I returned his wave, slid in opposite him, and helped myself to a cup of coffee from the old-fashioned tin pot that became a fixture on all the tables the day The Place opened, when the price was a nickel instead of a buck and a half.

He was working over a double cheeseburger and his

mouth was stuffed, his right hand clutching the burger and his left ready to shovel in onion fries thick with ketchup. He had already devoured half his side of coleslaw and about a third of his potato salad.

He mumbled something at me that made no sense with a full mouth.

Our usual waitress, Belle, paused to drop off a side of fried chicken livers and a chipped cereal bowl brimming with oatmeal on her way somewhere with a tray filled with orders: what passed for beef stew, a chili platter, spaghetti and meatballs in a white cream sauce, a hot dog, a burger with a side of fries, and a cottage cheese salad topped with pineapple slices.

"I thought for a minute Belle was bringing you the rest of your meal on that tray," I said, "except, of course, for the cottage cheese."

He wagged his head shoulder to shoulder and mimicked a silent laugh that made it look like he had golf balls stuck inside his cheeks while I brought the bowl closer to me and pulled from my jacket pocket a small plastic bag containing my wheat germ, which I mixed into the oatmeal.

His mouth momentarily empty, Fuzz said, "I don't know what's more disgusting, Supe, what you eat or you for always eating it."

"And you are sweating enough death-dealing grease to lubricate the heads of several hundred ballroom gigolos."

"In fact, grease is good for you. Adds years to your life. I just read that in a study somewhere."

"Where? In your favorite scientific journal—*Mad Magazine*?"

"Well, Supe, I see current reality has done nothing to squelch or interfere with your increasingly tenuous hold on what passes for a sense of humor."

"I hope it was something I said."

"Well, it's not nothing you're eating, like that pissant vulgar *secret formula oatmeal* of yours you insist is responsible for your depressingly fine physical shape."

"The *secret* is, it works, Fuzz. You really should try it yourself sometime."

His screeching laughter could have scared a charging rhino.

"No, thank you, and I never cared much for Jane Fonda or any of them exercise babes, either," he said, pouring another layer of ketchup on his fries. "Besides I got my own miracle weight loss plan going for me."

I waited for the payoff.

"Worry," Fuzz said, conspiratorially, after another moment. "Worry is the key, Duke. Find something to worry about. Worry about it. The pounds just melt away. Look at me."

I looked and wondered, "There must be *something* in the world for you to worry about."

He cocked his head and was giving me a one-eyed finger wagging when Belle returned to announce apologetically, "I gave you a dish too many, Chief."

Fuzz studied the table. "Looks right to me, you gorgeous, sexy creature, you."

Belle, who is somewhere in her late sixties and looks older in her Dutch serving girl outfit, a stained sometimes white apron over a formless yellow dress that ends about six inches above her knees and shows more working veins than the California gold rush of 1849, patted him on top of his head.

"Sorry, Fuzzball, but you still ain't my type and the fried chicken livers was for the other chief over there, at the counter; see 'im?"

"The chicken livers? Then it has to be Jordan Hardy," Fuzz said without looking.

I glanced over a shoulder, caught Jordan waving at us. He was in dress uniform and as cool and neat as Fuzz was sticky and unkempt. I waved back.

Fuzz looked, waved indifferently, and said, "Belle, I have a sudden passion for the fried chicken livers, since I can't have you."

"We're outta 'em, Fuzzball. This is the last of 'em."

He plucked one from the plate and took a healthy bite. "Oops. Please apologize to Chief Hardy-Har-Har for me." Fuzz waited for Belle to leave, before he cupped a hand by his mouth to hide his soft-spoken words. "You show me Jordan Hardy and I'll show you a chicken liver every time." He finished the one in his hand and went after another.

"Ease up, Fuzz. He's a good cop."

"A little less chicken and a few more guts would make him even gooder," Fuzz said, after rinsing his mouth with a long swallow of coffee. "The java's ass cold," he said, grimacing, and poured himself a fresh cup. "You know, Hardy-Har-Har still owes me a fiver from the last pussy pool. You interested in who she was and why?"

"No. Better you tell me what's new about Powell."

He threw away a hand gesture. "The usual crap calls and nothing real. I used to see better leads at my Arthur Murray dance class."

"How did it go with Nell Fontanne this morning?"

"Honestly? I think that your favorite actress is down to picking daffodils, Duke." While that sank in, Fuzz rammed some fries into his mouth and used a fork load of slaw for a chaser. "Soon as we hit her in the face with this Powell's name she started spouting poetry, for Christ's sake. Then that toady of hers, that colonel, Soulé? A pain in the ass zero I wanted to turn into a Roman numeral."

Jordan Hardy said, "Am I interrupting something?"

He had walked over to our booth and was hovering just behind me.

"If it's about the chicken livers, figure we're even for the pussy pool, okay?"

Ignoring Fuzz, Jordan said, "I wanted a couple words with you, if it's okay, Duke."

"Slide in." I moved to make room for him.

Jordan waved it off. "Thanks, but only for a minute."

He spent the minute saying nothing, as his face worked its way into a grim mask, his skin taut enough to add to the skull-like configuration.

He ran a hand nervously around his thinning white hair, one side, then the other, then smoothed out his thick mustache, which was more black than white.

"They want me to talk to the coroner's jury, Duke." There was almost a tear in his voice.

"They?"

"Crescent," he said, finally. I waited for more. "He hates your guts, Duke . . ." Fuzz grumbled something incoherent under his breath. "But he is my boss, so what the hell can I do?"

I said, "Do what's right for you, Jordan."

"I needed to hear that from you. Thanks, Duke."

I gave him a thumbs up.

He smiled, turned quickly and hurried away.

Fuzz Todd said, venomously, "And that sad son of a bitch wanted to be chief of police."

I pushed aside my oatmeal and went for the coffee instead. "So, did Crescent say something to you, too, Fuzz? You know, about a coroner's jury?"

"No matter," Fuzz said, grinning slyly. "The bastard only needed to say it once where someone was listening." He checked his watch, and then he changed the subject. "Meanwhile, you want to hear about Gustav Van Zandt?"

"Van Zandt?" Fuzz gave the air an underhand stab with his butter knife. "That was his name?"

"Maybe it was even his real one, in and among the aliases we compiled on the cross-referencing on the national system and with the Feds. He was wasted clean, Van Zandt. Not even a wishful thought on the Bowie knife. Clothing, nothing. His pockets empty. Prints gave him away, along with a record as long as your dong. Gustav was a journeyman anti-establishment noisemaker who's reportedly become a People's Militia mainliner. Tied him to a run of bank busts in a dozen states and the Doris Lee Pendleton hostage countdown in Iowa, some serial explosions on federal offices and the deaths that went along with them, before he dropped from sight about ten years ago and was peeled off of most of the post office walls."

Fuzz took a bite of burger and added what was left of the onion fries. He washed them down with a couple swallows of chocolate milkshake. "Nice company your dear old friend Bruno Guy keeps, wouldn't you say so, Supe? Proving it's not always the case that opposites attract."

I shook my head. "Something doesn't add up."

"How so?"

"Play it through, Fuzz. Whatever Bruno might be, he is no dummy. If Van Zandt was what you say, Bruno would no more have thought to have him deliver a message to me in so public a place, in so public a way, than he would think to show up himself."

"Ten years is a long time, Supe. The public forgets to remember."

"No difference what P. T. Barnum thought. Bruno Guy never underestimated the intelligence of the American public."

"Allowing for a minute that you're right, then why did he

set it up the first time to connect with you at the dinner for Nell Fontanne? I mean, Jesus in a Jag! How public can you get?"

"Maybe Bruno didn't. Remember, it's only what the Feds—Rupert Bachman—told me when I was invited in, that Bruno would surrender only to me and then only if certain conditions of his were met."

"Meaning?"

"The Nell Fontanne testimonial dinner made absolute sense. Bruno knows I'm a fan, and Anny. It's exactly the sort of thing I might expect from him, a personal signal that this situation is what it appears to be."

"So, if the government knew all they did about you and Bruno, they'd also know about that."

"Something like that."

"Okay. Bells and whistles going off all over the place. Conspiracy theory! Conspiracy theory . . . Why . . . ? Why after all this time . . . ? And what's the connection with Gustav Van Zandt?"

"I don't know. Maybe this line of reasoning is as far-fetched as it sounds on the face of it. But I don't have any better idea right now. You?"

Fuzz jabbed at the potato salad and followed a mouthful with another go at the milkshake.

He said, "Go ask him. Ask Bachman."

"If any of what we're talking about is true, you think Bachman would give me a straight answer?"

"Hell no, but it'll be some answer, and you never were bad at psyching out shit from shinola."

"Or shit from shit . . . What do you know about Clement McAllister?"

"The richer than shit guy?" I nodded. "You saying he fits somewhere?"

I told him about this morning's meeting and the offer McAllister had made to quiet Crescent, leaving out mention of the MacMurray Basin.

"Any scuttlebutt about the two of them, Fuzz?"

Fuzz considered the question. Shook his head. "Why would a guy with enough bread to start his own planet need anything from a guy who got into the gene pool when the life-guard wasn't watching?"

"Run it down for me?"

"Something that could reflect badly on our beloved chief? Absolutely not! I'll run it down for myself, thank you."

Chapter 13

Instead of heading straight back to the office, I made a long overdue trip that had been on my mind even before the whole business with Bruno Guy started, back to my old neighborhood. It had changed substantially since the last time I visited Bruno's mother a few years ago. Closer to five or six. So many? The realization brought with it a few sharp pangs of guilt.

Most of the billboards along Adams appealed to a black audience now and many of the buildings had been attacked by taggers in a crazy quilt of colors and gang symbols. The small, neat homes built in the twenties and thirties showed that their owners were waging proud but losing battles against decay.

I traveled a few side streets like a tourist, finding specific references to some of my best memories of growing up around here, before turning the Porsche onto West End and pulling into one of the vacant curb spots across the street from the Guys' Craftsman-style bungalow.

It was better tended than most of the other homes on the block, as it always was. The lawn and hip-high hedges enclosing the property were neatly trimmed and there was still a "victory" garden running down most of one side of the front yard, from a hedge almost to the stone walkway. The garden was a relic of World War II that Bruno's folks inherited from the previous owners.

At once, it had become Mama Guy's pride and joy and, heading through the gate, I noted that it still was.

Healthy crops of corn, tomatoes, lettuce, and lima beans divided by slat stakes and wrapping string.

Seed packets thumbtacked to some of the stakes for identification.

I smiled at the touch of my boyhood that hadn't aged a day.

The screen door squeaked open on rusted hinges. Mama Guy was stepping onto the porch to see who it was, one hand on her forehead, shielding her face, eyes squinting against the bright sun.

As ever, she seemed not to have aged, although she was into her early seventies now. I knew because she and my mom had been the same age, and I often wondered if my mom, had she lived, would have remained as well preserved as Mama Guy.

Mama Guy was a tall, large woman and stood ramrod straight, concealing her bulk inside a floral-patterned muumuu; feet sheathed in ankle-high black Reeboks; thin strands of hair the color of white rice curling out from under a Dodgers cap she wore with the bill backward, like some neighborhood gangsta.

I was halfway up the steps before she recognized me.

"Danny boy!"

"Hello, Mama Guy. I see your green thumb is good as ever."

"All the thumbs," she said, stepping forward to meet me.

She slapped her arms around my back, trapping my arms by my side. Squeezed tight enough to woosh the wind out of me. Settled her generous lips on top of mine for a long moment.

When she pulled back, I saw tears had formed in the corners of her large eyes the color of hazelnuts.

"Danny boy," she repeated, softer, but my name still outlined by traces of the European accent she'd brought here as a young girl, on the escape route her parents took from a country being overrun by Nazis, the voice still as sweet as her stuffed cabbage, the dish she often prepared with enough surplus for my family, whenever she suspected there wasn't enough money coming in to put our own food on our table.

This was often, and Mama Guy always had an excuse for the surplus she implored my mom to take, rather than have it spoil, she said. My mom played the game, too, too smart, eventually too defeated, to allow her pride to stand between her hungry brood and a meal.

"So, let me look at you," Mama Guy said, crossing her arms under her ample bosom. She nodded, shook her head, and frowned. "Anny, she ain't feeding you good enough. Ribs on you where I should be seeing meat."

There was no sense in debating the point. I was a good fifteen pounds heavier than the last time Mama Guy had seen me, and then, too, she complained about Anny's determination to starve me.

"I'll tell her you said so, Mama Guy."

"You tell her I said so," Mama Guy said, "and now you come on inside so we can do something about it, Danny boy."

The living room was unpretentious and neat, nothing out of place, everything where I remembered seeing it for most of the thirty years; the musty odor also familiar, but not quite as old as the furnishings; the faded couch and stuffed chairs protected by plastic and groupings of her needlepoint pillows.

"Make yourself comfortable cozy like you already know how," she said, heading past the arches to the dining room and on into the kitchen. "And don't go away until I get back, either."

Anywhere I looked, a memory was restored.

The one that grabbed me tightest was the eight-by-ten color photograph in the sterling silver frame that occupied a place of honor among assorted knickknacks on the fireplace mantle:

Bruno in a cap and gown.

His high school graduation picture.

Replaced at once by a smaller photo, black and white and slightly out of focus, but also in a sterling silver frame:

Bruno and Duke.

Teenage bodies in skimpy bathing trunks.

Flexing muscles and smiles.

The future too far away to ponder.

"You remember that one? From the camping trip." Mama Guy had returned carrying a tray, which she set down on the coffee table by the couch.

"Thanks to Bruno," I said. "I remember only because of your son, Mama."

She pushed aside pillows to make room and sat down, started to arrange a brew pot, cups, saucers, and a plate of chocolate chip cookies.

"Come and sit," she ordered, patting the place next to her. "Tell me everything so we catch up like a clock works."

I closed my eyes and traveled to the past, telling her, "We ate our lunches and the rule was we had to wait an hour before going back in the water . . . I ate too much . . . a lot of starch and carbohydrates in those days, Mama."

I took the photo from the mantle and carried it with me to the couch.

Settled alongside Mama Guy.

Placed the photo on the coffee table.

Impulsively leaned over and kissed Mama Guy on the cheek.

She pushed me off with a mock gesture of indignation,

then brought her fingertips to the spot I had kissed and let a smile tickle the corners of her mouth.

"Like a stick now," she said. "And you always telling me how that Anny of yours is such a great cook." She began brewing the tea. "You still like it strong, Danny boy?"

I nodded and continued with the memory. "I ate too much and I went back in the water too soon . . ."

"The two of you, always so impatient, like tomorrow would be yesterday if you didn't hurry up."

"I got a tremendous stomachache . . . it hurt too much too fight . . . I began to sink . . . drowning. I was drowning, Mama, and I blacked out."

"And next thing you know, Bruno—he jumps in to save you." She pushed a cup and saucer in front of me and poured. "He pulls you out like he was Captain Marvel, your favorite, more than Superman, and that's that. You think I don't know from that story? You think I don't not tell it thousands of times myself already? How do you think I got so many of my friends to vote for you?"

"Bruno jumped in to save me. He didn't even know how to swim." A sudden realization. "Mama, that's next week. I almost died twenty-eight years ago next week."

"A little before one o'clock, but you wasn't supposed to, Danny boy. *HaShem* had other plans for you, also for my Bruno, who probably still don't know from swimming, but anything for a friend or anybody. That was always my Bruno. Always my brilliant son, and also like his wonderful papa never so good in the common sense department." Mama Guy let out a heavy sigh. "Take a cookie."

"Don't eat them anymore, Mama."

She gave a look of horror that turned to fascination as I pulled a pink Sweet 'n Low packet from a jacket pocket and emptied half into the teacup.

She let me see her dismay, shrugged, and said, "So you really ain't going to eat any of my chocolate chip cookies that you and Bruno never could get enough?"

"My diet, Mama. You see—"

"Okay, okay!" She raised a hand between us. "Go on and hurt an old lady's feelings . . . and I had them nice and fresh for today, like I knew just in case someone comes visiting, you know?"

"I know, Mama. I know," I said, reaching for a cookie.

She waited until I took my first bite before smiling and nodding approval. "Such a good boy. Your own mama, may she rest in peace, she only knew, she'd be so proud from you."

"Did you know that Bruno wants to come home, Mama?"

The suddenness of the question seemed to startle Mama Guy.

Her chins sank into her chest as she arched her back. I noticed a slight hand tremor affect her teacup, almost causing it to spill.

She weighed the question, asked in an unsteady voice, "Meaning what, *come home?*"

"Bruno wants me to help get him back safely."

She settled her tea back on the table, took a cookie for herself, bit off a small piece, and started chewing it carefully. "Okay, so maybe a little surprised," she finally admitted.

By the time I'd finished telling her everything, we had moved from the living room to the kitchen, Mama at the sink rinsing the cups, saucers and silverware, me on a stool at the counter top, working another chocolate chip cookie, the cookie plate on my lap almost empty.

Mama Guy was saying, "—and so the government comes here once in a while, maybe more than you, but only to ask if I seen him, my Bruno. Have I heard lately from my dear, sweet boy? At least I can tell them the truth. No. I ain't got one word from him in years. He's also a fugitive from his mama." She looked across her shoulder and sent me a shopworn smile. "Not what I tell the chapter ladies, you know? For them I invent phone calls, letters on my birthday and cards on the holidays and that kind. They should only have sons as good as my Bruno."

"Some day, Mama. Some day you'll have him back."

She put the last of the dishware on the drying mat, toweled her hands dry, and crossed to me.

"Can you promise me that, Danny boy?"

Her eyes were wet and her voice had a tear in it, too.

"Not yet. For now, I can only hope. I'm doing what the government has asked me, what the government says Bruno wants, and I'm hoping that all goes well and—"

"A hope isn't a promise." She wiped at a tear. "It is something, though, isn't it?"

"Something, Mama."

"Bring him home safe to me, Danny boy. Please. Don't let my Bruno drown?"

"I promise, Mama," I said, finally, out of kindness, because it was something she had to hear, wondering at the same time if I also should tell Mama Guy she might have given me the answer to where I could find Bruno.

Next week.

If Bruno didn't find me first.

Rupert Bachman said, "How long did Marion stay with her?"

"Less than an hour, sir."

"And you got no sense she knows where her son is?"

"None at all, sir."

"Tell me again about this Captain Marvel business."

Bachman listened carefully.

He didn't know what to make of it beyond what the agent camped at Mama Guy's home was telling him, unless Duke Marion and Bruno Guy were supposed to meet up at some damned swimming hole, or—

—No, wait!

There was something familiar about—

"Tepper, have Washington scan the earlier tapes for anything she may have said to anyone about Captain Marvel. Meanwhile, patch me through to Stratton."

A minute later, he had Stratton on the line verifying Stratton was on Marion's tail.

"Goin' sweet as cider, sir."

"And you're still certain he doesn't know?"

"If he did and I wasn't catchin' signs, that would make him damned good, sir."

"He is damned good, Stratton, so you be sure to stay damned better."

"Yes, sir."

"Tell me again about this morning. Clement McAllister." Bachman listened intently. "But no internal infiltration?"

"Could only get so close, sir, because of the isolated location. Tried to penetrate, but distance worked against us with what gear we had on board."

"Upgrade first opportunity, Stratton. If something like this happens again, I want us to be adequately prepared."

"Yes, sir."

Bachman's next patch was to McAllister, on his private line.

McAllister personally answered after the first ring.

"Mr. McAllister, my name is Rupert Bachman, sir."

There was hesitation no longer than an eyelash before Clement McAllister said lightheartedly, "The Bug Man himself!"

Bachman would have instantly corrected anybody else, in a manner that let them know how he felt about the nickname pinned on him by that damned *Time* Magazine, but McAllister was too well connected where it mattered, in both Democrat and Republican party circles, to chance upsetting him.

"I hope I'm not calling at an inconvenient time," Bachman said.

"We going to talk about Duke Marion this afternoon?"

Bachman smiled to himself. It was true what they said about McAllister. He did know everything in the world worth knowing.

"Yes, sir."

"Then this time's as good as any, Rupert. You don't mind me calling you Rupert, do you, Rupert?"

"Of course not, Mr. McAllister."

"Clem," he responded. "Clem to my friends and Clem to you, Rupert."

Chapter 14

Another warm autumn afternoon. I was on a makeshift stage at the County Museum of Art sculpture garden, participating in ceremonies unveiling a new Rodin joining the dozens of Rodins donated a couple dozen years ago by some fabulously wealthy collector whose reach outdistanced the capacity of his own front yard, in a compromising squeeze between a pair of hefty blue-haired women in tea dresses and dated bonnets that might still be the rage in San Marino.

In the week since Van Zandt was murdered, the story had disappeared onto the back pages of the *Times* California section and was not even a footnote on the evening news.

No new message from Bruno.

From Rupert Bachman's secretary, whose deep pitched smoke-graveled voice duplicated the commanding tone of his boss, only his unassailable suggestion that all we could do was wait for the next contact.

R. D. Secunda, a deep pockets museum trustee who always reminded me of a supporting character in a Dürer engraving, was at the podium, gesturing elaborately at the tarpaulin-covered statue on the lawn, about five or six yards to the left of the stage and maybe fifteen feet tall, aiming his overwrought commentary at a sparse albeit enthusiastic crowd of eighty or ninety museum docent types spread over a dozen or so rows of folding chairs with a respectable clutter of TV news crews behind them.

". . . wonderful new Rodin sculpture adds further greatness to our world-honored and respected sculpture garden," Secunda was explaining. "This marble inspiration is très rare and, at last, it is here—courtesy of a selfless benefactor who puts his money where his marble is."

Secunda surveyed the audience to see who was enjoying the joke as much as he was and with a wink at the TV lenses, continued.

"Mr. Micah Delacroix as well as the Rodin stands as an enduring inspiration to our community as I expect we'll hear now, ladies and gentleman, in a last tribute, this time from our marvelous supervisor—"

Secunda aimed an eye and an arm in my direction, but—

—clearly, he had forgotten my name.

He angled to get a better look and relief soaked his face as he declared—

"Supervisor Daniel F. Marion."

Rising to polite applause, I reached into my pocket for the notes I'd scribbled on the way over, Abe Lincoln style, on the back of an envelope, having read and quickly rejected the reams of flowery dross prepared for me by Lewis Tully, using one of his fill-in-the-blank civic pride speeches.

It didn't amount to more than a few thank yous, testing whether this museum or any museum so endowed could survive without the generous spirit of people like Micah Delacroix.

Not much more than that.

More might have included the tidbit that Delacroix was under investigation for criminal fraud by the DA's office, and that might have ruined the tone of the celebration, certainly for Delacroix, a self-possessed sack of prime manure who was fidgeting in the seat of honor inside a two-day growth of beard and a two thousand dollar Armani.

I settled flat-footed at the podium, found my specs and geared them into place, pushing them tight against the top of my nose, acknowledged Secunda, and worked a smile at the crowd, giving it a few seconds more, so the leggy brunette standing off to one side of the audience could finish taking a Polaroid.

"First off, I want to thank Mr. Secunda and the members of his committee for inviting me to join with you here this morning . . ."

The brunette checked the photo and dropped it into the open-mouthed bag hanging from her shoulder.

Lined up another shot.

She was younger, better looking than any of the others here, and maybe that's why I was staring at her, or was it because she looked familiar?

"I don't know as much about art as so many of you here this morning," I said, "but I'm certain I love it as much as all of you, especially art that reveals the human spirit, by masters such as Dürer and Hogarth and, yes, Rodin . . ."

Familiar in a recent sort of way, but I couldn't place her out of context, the same way a supermarket checker or a waitress, no matter how many times you've seen her, becomes faceless somewhere else.

"Mr. Secunda tells me this new statue by Mr. Rodin is a real treasure, and I am truly pleased about that, for you and me and all of our city. So, Mr. Secunda, how about it? Time to get this show on the road?"

It wasn't exactly Abe Lincoln, but it got a favorable response from the crowd, including the brunette, who was on my face with a lip-licking intensity while the TV cameras turned to track Secunda as he glided over and hand-signaled three workmen in museum coveralls standing beside the sculpture, clutching pull ropes.

They tugged hard and the tarp fell aside, revealing the Rodin in its full glory, monumental and typical, reminiscent of his "Homage a Balzac" standing about twenty yards behind us.

More crowd applause.

The TV and still cameras catching the moment for the four, five, six, ten, and eleven o'clock newscasts and tomorrow's *Southern California Living* section.

And a man broke from his side aisle seat in the second row and sped toward the sculpture.

Surprising the crowd, then—

—freezing the crowd in disbelief—

—as he leaped onto the sculpture's base and began to hammer away with a sledgehammer.

His first blow, an overhead smash, cleaved the nose from the face of the Rodin. He gouged the head, then the neck, then an eyelid. His next smash snapped off a marble arm at the elbow. The arm hit the concrete pathway, causing fingers to snap away.

All this had taken less than half a minute.

The first murmurs and shouts had become a rock concert kind of pandemonium.

I had a clear view from the podium, but couldn't move off the stage fast enough to try to stop the screwball, unlike a couple men in the audience who'd foolishly jumped to their feet and were now charging him.

Screwball was not deterred by these aging, overweight and overwrought Good Citizens.

The first one to reach him, arms out for a grab, got the hammer in his head.

A geyser of blood erupted and he fell to the ground, critically wounded.

Two other Good Citizens wrestled with Screwball.

Both suffered a torrent of blows and crumpled to the concrete spurting blood like lawn sprinklers.

Jesus!

We were still in the first minute.

A matronly type who belonged at a charity bazaar, not here trying to control Screwball, caught the sledgehammer on her jaw, her shoulder, her head. Her sunglasses flew off and she sank to the ground in a scream.

Damn that nut case!

I yanked my .45 from the belt holster saddled at the small of my back and got off a shot without aiming.

The shot missed, but it slowed down Screwball for a fraction of a second.

His head snapped in my direction, his bug-eyes whirling like pinwheels. He wagged the hammer at me, almost as if to signal *The next one's for you!*

As I took two-handed aim—

—a woman shouted, "Kill him, Duke! Waste the son of a bitch!"—

—distracting me.

Cuh-rack!

The shot sailed harmlessly past Screwball.

A peripheral glance told me the shout had come from the brunette toting the Polaroid camera, who had moved closer to the stage.

I aimed and fired again.

Cuh-rack!

My shot caught Screwball in the arm as he brought down the hammer one more time on the Rodin.

The hammer sailed from his grip.

Screwball jumped from the statue and started running, making a path across an open expanse of grass between me and a gate exit.

I took aim and fired.

Cuh-rack!

I caught him in the leg.

He dropped and an instant later was smothered under a thousand pounds of security guards.

I drew a breath of satisfaction and relief, threw the safety, and watched as the camera guys elbowed each other for the best sightlines. I wondered if and how they really were different from the *paparazzi* who hunted a princess to her death.

"You should have killed the bastard."

The brunette with the Polaroid talking at me.

Approaching.

Maneuvering her lithe body like all the hinges were busted, although not nearly as well as she was. Watermelon breasts solid inside a long-sleeved, V-necked ivory-colored cashmere pullover that couldn't suppress hard nipples as big as six inch nails. No waist. Flat belly, long legs, a tight ass trapped inside tighter jeans that could just as easily have been painted on. Gleaming black boots with heels that added three inches to her height, maybe five-nine or five-ten barefoot. Magic brown eyes. Her brown hair falling loosely down her back. Her perfectly aligned teeth protruding a bit under a slight overbite. Barely any makeup and kid freckles on a lush face with laugh lines and a few other marks that made me put her in her early thirties.

Looking up at me from just below the podium.

Hands on the lip and leaning enough to make certain I didn't miss her breasts.

And, still looking familiar.

A rhyme without a reason.

"I know you, don't I?" I said, my chest still rising and falling from the rush that came with dropping Screwball. Or, was it because of her?

She ignored the question.

"I suppose you're fucking-A good enough to have gotten off a kill shot at that distance."

"Fucking-A," I said.

"I already knew. Bruno said so."

"Bruno?" I gripped the edge of the podium and stared harder into eyes that were trapping mine with a look that neither promised nor delivered anything.

"And you know Bruno, Duke. Bruno never lies."

"Who the hell are you? What do you know about Bruno?"

She pulled something from her shoulder bag and held it up for me to take.

"Go on," she said, a smile sliding up one side of her face, adding shape to a perfectly formed high-rise cheek. "It won't bite you."

I came around the podium and squatted, took it from her.

A photograph, but not one of her Polaroids.

This was an old photo, when you still had to get your negatives developed at a drug store and crinkle-edged prints came back in days, not sixty minutes.

Two young men.

Bruno Guy and Duke Marion.

An inscription:

Duke—Keep 'em flying. Bruno.

In black fountain pen ink, just like the other photo.

Bruno had developed a penchant for fountain pens and what he called "real" ink in grammar school, thereafter forever disdaining ballpoints.

The woman called up to me, joyously, "Catch you next time, Duke. I owe you one . . . . Shazam!"

"Hey! Wait!"

I rose quickly, but it was too late to jump from the stage and give chase.

In the last minute, the media had finished for now with Screwball and was making a concerted rush at me, their tape recorders and TV cameras targeting my face as a tossed salad of voices scrambled one question into the next:

"Why'dja shoot, Duke?"

"Didn't trust those security guards, Duke?"

"Afraid you might endanger innocent lives with your gunshots, Supervisor Marion?"

"Pull out the weapon, Supervisor? Need a shot of you with the weapon!"

Screw them all!

I sidestepped left, then right, looking for a jumping off point, struggling to keep the brunette sighted.

She was past the rows of chairs, running with the ease of a marathon racer.

She stopped for an instant.

Turned and smiled at me.

Fired an imaginary gun at me.

Started running again.

Past a Rodin.

Another Rodin.

A Renoir.

A David Smith.

And, half-shadowed by an immense, Surrealistic Henry Moore bronze, one of Rupert Bachman's boys in dark glasses and a Brooks Brother suit, his head bent, hand cupped against his face, mouth chattering into a cell phone.

★ ★ ★ ★ ★

Stella Ivers moved swiftly through the gated museum exit.

She hurried across the street with a disregard for any traffic, used to stopping traffic, and didn't even hesitate at the sound of screeching brakes.

She turned north and, at the corner, made another left.

The white Mercedes was parked in a two-hour zone and the red flag on the meter was showing, but no ticket.

She smiled at her good fortune, sent a laugh into the light breeze as she unlocked the door and slid behind the wheel.

Checked her watch, smiled at the time, and turned the ignition key.

Thought again, *Catch you next time, Duke,* while she checked for traffic before moving the Mercedes away from the curb and into an eastbound lane.

Chapter 15

I called Anny from the car to let her know what had happened, then Rita with the same advisory and to explain what I needed her to do. She didn't question the request, she never did, and she had answers for me by the time I'd slipped through the private door to my office, delivering them before I finished crossing over to my desk and slumped into the high back, physical and mental exhaustion finally racing ahead of my adrenaline.

"All affirmative," she reported from her desk, holding up her logbook, "and all but one of them with the condition you predicted."

"Exclusive interview with me."

"Exclusive interview with you."

"What did you tell them?"

"What do you think?" she said, sharply. Something was bothering her. "What you told me to tell them!" Like I had accused her of incompetence. "I told them 'no deal.' How you already said all the No Comments and Go Screw Yourselves you were going to say at the museum. The lone exception was—"

"Jack Lipton."

"Jack Lipton." Rita put more attitude on her face. "He said give it an hour before you head on over. His crew won't be back much before that. They went straight from the museum to a star planting on Hollywood Boulevard in front of Frederick's."

"Anybody who matters for a change?"

She told me who.

"I have to admit she's always looked good in their see-through lingerie or less, but a star?" I said, trying to pry a smile out of her. "What did she ever do to deserve a star."

"Have someone cough up the fifteen thousand that it takes nowadays," she replied harshly. "And whatever she did to get that kind of money . . ." She let the thought trail off.

"That's all, fifteen thousand? At that price, maybe I'll just go and order up a star for you, Rita."

She refused to acknowledge I was teasing, shot me down with a look that said *Lay off,* and swiveled away, so that I was left staring at her back.

Something definitely wrong.

"Was it something I said, Rita?" I made it sound like a joke, but she knew better.

She inclined a hand left and right.

Choked on some broken words.

I moved to her desk, where I could look at her.

She tried to hide from my inspection, but it was too late.

Her face was tear-stained.

I started to apologize, figuring maybe she was overreacting to the museum crisis and a picture of Screwball hammering me into a coma the way he had three of the people who'd try to stop him.

Her head and hands signaled otherwise and I realized how stupidly self-important I must have sounded.

Rita removed her oversized frames and placed them on top of a stack of files on her desk. Reached for a Kleenex from the box she kept in her lower drawer. Wiped her eyes.

They had been clear and fresh with the new day when I left her a few hours ago. Now they were red-rimmed. This wasn't the only cry she'd had.

I challenged her with the observation.

She didn't deny it.

She looked up at me like a wounded animal, a whimper or two away from a total breakdown.

And—with a mental snap of the fingers—I knew what this had to be about.

I said, "Benny's ex strikes again?"

She moved a hand over her mouth, not trusting herself to speak, and nodded.

Benny was Rita's husband of seven months, after a year-long courtship that had started in the technological version of a singles bar, an America Online chat room.

Their computer-inspired relationship only came to light after the marriage was revealed, taking by surprise most of her coworkers and the few friends workaholics ever seem to have time for.

This private, unprepossessing, plain-featured woman in her mid-forties, always hiding behind a gruff pose and trenchant observation, had surprised everyone who had figured her for the eternal spinster—and that was just about everyone—when she revealed their computer-inspired relationship and elopement to Las Vegas.

Over a three-day holiday weekend, Rita explained, because she didn't want me running the office without her presence for a day and making an unholy mess of things.

She had kept her maiden name as a symbol that marriage had not entirely robbed her of her independent nature, but otherwise had quickly and enthusiastically taken on all the trappings of devoted wife and mother to Benny's eleven-year old son, Coop.

Benny's ex-wife had dumped Coop on their doorstep when she heard about the wedding and gone on a month-long, cross-country bender with a trucker she'd picked up in one of the bars on her nightly circuit.

She called Rita four and five times a day, at home and at the office, screaming threats and swearing revenge.

Rita shared that ugly story with me only after the ex took her next swing, getting the court order that restored Coop to her custody.

I helped her get the best lawyer around for these kinds of cases, Molly Deering, who took it on as a *pro bono* favor, and also stepped up as a character witness on the day of the hearing.

The odds as usual favored the natural mother, even here where she was shown to be a chronic drunk, a sometimes hooker, and a likely threat to the safety and well-being of her son.

Old Judge Ernie Rappoport, "Right Wing" Rappoport, was moved to rule by the ex's tearful allegation under oath that Rita was a home wrecker who slept with Benny for at least a year before the couple divorced, although, in fact, Rita and Benny hadn't found each other on America Online until about a year after Benny's divorce was final.

"What has she done this time, Rita? Tell me."

"She's demanding an increase in her alimony and child support," Rita finally volunteered, chiseling each word from granite. "We were served this morning."

"Did you call Molly Deering?"

"Chief, she only wants the money to support her habits and this actor twenty-something years her junior we hear is living off her. Is that fair? Not to Benny and me, I mean. I mean about Coop?"

"I said, 'Did you call Molly Deering?' Does Molly know about this?"

"Coop calls us all the time, you know? Crying. Crying because he hates it there, hates his mother, hates the creep who's screwing her for room and board. Coop says he misses us, wants to come home where he belongs and—"

"Rita, answer my question, damn it."

She reached for another Kleenex.

"It wouldn't be fair, Chief. We couldn't afford Miss Deering the last time and—"

"I did not ask you if you could afford her, Rita. I asked you if you called her."

Her head shook spasmodically left and right.

"I want you to get Molly on the phone for me before I go to the Board meeting, whatever's left of it. If you can't reach her, leave my private beeper number."

"Stay away from the Boardroom," Rita said, abruptly, all business again.

"Meaning what?"

She motioned me to wait a minute while she caught her breath and popped the tissue in the wastebasket.

"Pearce Dickson passed the word through Lewis a little before you came in. He says it's chaos out there. Citizens group came marching in demanding you quit or face a recall, saying you're a danger and a menace to decent people because of the business with Powell and Van Zandt and, now, at the museum today. He says there's no percentage in showing your face and playing into a scene he's certain Chief Crescent is behind."

"When was the last time I ran away from a fight?"

"This time, Chief."

Her tone defied me to disagree.

I took a deep breath and shot it into space.

"Get me Molly Deering," I said, and started back for my desk.

"I truly don't think you should. You really don't—"

"This one you can't argue me out of, Rita."

★ ★ ★ ★ ★

A short time later, Jack Lipton was telling me, "We already got two minutes on the air, satellite feed from the truck, so we wouldn't have been editing this B-roll shit until after the sports montage, but if she was at the unveiling, Duke, she's bound to be in there someplace."

Jack was the assignment editor at *Cable News Extra*. He owed me one for a few leads I slipped him while I was still on the force, stuff that actually needed some media prodding if I was to ever score the busts I wanted. The breaks had led to Jack's promotion and he'd often said a payback was mine on request.

"I appreciate this, Jack," I said.

Images popped onto a bank of eight TV monitors in Jack's cramped editing bay, where we sat at the console alongside an editor working a computer keyboard and enough buttons and levers to launch a space shuttle.

The stage.

Speakers at the podium.

Sleazy Micah Delacroix giving the crowd a politician's wave.

R. D. Secunda oozing sincerity.

Duke Marion playing at supervisor, looking uncomfortable.

Crowd shots.

The attack on the Rodin sculpture.

Pandemonium.

Duke Marion taking serious aim at the Screwball, looking comfortable.

I gave the passing images intense concentration, most especially the crowd shots. Jack ran one cigarette after the next—a convincing argument against second-hand smoke—and sometimes called instructions to the editor.

Lower the sound level.

Slow down the visual.

Back up and give the supervisor another look at that crowd overview.

The editor did as he was told, occasionally stifling a yawn behind his fist, followed by a swallow from the coffee mug at his elbow and mumbles about the channel's cheapskate policy on overtime, which Jack ignored.

Finally—

"Jack, there, the third monitor over from the left!"

"Chick, you heard the man."

Chick froze the image.

A crowd scene.

He punched some keys and sent the visual into slow reverse.

"There, way back there," I said. "Back of the seats, near the tree."

"I can bring it up, you like," Chick said.

"Yeah, please."

Chick hid another yawn, then typed out instructions to the computer.

"The pretty one standing with the Polaroid camera."

"Got her," Chick said, and the image froze. "Some babe. Nice titsiks." The most alert and interested he'd been since I got here. "She can sit on my face anytime she likes."

"Jack, you think you could break out a photo for me?"

"No problem, Duke. Compliments of management. It'll take maybe a couple of hours?"

"I'll send someone over to pick it up, probably Lewis Tully."

"Works for me."

"I appreciate this, Jack."

He looked away, like something was bothering him, then turned a contrite face back.

"Schneider knows how we're friends and didn't want me

saying anything," Jack said, "but I don't feel right doing that." He was referring to the station's general manager. "Schneider takes the whip to you in his editorial tonight." He turned over a hand to signal his dismay and studied me for a reaction.

I shrugged. "Schneider's not the first and we both know he won't be the last. What took him so long?"

"Honestly? I got Schneider to look the other way over Edwin O. Powell's death at the Nell Fontanne dinner, but he thinks you were far too fast on the draw today. He's on the museum's board of trustees. Somebody called up screaming. I worked on his head as long as I could, but that's like trying to crack open a coconut using a can opener."

"I don't suppose Schneider mentioned who it was that called up screaming. Maybe someone wearing a badge and a blue uniform?"

"I asked, but he wasn't telling?"

"Did he tell you why his editorial won't also blame me for a dead man at the Board of Supervisors?"

Jack shook his head. "Fuck. Didn't I mention that? It will."

The memorial park rose majestically above the city of Glendale, the highest point on the highest hill topped with a magnificent Hollywood Sign of a cross that Stella Ivers used as a guide after exiting the Golden State on Los Feliz Boulevard.

She traveled east and, where the boulevard dead-ended— *How appropriate*, Stella thought—she steered the Mercedes through the impressive archway and up a winding road to the main building, found tree-shaded parking in the visitors' lot, and headed for the building armed with an elaborate bouquet of flowers.

Robert S. Levinson

Stella announced herself to a receptionist and was shortly escorted to an immense building out of early Greece by a buoyant tour guide in a royal purple and gold uniform with silver epaulets, who seemed like he'd be equally at home guiding tourists past all the movie star hand and footprints into the make-believe majesty of Grauman's Chinese Theater.

As they made the steep climb, the guide wondered in a quietly impish manner and the slightest trace of an Irish accent, "Did you notice everyone's astonishment when you pulled out the original receipt. The original, mind you, after all these years. Imagine."

"Imagine," Stella said, to be polite, wishing he would shut up.

She liked small talk only slightly less than the people who made it, usually hoping to strike a vein of information they could add to their next summaries of meaningless pap.

"We thought it a mystery never to be solved," he said, "and that includes the likes of me. But here you are, a blessed saint's sight lovelier than Howard Hughes, who was a favorite choice of most."

"Yeah."

"Relatives of yours, I suppose?"

Stella ignored the question.

He seemed to be getting her message, for his elastic smile diminished, then disappeared entirely.

They passed inside the building, under an arch whose chiseled marble sign overhead identified it as "The Great Sanctuary."

"The crypt, suppose you already know it was built to specifications and never ever occupied. Until this week part of a glorious puzzle lasting a quarter of a century. People taking our tours? Some actually weep upon hearing the tale."

150

He stopped and introduced her to the massive crypt of multicolored marble with a slight bow and a generous sweep of an arm. An imposing wrought-iron gate protected an inner courtyard facing a marble wall from intruders.

Stella studied the tomb while the guide unlocked the gate and pushed it open. Not so much as a squeak. The crypt was being looked after.

Before stepping inside, she drank in the marble legend carved in stone:

FOREVER IN LOVE,
FOREVER IN LIFE, FOREVER AFTER.

She knew the guide was studying her and wondered if he saw the melancholy hiding inside her tight-lipped smile as she knelt in front of one of the two marble doors in the wall and, after confirming the engraved plaque—

ARCHIE PRATT

—placed the bouquet of flowers.

He started to speak: "I must confess, this is becoming quite emotional for me. You see, you are the first person—"

Stella quieted him with a look that carried its own snarl.

Rose.

Moved to the door on the right side of the wall, where the plaque read—

ESTELLE RITOLA

—and reflected quietly.

The guide began explaining in an almost reverential voice, "The marble, you see, was imported from Spain, Italy,

France. It came here from many of the same quarries that Michelangelo himself specified . . .”

Stella stepped back.

“All in all, the cost exceeded fifty thousand dollars. No mean feat in those days, a quarter century ago. Three times that today. Maybe four.”

She removed the Polaroid camera and took aim.

A small dot of light bounced off the marble as Stella snapped the shutter.

The print whirred out of the Polaroid and she dropped it into her handbag.

Her work done, she turned on her heel, rushed from the crypt and started down the corridor, her steps feeding an echo loud enough (she thought, as the smile angled up her face) to wake the dead.

The guide locked the gate, tested it, then skip-stepped to catch up to her.

“If it’s not presumptive of me, miss,” he said, “may I wonder about the gentlemen newly laid to rest here?”

Stella ignored him and picked up the pace, keeping her eyes straight ahead.

His labored breathing joined the echoes and made for a curiously eerie symphony of sound.

He spoke anxiously to her back: “I don’t suppose you’d consider sharing your secret with me, miss? I’d be eternally grateful. Archie Pratt? Who he was and the lady, too, if you’re knowing that as well? Estelle Ritola?”

Stella glanced over her shoulder and, after a moment’s hesitation, gave the guide a sweet look and urged, “Go blow yourself!”

The guide stopped at the head of the stairs and watched her sail down, hands on his knees, chin touching clouds, angling for breath.

Neither had noticed Rupert Bachman, who'd followed them out of the building and now was paused invisibly behind the guide, while he carefully inched a cigarette into his ivory holder.

Chapter 16

I finally said, "You're looking great, Molly."

"Thank you. You, too."

Molly Deering smiled.

I smiled.

"How long has it been? Forever?"

"Forever. Yes. Or an eternity, whichever is longer?"

"A long time."

"Long time."

Long pause.

Two people struggling with small talk.

"We could have left it at the thank you on the phone," I said.

"Except I wanted to see you and since here you are— maybe you wanted to see me."

"Here" was the Derby on Los Feliz near Vermont, the bar where we usually met, away from downtown, close to Molly's place, an easy hop back onto the freeway for me in the long-long ago, when our meetings were rendezvous full of passions and pitfalls and words that slashed through the inanities to the heart of two desperate people who thought they were in love, in one of the wall booths where a drawn curtain shuts out the world.

"I had to be in your neighborhood, so I figured—"

"You didn't answer my question, Duke."

"Should I lie, Molly?"

"If it makes it easier for you."

I shook my head. "When I called to thank you for taking on Rita again, heard your voice, I realized how long it had been, wondered if you had changed, how you looked. It made accepting your invitation easy."

"If I hadn't, would you have suggested it?"

"I don't think so."

"You don't think so, but are you sure?"

"Is this a cross-examination? Am I under oath?"

"Are you sure?"

"I'm here, so what difference does it make, and you do really look great, by the way."

Molly did, always, not just to me, although she never intentionally drew attention to herself.

She shunned makeup, except for a dab of lip gloss matching her natural red hair, which she kept short, and generally packaged herself in one of those pin-striped power suits women lawyers like to wear, but in her case it was impossible to suppress the sex appeal oozing from her like sap from a maple tree, yet Molly seemed genuinely unaware of her impact on men.

She was always fifteen or twenty pounds overweight, a family curse no amount of dieting would overcome, but naked she was nevertheless a thing of beauty. Alabaster skin as delicious to the eye as to the touch. Breasts that demanded fondling. A look that was no more irresistible in bed than any glance she lavished on a judge or jury.

I was always being introduced to her at testimonial dinners or politically-correct fund-raisers for the charity of the month, so often that it became our running gag, but it didn't get beyond the good humor until a golf tournament to raise bucks for the families of LAPD cops who buy it in the line of duty.

She was on the rebound from a three-year live-in with a

criminal lawyer who, it turns out, was trading services with call girls and street hookers who comprised a large percentage of his clientele.

I was going through my own cop crisis, the kind that's too common and too often ends in divorce or with a mouthful of gun barrel, some premature male menopause, and blaming Anny for miseries of my own making.

We sort of fell into each other. Mutual need. While it lasted. Three months. Four, maybe. Actually, three months and eleven days. Until I relocated my sanity and moved back home.

Molly, who had predicted often the day would come, was able to take the news philosophically and the lovers parted friends. We still bumped into one another at the occasional public event—she always had a new boyfriend to introduce—but the last one had been about a year and a half ago and, except for sending Rita to her, Molly and I had lost touch.

We talked a little more about Rita and Benny.

She said, "They really have their hands full with that ex of his. She's a certified tramp with low expectations and drug highs. I worry for the boy if we don't get him out and away from her."

I reached over and put a hand on hers.

"You will, if anyone can. You're the best, Molly."

"Or the first runner-up," she said, her hooded green eyes rooting into mine. She topped my hand with her other hand and said, "I also worry for you, Duke. This business I've been reading about and seeing on TV. That fuckface Paul Crescent. He just won't let go or let up, will he?"

"That's why they're called vendettas."

"And nothing you can do about it?"

I told her about Rupert Bachman and Clem McAllister.

Molly drew a heavy breath and blew it at the curtain. Retrieved her hands, laced her fingers and, elbows on the table, hammered thoughtfully on her mouth for a moment.

"Since the Bug Man can't seem to stop him, why not let McAllister do it for you?"

"If I wanted to owe anyone, it wouldn't be him."

"But you're leaning his way anyway on the MacMurray proposal, so let him think whatever he wants. *Quid pro quo.*"

"And what do I do the next time?"

"Who says there'd be a next time?"

"With people like McAllister there's always a next time."

"And people like me?"

"See the kind of problems a *first* time can create?" I smiled at her.

She looked away from me and for a minute the booth grew oppressively quiet. When she turned back, a smile was fixed on her perfectly shaped oval face, an inch off center, and I suppressed an urge to reach over and make the adjustment.

She said, "I saw you on television, at the dinner for Nell Fontanne. She was one of your favorites, wasn't she?"

"Yes."

"I remember. Your wife, too. She's beautiful."

"Thank you. I won't tell her you said so."

Molly smiled into her coffee cup. "What will she say when she hears we were together?"

"Are you going to tell her?"

"Aren't you?"

I shrugged.

"Tell her, Duke. Lying never came easy to you, and if you try she'll only guess."

"You always were Miss Practical. Miss Common Sense."

"Miss Fucking Miss You Like Crazy." Her eyes misted. "But you know that."

"I thought we—"

"Sometimes I wake up in the middle of the night, my hand fondling my latest fling and catch myself wishing it were you, so bundle up your thoughts, trash them, and think again. I don't know if I'll ever get over you."

"You have to try harder."

"The story of my life, honey. The story of my life."

I looked at my watch.

"I know, I know," she said. "Go ahead. I don't want to make you late for wherever it is you're going that isn't back to my place."

I left Molly after she gave me a kiss on the cheek that she managed to move to her lips, and told the server she wanted to trade him a Chivas rocks for her coffee cup.

Figured I'd be at Barnsdall Park in five minutes.

Tipped the parking kid after checking out the Porsche.

Climbed in wondering if Bruno would be there, too.

Twenty-eight years ago to the day since Captain Marvel saved his best friend from drowning.

Trying, Mama Guy, trying.

Not even remotely expecting the surprise that awaited me in Barnsdall Park.

Chapter 17

Hollyhock House has always looked to me more like a Mayan tomb than the pre-Columbian home the legendary Frank Lloyd Wright designed and built over a three-year period in the late teens for Aline Barnsdall, one of the city's most esteemed and generous benefactors.

Her residence was the centerpiece of a sprawling private estate that rose above the intersection of Hollywood and Vermont, a popular showplace for the moneyed elite who never tired of finding new ways to look down their noses at everyone else, so my socialist leaning best friend, Bruno Guy, used to lecture me whenever we went poking around there as kids.

By then the estate had become a Barnsdall Park that included an art museum and an arts and crafts center for children, with Hollyhock House a Mecca for architects and art prowlers who took the regularly-scheduled guided tours for the opportunity to inspect and absorb Wright's genius.

After a long period of decline that coincided with the neighborhood's fall from grace, the landmark was restored to its original brilliance, enough to pretend away the homeless unfortunates and outright bums who found nightly shelter in various brush areas off the winding road up from the boulevard.

I traveled it now, after passing ground level acres of dirt and the heavy equipment still camped there after the city's long and costly struggle to construct an underground rail system that includes a station across the way.

The quarter moon gave the sky an eerie quality matched by the quiet rush of night sounds as I parked and locked the Porsche in the slot nearest the locked security gate.

I intended to track the fence down slope about fifty yards to the jump-over point Bruno and I had used again and again, except—

—the gate wasn't locked.

It hung half open, a padlock hanging from the chain link.

A security foul-up or—

—somebody else here late and illegal?

Still here?

I proceeded cautiously along the dimly lit concrete trail to the gate surrounding Hollyhock House.

Also unlocked.

I smiled at the possibility of *Who* crowding other thoughts from my head.

The front door.

I tried the handle.

Locked.

A red security dot blinking ominously. I wondered if I had already walked past a laser beam or triggered some other type of security device that would have cops racing here any minute.

I waited anxiously for a few moments, for the sound of wailing sirens, although a silent alarm, a Code Two, was the more likely call.

Nothing, only coyotes wailing in the distance.

Dogs taking up the call.

A slight, drifting odor of skunk in the welcome breeze of another pleasant moon-fed evening.

Night rumblings that'd dissolve by sunrise into the sounds of a city awakening.

And I studied the door and called, "Shazam!"

Shouted, "Shazam!"

Challenged, "Shazam!"

And got nothing back.

Until—

—a click and a burst of flame to my right, barely within my vision.

I turned in that direction and opened my mouth to call Bruno's name and—

—caught myself staring at Rupert Bachman.

"Shazam, Duke?"

My face turned to stone.

Bachman finished lighting his cigarette and slipped the pearl-plated lighter into a jacket pocket.

"Don't say it," he suggested, his voice as slippery as his smile. "You can imagine how often I've heard it already: *Mr. Bachman, please don't smoke . . . Mr. Bachman, to start up again after so many years . . . ? I hope you don't think that you're immune to cancer, Mr. Bachman.*" He made his arms a pair of wings, palms up. "What's a man to do? Plain and simple, I missed the bloody things and am quite prepared to take my chances."

"What the hell are you doing here, Mr. Bachman?"

A laugh jumped from the base of his throat; more like a cackle. "I thought I would venture by to ask you the exact same question? Only—I got here first." He held up a set of keys for me to see and advanced on the door. "Shall we go in-side?"

He led the way like a soldier on point who already knew the terrain, augmenting the ghostly light that broke through drawn curtains with a pen light and matter-of-factly sharing points of Hollyhock House's history, like a student who had crammed for orals and was intent on getting it all out before a memory lapse.

"You sound like quite the expert on the subject of this place," I conceded as we took a bathroom passage connecting one starkly furnished bedroom to another.

He nodded curtly, but otherwise tried not to appear pleased, as if my compliment might cost him some advantage.

"And you, Duke?"

I shook my head. "This is my first time inside."

Bachman feigned surprise.

Waited a beat or two before making what he meant to sound like a naïve inquiry.

"Your best friend, Bruno? He has been into Hollyhock House, correct?" He gave me a look that said he already knew the answer. "Not with you?"

I answered with innocent history of my own, hoping it would help me see where Bachman was trying to lead me. "We often wandered up here, but we never got inside."

Bachman glided his penlight from a simple cherrywood vanity chest at the foot of the small bed frame to one of the nightstands.

He said, "Both items the originals, painstakingly handmade by old world master craftsmen to Frank Lloyd Wright's exacting specifications. So, never, you say. Amazing."

"You know the comic book hero, Captain Marvel?"

He shook his head. "Duke, the only heroes I know are presidents, premiers, and prime ministers. Real presidents. Real premiers. Real prime ministers. I also know real terrorists and traitors and would-be despots, dictators, and tyrants." His face tilted and his right eyebrow inched up.

Not knowing what Bachman expected to hear, I continued

with my own piece of Hollyhock House lore: "Bruno and I were positive the old man who gave Captain Marvel his super powers lived at Hollyhock House. We'd stand outside those gates, hoping to get through to him by calling out the secret word he gave Billy Batson, that Billy spoke when he needed to turn into Captain Marvel. Or Captain Marvel spoke to turn into Billy again."

"*Shazam!*"

"Right. *Shazam!*"

"Quaint."

"Sometimes we jumped the fence, but we never could get inside past the front door. Wright knew how to build a house that kept out anyone who didn't belong."

"All of Wright's roofs tended to leak during a heavy rain."

"Nobody's perfect," I said, grinning. Bachman's look said he had other ideas. "Years afterward, I had plenty of opportunities to visit, to take the tour, but I didn't. It didn't seem right—"

"Making it inside Hollyhock House alone? Without your best friend Bruno Guy?"

Questions spoken like two answers Bachman needed to win the prize.

I said, "This tour has been informative, even educational, but don't you think it's time to tell me what your real game is? What you're doing here?"

Bachman angled back his head, chin up, and studied me over the sharp bridge of his nose, through eyes that had shrunk to impenetrable slits.

"The picture Gustav Van Zandt passed to you during your Board of Supervisors meeting—it did say *Shazam!*, didn't it, Duke?"

I don't know what amused him most, his question or the startled look on my face.

Smug, smart-ass son of a bitch.

"I don't recall showing you that picture or telling you—"

"You might be meeting Bruno Guy here tonight? Were you meeting Bruno Guy here tonight? Were you, Duke?"

"Were you following me, Mr. Bachman?"

Bachman took aim and fired a finger gun at me.

"*Shazam!* Duke."

The gesture instantly recalled a memory of the woman at the museum sculpture garden who had said "Shazam!" and made me even more certain than I was that he had intended to meet me here tonight.

Bruno, not Bachman.

On an anniversary night.

On this date twenty-eight years ago, Bruno and I had arrived home from camp and scrambled through dinners, then sneaked off to Hollyhock House, hoping to connect with the old man and thank him for letting Bruno turn into Captain Marvel and know how to swim long enough to save a drowning boy.

"Don't tell me, let me guess," Bachman said. "Tonight, a commemoration of some type." He held a palm to his forehead, shut his eyes. "I see water. A young boy in over his head, struggling to reach the surface. Why, Duke, he looks like you might have looked as a boy."

"How did you know?"

He opened his eyes and said merrily, "There's a reason why they're called secrets, Duke."

The question deserved the answer.

He was having me tailed.

Bugged, probably.

"I'll have to be more careful," I said.

"Be anything you choose, but understand something," he said, darkly, "This stupid game of cat and mouse aside, I aim to have your friend Bruno Guy no matter what, Duke. With or, if necessary, without your assistance."

Maybe it was because of the way Bachman stood or the way the words spilled out. I snapped. "Bachman, just being this close to you makes me feel like a rock. I have better things to do with my life than help you crawl out from under—"

"Help me? Me?" A repellant laugh. "I have told you this before, Duke—this is a task you are doing for your country. Not for me or for your friend Bruno Guy. For your country. Preventing death and destruction from bombs set off by un-holy men committing unconscionable acts. And all else— God. Mom. Apple Pie—all else must wait in line."

"Then, damn it, help me a little. Answer me. Tell me about the photograph. About Gustav Van Zandt."

It was a standoff.

For about a minute.

Until he turned up his palms.

Fumbled for his cigarette holder as he spoke.

Found his cigarette pack; a blue and white wrapper I didn't recognize.

Fumbled for a fresh smoke.

"Gustav Van Zandt was an intermediary. Bruno trusted his revolutionary running mate to make contact with us and through us to get to you. He did. Then somebody got to Van Zandt." Bachman zapped the mouth end of the cigarette holder across his throat. "And, so, here we are, Duke, pegs back at square one. Waiting for Bruno?"

"Who got to Van Zandt?"

Bachman shrugged.

"That's not for us, Duke, not our business. You are not a cop anymore and I never concern myself with local police matters. It seems our mutual need now is to determine who replaces Gustav Van Zandt and leads us to your friend. Can you believe it? A blood-stained upstart like that dreadful quasi-human being dies in the service of the country he swore to destroy." Ugly laughter again. "Tell me. Is there possibly any treasonous blood in *your* background?"

My look cut off his head.

"Joking, Duke, merely joking. I read all the files before coming into this matter, of course. I was damned impressed. You certainly proved your patriotic mettle on more than one occasion. Suffice it to say, you and Bruno make strange, strange bedfellows. He got right in with those ranting, self-proclaimed liberators. Idiot revolutionaries. Migraine militias we call them, for the obvious reason. They're a persistent headache to us. First he followed, then Bruno led. Soon, Bruno learned he was smarter than all of them combined, that he could rant a damned sight louder."

We were back at the main entrance.

Bachman pointed me out in front of him, locked and gave the door a shake, drank a load of night air before jamming the loaded ivory holder between his back molars and lighting up. He took a hard drag and pushed it into the air, crisper than when I'd arrived.

I wondered to myself if I was hearing the same howling coyote I'd heard earlier.

"Because of that, Bruno can now walk away free, knowing what he knows and knowing we need to know it all—more than we need to try Bruno Guy and send him to prison for the rest of his despicable life. Damn shame, that part, Duke. Bruno Guy is like all those commie bastards—"

"Haven't you heard, Mr. Bachman? The Cold War ended a lot of years ago, and so did Mother Russia. Besides, Bruno is no *commie*, never was."

If he heard me, he chose not to show it.

He said, "And the redneck warriors and mad bombers,

who know every angle and loophole. Communism does not work for you anymore, you move on to something else." We had reached the outer fence. "Don't worry about the gate. Someone will come along to lock up after us."

I said, "For as long as I have known him, Bruno Guy has only fought for what he believed in. But never once *against* his country."

"A finite distinction. A friend's excuse. He murdered and caused other innocents to be murdered. The record speaks for itself and far more eloquently than you, my friend. You are living in your childhood. The man became unworthy of you a long time ago."

"The press convicted him, not the courts. Do your files show that, Bachman?"

Bachman's expression hardened and he stepped up to me, pushing his face into mine. He gave me the kind of look a teacher reserves for slow students.

"Maybe I should reread the files on you, Duke," he said, struggling to control his anger.

"Do that. While you're at it, the Constitution of the United States of America."

"Yes," he spit back. "And the Bill of Rights. They're my bibles, Duke. I worship good government."

"Think about freedom sometime."

Bachman snapped around on his heels and strutted down the path, heading for the dark-colored Ford parked near my Porsche with its motor running.

One of his Brooks Brothers stepped out and around and opened the rear door for him.

Bachman turned and called to me. "Oh, and Duke! The woman that you met with earlier. The attorney. Molly Deering? She's quite the looker, Duke." He weighed a pair of invisible breasts. "My sincere compliments." He saluted and ducked inside the car, before I could tell the smug bastard what I thought.

The Ford made a fast half U out of the parking space and was out of sight by the time I reached my Porsche, not bothering to do anything about the padlock on the park gate.

A raggedy tramp was half-hidden against a shade tree ten or fifteen feet away, alongside a shopping cart loaded to the brim with a life he had lost somewhere.

What society allows to happen to its own is the biggest crime of all, I thought, feeling like Bruno's surrogate.

He'd expressed that sentiment on more than one occasion over the early years, before he became a fugitive.

Sometimes I agreed, to avoid a debate that could rage for hours.

Sometimes I didn't, arguing that people do it to themselves.

Bruno always responded the same way:

"If society is not part of the problem, grant me it's also not part of the solution."

"So, work inside the system to change it."

"No, Danny boy. Work outside the system to change the system. All follows."

Impulsively, I pulled a five from my wallet and started for the tramp, who bound to his feet, maybe misunderstanding my intention, taking me for security, and fled on legs as thin as rails but surprisingly swift, his pants half-staffed and showing a flash of crack, sending out a strange hooting sound that stirred other park animals into noisy response.

I left the bill sticking out from the dog-eared paperback on top of the shopping cart, *Paradise Lost,* and headed back to the car wondering if the tramp had to read the truth to understand it.

★ ★ ★ ★ ★

The tramp let ten minutes pass, to be certain the Porsche was gone and would not be coming back. It would be just like a cop, even an ex-cop like Duke Marion, to circle around for a look-see, and—

—hey!—

—what if Marion parked the Porsche down below in the MTD's storage lot and was hoofing it back here to the park?

The tramp tensed at the thought.

Shifted his eyes into high and strained his ears listening for any sounds out of the ordinary.

A twig snapped, startling him off balance.

He hooted and slapped a hand to his heart.

Unseen creatures answered the noise.

Holy Fucking Laugh! It was of his own doing, his cracked and shit-soled Nikes had done the deed here in this damp grassy hideaway.

The tramp muttered, "Calm down, calm down, calm down, Raymond. You were just another bum to him."

After another five minutes—you can never be too safe, experience had taught him that even better than Bruno—he slipped back to the shopping cart.

What's this?

Marion had left him a fiver.

The tramp hooted.

Cheap S.O.B.

Money he must make, a ten or even a twenty would have been more like it.

Cheap S.O.B.

Another reason to wipe him off the face of the earth.

Shame it couldn't be tonight.

Except for the Feds snooping around, would have been as

169

easy—easier—than the moment of truth putting the knife to that miserable rat Gus Van Zandt.

Okay, Raymond, so okay.

Everything in due course.

One by one they all go, all the miserable rats.

The tramp pulled the bill from the paperback and stuffed it in his billfold.

Maneuvered the cart onto the drive.

Started downhill.

Chapter 18

I checked out the kids' rooms on my way to the bedroom.

John's, the way it was before he left us.

Alicia's, the mess you know to expect from a girl who is not quite a woman, sixteen going on seventeen, and still passing through a world in which she's the only inhabitant.

I pressed lips to fingers and blew the kiss across to her empty pillow, as I'd done a few moments ago in Johnny's bedroom, at Johnny's empty bed.

Kicked myself again for letting one more day get by me without time for family.

Real time. What's come to be known as *Quality Time.*

More than brief snatches of faces dipping into cereal bowls in the morning until, one day, they're gone or going.

And you're left with a hole in your life the size of the sky.

"You remember to eat some dinner?" Anny wondered as I entered our bedroom.

She was propped up in bed, reading a cookbook, which she does the way some people can read a musical score and hear a symphony note for note. Anny tastes every ingredient and knows precisely how the dish will taste. Sometimes, she mentally adjusts the recipe to enhance the flavor, a claim not disputed by anybody who's ever sat down to one of her meals.

"Grabbed a burger on my way over to Hollyhock."

"Fries?"

"Super-sized."

"They'll kill you, you know."

"I needed something to offset the oatmeal. Too much health can kill you."

"They'll clog your veins and your arteries and—" I settled on the edge of the bed. Smothered her lips. Tickled her tongue furiously with mine. "—meaning I'll have wasted the last almost twenty years on you."

I said, "Pass on all I've taught you to my replacement, with my blessing."

"Only one you in my life, Sailor," she said, "and maybe we should review that part about who was the teacher and who was the student?"

I smiled and stroked her cheek.

Anny, my island. My rock.

"Where's Alicia this time?"

"A sleepover. Josie's. Studying for a geometry test."

"Or so she says."

"Or so she says. Alicia also said to give you a kiss and a hug from her." She did. "Now, get yourself ready for bed and get a kiss and a hug from me."

"I was hoping for more."

"Hope springs eternal."

"Me, too."

I eased off the bed, dodging her playful grab, and began undressing.

She said, "Did you ever talk to Molly Deering?"

"Yeah. Hung around the office until she called. Told her the situation, then put her on with Rita."

"She think she can help?"

"She's more than willing to try again, especially when I told her about Coop and his phone calls. Molly still feels guilty for screwing up last time."

"But she didn't screw up."

"Of course not. She knows that, too. But Molly is not a good loser and that's what makes her such a great lawyer. She remembered Benny's ex and what a frightening bitch of a woman she is, an alky and a junkie using the boy to mind-fuck Benny and Rita every chance she gets, as well as for alimony and child support. Said she's been concerned ever since for Coop's well-being."

"I'll bet she doesn't lose again."

"I said the same thing later."

"Later?"

"I one-stopped for coffee with her at the Derby, before going on to Barnsdall."

At once I felt relieved I had told her, even if I would never know if I had because I wanted Anny to know or because of some back-brained concern she might hear about it through Rupert Bachman and think the worst.

I said, "It was her suggestion."

"It would have been mine," Anny said.

"The big disappointment was at Hollyhock House."

Anny exhaled, a mother's sigh, and seemed relieved that I'd changed the subject.

"No Bruno."

"Did you really expect him to be there?"

I shrugged.

"Even more than I figured he might show up for Nell Fontanne. It said Shazam! on the photo I got from Van Zandt, and today from the woman at the museum. Shazam! If Bruno was using *Shazam!* to send me a message, then Holly-hock House made sense, especially tonight, but instead of Captain Marvel I got Rupert Bachman."

"Bachman was there?"

"A tail so good he arrived before me."

"He's bugging you."

"Of course. In more ways than one."

"If Bruno is giving himself up to the government, what difference if Bachman is there or not, just as long as you are there to guarantee his safety? That's how this started, isn't it, what they said when you were contacted?"

"What Bachman told me, exactly, but nothing I've heard from Bruno himself."

"You're having second thoughts."

"Like, maybe, Bruno also had second thoughts about making Bachman part of his Welcome Back party, assuming Bachman ever was part of the plan."

"Ever? How else would Bachman know to involve you or even know how much you idolized Nell Fontanne if he didn't learn it from Bruno? It sounded absolutely like a signal from him."

"Only Bruno didn't show. And *Shazam!* was an even better signal. Bruno wasn't at Barnsdall, either."

"How about the woman?"

I opened my Day Runner and pulled out a copy of the photo Jack Lipton had supplied, walked it over to her. She studied it and nodded approvingly, handed it back.

"Beautiful. And an upscale dresser."

"And carrying a photo of Bruno and me. Where does she fit?"

"Did you ask Rupert Bachman?"

I crossed back to the dresser and returned the photo to the Day Runner.

"He brought up Gustav Van Zandt, but didn't mention her. So, I didn't mention her."

"A regular Mystery Woman."

"Not to Bruno, it seems."

She smiled one of her delicious smiles. "Then maybe the thing to do is ask Bruno when you see him?"

"What is it about your sense of humor I like the most?"

"Me?"

"Oh, that answer you have."

"I phrased it in the form of a question."

"Were you practicing for *Jeopardy!* or priming me for the coroner's jury tomorrow morning?"

"One and the same thing if you've been paying attention to any of the newscasts, including I might add tonight's *Cable News Extra* editorial by your friend Jack Lipton's boss."

"Jack warned me it was on the way from old Pooper Scoop Schneider. That bad, huh?"

"Put it this way—You can be happy the lynch mob hasn't formed outside yet. He all but ordered the jury to carve you up and name you Cadaver of the Month."

"Making Paul Crescent a happy man tonight."

"Paul Crescent will *never* be a happy man, but step back over here, Sailor, and you'll learn what I can do for you."

Later, not even thoughts about becoming a sitting target for a coroner's jury in the morning kept me from enjoying a sound night's sleep.

In my dream, I was Captain Marvel.

Chapter 19

The coroner kept me at the witness table for almost an hour, tossing questions in a dispassionate monotone belying the idea anyone might have—especially me—that he held more than a professional interest in the matter of what the media had reinvented as "Duke Marion's Century City Showdown," which pitted a trigger-happy ex-cop turned county supervisor against an unarmed man old enough to be his father.

It was a theme the coroner seemed only too happy to replay for the stone-faced jurors, who scribbled away in notebooks and frequently responded to a harsh question with hard stares in my direction.

About forty members of the news media filled the six spectator rows in the small hearing room, kept as cold as one of the department's walk-in body lockers, including a few reporters I recognized as favorites of the coroner's own good buddy, Chief of Police Paul Crescent.

Who said life was fair?

What comedian?

I kept my composure, answered every question in a straightforward manner, didn't raise a sweat, and left with a nod that told the coroner my memory was twice as long as his dong and an appreciative smile for the jury members, most of whom shied their eyes; nothing I could take with me as a good sign.

Crescent had arrived sometime after I was called inside to testify and was sitting taut with anticipation, his legs crossed at the ankles, his arms locked inside one another, waiting for his turn.

An unpleasant grin briefly ate up both sides of his face when he saw me exiting the room, before he looked away and resumed talking in a hush to the lip-wetting chief public information officer seated by his side.

Crescent had inherited Hal Everest from me.

Hal, always letter-perfect at delivering the official department spin to the media, was an outrageously flamboyant personality, who did his best work anywhere he could pick up a round or two, although his drink was never headier than a double espresso. He had an acerbic wit that let him get away with proclamations like, "The shortest distance between two points is a straight lie," or "The truth's like Halloween. It always comes back to haunt you."

I ordered him to tell the truth most of the time.

Hal never liked that.

He showed it now by not returning my finger-tip-to-forehead salute.

Rounding the corridor intersection, I almost collided with Jordan Hardy, who looked embarrassed and was about to say something when Crescent squawked out his name, the way you summon a pet dog.

Jordan gave me a pleading look and hurried past.

"Supervisor Marion!"

The portly man in the Rodeo Drive costume calling my name was trotting up the corridor like his next step would bring on a heart attack, weighted to one side by a Gucci briefcase and watering the linoleum with his sweat.

He stopped three feet from me, dropped the case, and held a hand in front of my face while he gulped for air.

He mopped his pimpled brow with an oversized silk hand-kerchief and swept it over his baldhead to the nape of his neck.

I knew who he was, although we had never met:

Thompson Ehrlichman.

Ehrlichman, Wright, Bernstein, and Block, Esq.

Century City high risers with the highest rates west of the Mississippi.

The legal brains behind the MacMurray Basin proposal.

He rubbed his palms dry and pocketed the handkerchief, checked his hand for sweat and said apologetically, "Excuse me if we don't shake, Supervisor." Stashed the hand in a pocket. "I'm Thom Ehrlichman of—"

"I know who you are, Mr. Ehrlichman. If it's about the MacMurray, a hallway is no place for a conversation. Call my office and ask for Rita Gossage. She'll be happy to make an appointment."

"Not that whatsoever," Ehrlichman said, arrogantly, in a deep voice thick with asthmatic wheeze. "I have four-hun-dred-dollar-an-hour lawyers for the grunt work." I saw he wanted me to be impressed. "May I have five minutes of your time?"

"What's that worth in your time?"

"One hundred sixty dollars" he said without hesitation. "Plus travel time, both ways. It could be worth as much to you, Supervisor. You mind if I sit down?"

"You mind if I don't join you?"

"You mind your manners." He took my hand and, before I could pull free from what was a surprisingly strong grip, coaxed me to one of the empty slab benches. "The only reason I'm here is for your own good." He pushed a shoulder against mine. "There, isn't this better?"

"Four minutes to go."

178

"I've won million-dollar settlements for clients with summations that required less time," he said.

"Only I'm not your client, Mr. Ehrlichman."

"You can be. Say the word." The look on his face said he wasn't kidding.

"If I needed a lawyer, the county would provide one, or if necessary I'd hire one I could afford."

"The ADL pool is full of them and the jails are full of their clients, but there are only a few lawyers like me, and do not for a fractured second think I am here because I feel any sympathy for you, any emotion. Now that we've met, any rapprochement."

"Somebody sent you."

"Somebody upset with how the chief of police seems to be carrying on against you called this morning, asking me to be here and make myself available to you. I apologize for my lateness. Traffic. And a driver who foolishly ignored my instruction to stay off the freeways. The imbecile's next trip after returning me to my office will be to the unemployment line."

"Clement McAllister."

Ehrlichman looked around as if he feared I might have been overheard.

Dropped his own voice.

"A client who seems to have taken a position in this, on your behalf, although for the life of me I don't . . ." He let the thought disappear, as if it might offend McAllister if he knew. "My client has asked me to remind you he is well prepared to intrude himself in this matter now or at such a time as you might find it prudent."

"I've already made it clear to your client how I feel."

"If so, I would speculate he didn't like your response and, being the kind of person he is, is giving you a second chance to make a wise decision." A false smile. "Guessing at your response, he also asked me to remind you that the offer comes without obligation."

"No echo."

His look questioned me. "I don't understand the word."

"Grunt talk for *obligation*."

"You're toying with me, Supervisor."

"Trying to save your client an expensive minute or two."

"I'll report about your generosity," Ehrlichman said, using his hands to push up from the bench. "And that's your final answer?" he wondered before stepping over to his Gucci case. "I want to be certain."

"Yes."

"It could cost you mightily at election time. Maybe, earlier than that."

"Any other answer could cost me more."

He shook his head at me. "Then here's a free piece of advice, Supervisor. Be careful. My client is not a man to fool with. He doesn't take well to disappointment."

"Exactly what does *Be careful* mean, Mr. Ehrlichman?"

Ehrlichman shrugged.

Bared his teeth.

"Grunt words, I believe, and you've made it eminently clear you're familiar with them."

Chapter 20

Within the hour, I was on the first hole at Rancho Park and had reported all of this to Charlie Temple and Pearce Dickson.

Charlie, my predecessor as chief of police, gave the golf ball a whack and ordered it, "Sail through, you little cocksucker." The ball obeyed, the way his guys always did when Charlie was running the show, and dropped in great position halfway to the green. "One helluva shot, Duke! Tell me! Let me hear it from you!"

"One helluva shot, Chief. I see the improvement."

Pearce chimed in, "*Improvement.* Goddam. Hear that, Charlie? Sounds like our boy Duke is finally becoming a politician."

"It was one helluva shot, you son of a bitch!"

Charlie's thick, staccato voice was as coarse and gutted as his seventy-two-year old face, hidden under a vanity bowl of scarecrow orange hair. Nothing could hide the worry lines and furrows built over more than a decade of battles won and lost, but always fought fairly.

I never hesitated saying that the toughest part of my tenure was trying to be as good a chief as Charlie Temple, who had rooted corruption out of the LAPD and, by putting more cops out on the mean streets, reduced the crime rate, raised L.A.'s level of confidence in the police department, and put to rest the sad history of minority riots and the Rodney King kinds of incidents.

Charlie, of course, never hesitated in agreeing with my assessment, but he always made it clear I was his boy and carrying on the *Charlie Temple Tradition,* an expression of support he'd so far failed to extend to Paul Crescent, about whom Charlie said nothing publicly and privately called a turd. Nothing in the world was worse to Charlie Temple than a turd. After he started having bowel problems, he took monstrous delight in sharing with friends in extreme graphic detail.

Charlie gave Pearce a decapitating look, slid into the back seat of the golf wagon, flicked the remains of a butt onto the green and, after lighting a fresh smoke, parked it in a corner of his generous mouth.

"Tell me, Supervisor Dickson," he said, treating the word *Supervisor* sarcastically, "In your most official and experienced view, does learning to be a politician explain why Duke let the prick coroner pee on his leg this morning?"

Pearce took the seat next to him, leaving me to drive, made a thinking noise and decided, "Pee is a lot better than puke and, besides, the hearing was strictly procedural. The trappings of good government cloaked in bureaucracy. Just a little display for the public in an election year."

Charlie made a sneering noise.

"Plus an old grudge to settle. The coroner never was Duke's biggest fan and don't try telling me he's not playing footsie right now with that turd Crescent, who has his own agenda against Duke for reasons that all three of us know better than a guess. That not so, Duke?"

"Better than a guess, Chief."

"Toldja. Your disciple's growing political balls, Charlie. Although you have to ask yourself why he'd refuse a helping hand from a power broker like Clement McAllister."

At once, Pearce looked like he regretted the comment.

I wondered, "What would you have done, Pearce. Taken McAllister up on it?"

Charlie also looked interested in having an answer.

Pearce hesitated, then said, "I'd have stalled Ehrlichman," and shot me a cautious grin. "Always put off until tomorrow what you don't necessarily have to do today."

"Hell, I would have said yes," Charlie decided, taking back the conversation.

It was not a response I would have expected from him.

I said, "You're kidding, aren't you, Chief?"

"Man's got money, power and influence. Never hurts to have that combination working for you and who was it once said to keep 'em where you can see 'em coming, even the bad guys?"

"Maybe you should have run for supervisor, Charlie? I can see now who the real cop politician is, and I don't mean Paul Crescent."

"Not a politician, Pearce. Call me a survivor if you need a word for it, and don't ever again put me in the same breath with that turd." Charlie plucked the cigarette from his mouth and a stream of smoke escaped. "What did you say the body butcher called *you*, Duke, a *fucking vigilante?*" he said, changing the subject.

"Just *vigilante*, Chief. The fucking was in the coroner's pronunciation."

"*Trigger happy*, too. Duke, I hope you took that one as a compliment. When you were chief of police, I heard him call you a whole lot worse. . . . Come to think, I also called you a whole lot worse."

He laughed at the recollection.

Pearce said, "Charlie, bottom line—it's not the Duke's fault that he blasted a man who was aiming an empty gun." He was trying to make up. A wink. "No way Marion the Barbarian could have known when—"

"Not *empty,* Pearce. *Loaded,*" I said. "The damn gun was loaded, only the bullets Edwin O. Powell used happened to be blanks."

Charlie said, "Not the issue, for Christ's sake." He patted my shoulder. "Duke, you did absolutely right what you did, taking out that old hambone, and I don't say so because I never was a fan of his. Only, you went and did it cop right. That's a no-no if you ain't a cop. You ain't. Sure, you still get to flash a badge and carry a weapon. Courtesy. It's only the uniform you abandoned—off the totally misguided notion mankind is better served by the law than by law enforcement."

I pushed my hair back and adjusted my cap, buying a few seconds of relief. "And you retired and became a philosopher. Where's your long white beard, Charlie?"

"Tickling your asshole, Danny boy. Tickling your asshole. And don't you be so damned holier than thou."

"Charlie, c'mon," Pearce said. "Lay off the kid."

Charlie held Pearce off with a palm.

"When Duke was chief he was one of a kind. Now, he's one of the other kind, Chairman Dickson. One of your kind. He made a little manslaughter and that made a lot of little people unhappy."

"I keep telling him to kill them with kindness," Pearce said, trying to lighten the conversation, but neither of us could get Charlie onto a new topic.

A half hour later we were at the second hole, Charlie still refusing to let go.

He'd never entirely forgiven me for putting on a pinstripe and running for office and was relishing this opportunity to rub it in.

Pearce hit a solid drive that soared onto the green and earned a sour look from Charlie, who poked a divot into the tight grass, set his ball, and taunted, "Before this business with Edwin O. Powell, you should've been well into the new life you picked for yourself, Mr. Supervisor Marion, outside in the real world, where guns are only for target practice and badges are for traffic tickets."

Pearce said, "For Crissake, Charlie. You know damn good and well that Duke thought he was saving a life, saving Nell Fontanne."

Charlie fieldstripped his butt.

Turned his back on a light breeze while he lit a new one.

Began lining up his shot and, meanwhile, took another swing at me:

"It's the life he took, not the one he saved, made the eleven o'clock news. When will your kind ever learn that our jails and prisons are full of bum raps from bad juries?"

I said, "Chief! If it ever happened the same way, I'd do it again."

"Of course you would, or I'd spank you," he said. "And shame you don't have Hal Everest slobbering for you instead of for the turd. A real pissant, Everest. I don't know how he's lasted so long. He lies like a bad drive and the news boys lap it up."

"He saved your hide more than once, Charlie."

"Pearce, that was different."

"How was it different?"

"That was my fucking hide he was saving. I was worth it. Duke, for all the aggravation he gave Hal, he was worth it, too, on those, how should I put it?—special occasions."

"You mean when the department fucked up?"

"The department never fucked up," he said, blue veins growing at his temples. "That was the public's perception, so it didn't hurt to have Hal around to square it with them while we did the rest internally."

"Isn't that all he's doing now, for Crescent?"

"If Crescent was worth it, but Crescent is only worthless. Crescent should be a supervisor, like you, Pearce."

"He's out for bigger game, Charlie."

"I think so, too. And you can't blame Hal for wanting to protect his pension, but that doesn't keep him from being a pissant, same as Jordan Hardy. Why you ever pushed him up in rank stays one of life's great mysteries to me, Duke."

"Jordan's a fine cop, who deserved it. My choice after Fuzz Todd."

He made a scoffing sound. "Shows how much weight you were pulling by then with the City Council and, p.s., I think Fuzz is a lightweight. Never pretended otherwise with you."

"Fuzz may come across that way, but he knows the book, he goes by the book, and everybody in the department loves him."

"That explains why we got the turd instead, doesn't it? Three strikes and Fuzz was out. Last thing any City Council wanted was someone who measured up, especially after you and me, Duke."

His swing arced off the fairway. He tagged an inventive storm of cursing with an accusing finger and another poke at me. "It's handicaps like you keep me off my game," he said, then almost fatherly, "You should have stayed a cop, in a uniform, I mean, like your dear, late father, God love him. In your head you'll always be a cop, God help you."

Charlie crossed himself. Looked at my face and saw he'd peaked my anger with his reference to Pop.

Impulsively, I grabbed his club away, set my ball, and whammed it onto the green. Pushed the club at him. Stalked after my shot.

Charlie called after me, "No offense, Danny boy. No offense."

Chapter 21

Colonel Karl Soulé was standing on the entrance portico of the Beverly Hills Hotel, an impatient look on his face, as Stella Ivers glided the white Mercedes up the lane and paused under the canopy only long enough for him to ease sideways into the passenger seat.

"You are late, Miss Ivers," he announced over the radio music.

Stella ignored him, easing the car to a stop at the driveway light off Sunset Boulevard, moving her lips to the music.

Soulé raised his voice over the music. "You know I don't like to be kept waiting, Stella. It smacks of rudeness."

"Them's the fucking breaks."

"Must you always use that word?"

She ignored him.

"You use the word the way most people use periods and commas."

She threw him a glancing smile.

"It offends me. You know it offends me. And, God forbid, were the princess to hear you."

She gave him a look and a signal indicating she couldn't hear him over the radio.

Not so, but maybe it would shut him up.

Soulé reached over and turned down the volume. "Just so you understand I am here now because I have no choice in the matter. It was the princess's wish for me to accompany you this evening, and—"

"Blah, blah, blah, for Christ's sake! Tell me what I don't know!"

She turned up the volume, higher than before, as the light changed.

Soulé, his eyes still closed to the insult, said above the blare, "You do not have consideration for anyone but yourself!"

Let the prick stew, she thought.

She eased the Mercedes into the traffic flow heading east, toward the ocean.

"Where are we going, Stella?"

She ignored him.

"I don't care for surprises!"

"Maybe you should have asked the princess," she said, finally, her eyes tracking something curious in the rearview.

"I did, of course. She didn't tell me," he said, shouting at her.

"Maybe she didn't want you to know," Stella said, shouting back.

"I don't care for secrets, either!"

Within a half mile she was certain she had a car on her tail.

A late model, dark-colored Ford.

Driver plus one.

Alternating lanes and positions from a reasonable distance, not so far back as to risk losing her to a changing signal.

She had no idea when the Ford had picked her up. Probably was about the time she reached the hotel. She had been too careful before that not to notice.

"You got your seat belt on, Karl?"

He showed he could not hear her over the music.

She reached for his belt, tossed it over his lap.

He nodded and cinched himself in.

Twelve minutes later, she'd reached the southbound entrance ramp to the San Diego Freeway.

She edged into the traffic flow, the Ford still with her, and shouted at him over the music, "Hold onto your balls, Karl!"

He looked at her curiously, not quite certain what she meant, then with alarm as Stella floored the pedal and began streaking forward, in and out of the medium flow of traffic.

"Stella!"

The Ford copied every maneuver, not pretending to be anything but what it was, a pursuit car.

That fucker can really drive, she thought.

Closing in on LAX at eighty and ninety miles an hour, the freeway traffic had grown heavier.

Stella maneuvered from the exit lane to the inside lane and back, filling cracks in the flow, ignoring the honking horns, oblivious to braking lights and the skidding noises, singing along with the radio to drown out Karl's demands that she slow down.

She fled the freeway, ignored the stop sign, tore across the exit street and back onto the freeway.

The Ford stuck with her.

The cocksucker majored in Indy 500, she decided.

She ran the lanes for another two or three miles, waiting for an opportune moment and—

—when she found it—

—swung the Mercedes a hundred eighty degrees.

Traffic splintered to avoid a head-on collision with her.

She shifted the wheel and jammed hard on the gas pedal.

Karl was screaming, his spittle raining on her face, the messy pig.

The Ford tried the same maneuver, either that or lose her.

It fishtailed into the rear of a Jeep.

Was broadsided by a van and a Cad.

Torched by leaking gasoline.

Exploded.

Karl was sucking air, wailing indiscriminately at her, covering what was probably a wet spot on his pants with both hands.

She shouted exuberantly, "So much for them, Karl! We showed those fucking motherfuckers, did we fucking ever!" as she worked the brake and gas pedals trying to get the car back under control and facing in the right direction, but—

—an SUV's brakes had failed.

It pin-wheeled into the back end of the Mercedes.

The entire rear end of the Mercedes blew apart.

The force of the explosion propelled it forward, totally out of control.

The Mercedes jumped a barrier, hurtled off the freeway, and did a twisting roll down a jagged, hard-shelled slope.

Slid.

Banged against an abutment and came to an ugly stop on its side.

Chapter 22

"I knew you'd wanna know," Fuzz Todd said, leading me into the Intensive Care unit at Marina Emergency Center. "Why, I told Rita to go yank you out of your meeting or conference or whatever the hell she said."

The MacMurray wouldn't have meant anything to Fuzz, so I told him, "Another gang of hit-and-run developers trying to rescue a few more street corners in my district from the dreaded strip malls."

"7-Eleven heaven. For the longest time I thought strip malls meant topless joints, you know? Not a gathering place for beggars and dime-drops."

He pointed to one of the rooms with glass windows that faced a central area occupied by medical staffers who played around the clock with lives teetering on the brink. "Over there, Supe," he said, pointing to the room where a somber-faced coffee-skinned nurse was checking a readout from a monitor parked immediately outside the door. "Hey, Graciela. How's it cookin', good-lookin'?"

Graciela raised her narrow shoulders closer to her ears and turned her palms up.

"Is that a good—(Fuzz imitated her gesture)—or a bad (Fuzz did it again)?"

"It's a so lucky to be alive," Graciela said, crossing herself.

"You mean it ain't cable television the poor fuck is wired for?"

Graciela made a clucking sound and an indignant face, crossed herself again, and resumed interpreting the monitor readout.

I glanced inside the room.

Col. Karl Soulé was the bump under the bed sheets, at the core of a tangle of tubes and electrical connections sending out medications and green skizzy lines of information.

"What's the prognosis, Graciela?"

She shook her head. "You gotta ask doctor."

"The doctor around?"

Shook it again. "Anytime soon."

I turned back to Fuzz. "Somebody advise Nell Fontanne?"

"Tried like hell, but weren't able to crack the hotel switchboard. Like she's got a Do Not Disturb on her life. C'mon." He grabbed me by the jacket sleeve and tugged me to a room at the end of the corridor, where a uniform stationed outside the door was gabbing it up with a well-endowed nurse who didn't seem to mind the attention. "I finally ordered a car on over to make it a command performance for your beloved princess."

The woman in the room appeared to be sleeping fitfully underneath more modern medical technology than Soulé. Like Soulé, her face was masked by bandages and tubes. Brown eyes half open inside the slits, brown hair piled inside a shower cap.

Fuzz said, "Fire Rescue says she was driving, based on who was warped where, and probably saved by the seat belt."

We moved around for a clearer look.

"She have a name yet?"

"Not one I know. We made Soulé from his billfold, but no such luckaroonie with her. Sporting no ID whatsoever, unless that was her name on the clothing labels. Giorgio

Armani? She pulls through and the least we got her on is driving without a license."

"Prints."

"Not yet."

"If she was with Soulé, Nell Fontanne might know."

"Thought already occurred. The other thought was—*you* might also know." His face went mobile, taking smug delight in knowing something I didn't.

"You swallow a canary, Fuzz?"

"Fat one, and here's something for you to jaw on," he said, pulling out of an inside jacket pocket what I thought for a moment were postcards.

The two Polaroid photos taken of me at the museum unveiling ceremonies.

"You look like you were overdue for a haircut." Fuzz bobbed around. "Still are."

"Where'd the pictures come from?"

"Handbag in the Mercedes. She the president of the Duke Marion Fan Club?"

I threw a thumb over my shoulder. In a minute, we were outside ICU on our way to the elevator, me explaining how the pictures had come to be taken.

I dug into the file pocket of my Day Runner for one of the freeze-frame prints Jack Lipton had sent over. "Here's the photographer."

Fuzz arched his eyebrows, studied it hard enough to suck off the emulsion. "Some dish."

"Keep it. Send it up through the national system and see if it delivers a name."

"I can do that, but if there's some connection between her and Bruno Guy, maybe the first order of business is to run it past the Bug Man and his gnats?"

"Not yet, okay?"

He tried to read my face. "I suppose you got a good reason?"

"Not really."

"Works for me," he said. He stretched his mouth dumbly, working his lower lip over his upper lip, and scratched the top of his head. "Maybe a clue?"

"Something I feel in my gut."

"Maybe consider eating a healthier breakfast than all of that oatmeal? A couple of dried prunes always work for me."

I still had the Polaroids. I started to hand them over, but Fuzz shook his head.

"Hold onto them for the duration. Saves me the trouble of logging them in for what so far is Stupid Driver Tricks and, besides, if word leaked, the lovable coroner's jury might get more stupid about you than it already is."

It was nothing Fuzz should be doing, against every rule governing suppression of evidence, and I reminded him.

"Thanks for the tip. And, you wanna hear what else is our little secret for now?"

"Why do I think I do?" I said, slipping the photos into my Day Runner.

"Ran the plate on the Mercedes . . . Turns out our Jane V. Doe was playing kamikaze in a vehicle registered to—" Fuzz hesitated, like a stand-up comic about to deliver his best punch line: "—Edwin O. Powell."

We exited the elevator, padded through the busy main lobby past the automatic doors to the No Parking area directly out front, where I had parked the Porsche behind Fuzz's unmarked.

I said, "Let's assume the mystery lady up in ICU is the same mystery lady who took my picture at the museum and dropped Bruno's name on me."

"Assumed."

"Then she cracks up with Nell Fontanne's major domo, Colonel Karl Soulé, in a car belonging to the guy who pulled the trigger on Nell."

I'd been ticketed. I pulled the citation from under the wiper and handed it to Fuzz, who took it without comment and jammed it in a pocket.

"You bring such clarity to the situation," he said. "I should have seen it myself. It's a clear, open and shut case of confusion!"

Just then, his beeper went off.

He used the car two-way, sitting behind the wheel with the door open and his feet on the pavement. His head stopped nodding and started sliding left and right. He hailed me closer.

"Get a load of this, Supe. My guys couldn't find Nell Fontanne over at the Beverly Hills. She's gone. Checked out of the hotel without checking out."

Chapter 23

I followed Fuzz to the Beverly Hills Hotel, where another surprise was waiting:

Rupert Bachman.

He was standing at parade rest in the center of Nell's sitting room, hands gripped behind his back, ivory cigarette holder tilted at a jaunty FDR angle, smiling grandly, as if he had been anticipating our arrival.

"Hello, hello, hello," he called to us. "Your men are finishing up in the master bedroom, Chief Todd." He pointed to the connecting door.

I sent Fuzz a look that said I wanted to be alone with Bachman.

Fuzz excused himself and headed for the bedroom, while Bachman crossed to the bar, set the holder carefully on an ashtray, and proceeded to mix a drink calling for several shots from an old-fashioned seltzer bottle on the sink bay.

"Something for you, Duke?"

"You turn up in the strangest places at the strangest times, Mr. Bachman."

"Really? I've always felt extremely comfortable in a two-thousand-dollar-a-day suite. And, more than you, I'm here minding my own business."

"How is Nell Fontanne still your business?"

"You sure I can't make you something? Stocked as you

might expect from a first class hostelry. Chivas and water? Rocks? Tall?"

"Is that what your file on me says?"

"That's what my file on you says."

"Beer is fine."

"The preferred option before the dinner hour. Also in the file."

"No more bullshit, okay? What's really going on here?"

"You know already." His head disappeared below the counter while he checked the fridge. "The aging albeit legendary and beautiful Princess Nell is gone, *pfft!*, vanished like a character from one of those Ross Hunter movies late in her career—leaving behind more Jean Louis clothing than clues. I know—something cold in a domestic brew."

"Where?"

"With her Prince Charming, do you suppose?" Bachman reappeared and displayed a bottle. "Budweiser?"

"Fine."

I stepped up to the bar and eased onto a stool.

"I hear tell it is the *champagne* of beers," he said, dripping sarcasm, acting as if holding the bottle were a concession being made exclusively on my behalf.

I took it from him.

The bottle and the sarcasm.

Chances were excellent that telling Bachman what he could do with the bottle would not improve the quality of our relationship or inspire him to share information.

"Shazam!" he toasted with his glass.

Winked.

We clanked and drank, his sip to my swallow.

"How's your *champagne?*" he said, drolly. "My drink is brandy and soda. Centuries old and civilized."

I tried my question again. "What is it that makes Nell

Fontanne your business? The fact that Bruno Guy picked her testimonial dinner as our rallying point?"

"Part of the equation, yes, you might say."

"Do I get to hear the other parts?"

Bachman flicked a smile.

"You said she was with her Prince Charming—"

"A supposition."

"But her Prince Charming would be Edwin O. Powell. You did know Nell and Powell were lovers?"

"The *late* Edwin O. Powell, and shall we take it on face value that if you know I know, too? Especially a piece of old news resurrected in lavish detail by the tabloids even as the newly departed was being readied for his final rest."

"And you knew before me," I said, playing to his ego.

"Quite likely." He toasted me again. "You on the other hand—Did you know the *late* Edwin O. Powell was more than Nell Fontanne's long-term lover?" He said casually, "Powell also was the father-in-law of your comrade, Bruno Guy."

I almost fumbled the bottle of Bud.

"Nothing you'll be reading about in the checkout line any time soon, Duke . . . Or that Powell's daughter is the woman you just visited at the hospital."

He enjoyed my astonishment for another moment.

"Mrs. Guy's name is Stella Ivers. Stella Ivers Guy? Or, isn't that done in common law marriages? Or where the woman could not look less like a guy than Stella Ivers."

He filtered a laughing sound through his lips.

This wasn't the time to tell Bachman he was no sure bet for a gig at the Comedy Store.

"Have you caught on yet, Duke?"

I continued playing ignorant disciple to his Lord of All Knowledge.

"Why would Edwin O. Powell want to kill Nell Fontanne? They were lovers."

"Exactly. Lovers. And some damned prince from a kingdom that survives by issuing souvenir postage stamps took Nell from him, infecting him with a desire for revenge that built up over the years. When she returned here to be honored and Bruno Guy, his son-in-law, decided to use the occasion to surrender to you, his old and loyal boyhood pal, Powell seized the opportunity for himself. He decided to go out in grand style, taking with him the one true love of his life."

"After all these years?"

"Time marches on, but love is eternal."

"You're saying Powell was Bruno's contact. I can see it on your face."

"And I recognize the doubt flashing from your eyes, Duke, so this is an excellent time for you to see—"

Bachman pulled a folded piece of paper from somewhere and offered it to me.

"It's a scan of something my agents were able to remove from Powell during the screaming pandemonium that followed the shooting incident. Bruno meant for him to pass it on to you, but Edwin O. Powell's desire for revenge was stronger than any obligation he felt toward Bruno or, sadly, even his own beautiful daughter, Stella."

I put on my specs and unfolded the paper.

The note was brief, in handwriting familiar to me:

Duke—Forgive and forget. Trust the bearer of this message.
Bruno.

Bachman said, "From Bruno, correct? I see you recognize the handwriting."

"Computers can create or duplicate anything nowadays."

"Long before computers, Duke, trust me." He noted how that concept amused me by turning up his hand and spreading his fingers. "Fine, don't trust me, but trust that it's most definitely a note from Bruno Guy—in his own hand."

"Why wouldn't Bruno write: *Trust Edwin O. Powell* or *Trust my father-in-law, Edwin O. Powell?* Why the bearer of this message, not Powell?"

"Questions where, I fear, you will need to get your answers from him, but here are some for you." A smirk. "Why did Bruno urge you to forgive and forget? Did the two of you have a falling out along the way? Is that it?"

"All Bruno and I ever fought over were trading cards and comic books."

"Powell? Forgive Powell? Is that what he wanted then? Forgive and forget. Trust Powell?"

"I never met Powell in my life. I only knew him from motion picture screens sixty feet tall and the shelves at Blockbuster Video. The movie channels."

"Curious, then, so curious." He paused to study his nails. They'd been chewed or picked almost to the quick. "How can you explain why Colonel Karl Soulé would suggest otherwise to the coroner's jury?"

"What's that supposed to mean?"

"The obvious. Either you just told me a naughty fib or Colonel Soulé lied under oath to the coroner's jury yesterday, mere hours before his unfortunate accident."

Bachman was playing cat and canary with me. He was leading up to something. I could have kicked myself for not spotting it earlier.

The bedroom door opened noisily.

Fuzz stepped through to inquire, "You boys okay?"

"A few more minutes, Fuzz."

"Sure, no problem-o. Still a whole mess of nothing else to find going on in here."

He stepped back into the bedroom and closed the door.

Bachman waited a moment.

He cleared his throat and continued, "Colonel Soulé explained to the jury that Edwin O. Powell was meant to deliver a note to you, however, you and he had had quite a nasty disagreement some years ago—"

"I said I never met the man."

"A number of years ago, over Stella."

"I never met the woman, either, his daughter."

"Except at the Los Angeles County Museum, when you shared a few surreptitious moments amidst a shoot-out that endangered innocent civilians, but that's not here or there for now."

My heart started pounding at my chest, like tidal waves smashing the beach.

"Maybe it had to do with Stella's intention to wed your dear comrade." He said the word dear like Bruno and I belonged in a Gay Rights Parade. "More likely, you had your own eyes on Stella even before Bruno, and her father stood in your way."

"I had a wife . . . I have a wife."

"Exactly. What father would want his beautiful young daughter taking up with a married man? It might make even a murdering terrorist seem preferable to someone like Edwin O. Powell. An old-fashioned man with old-fashioned principals. Say, Duke? You ever wonder about Molly Deering's father?"

My body vibrated angrily. I felt blood coursing through the vein at my temple, the one Anny called my Clint Eastwood vein.

It felt ready to burst.

I pushed at it with my fingers.

"You are some piece of work, Bachman."

Bachman pretended not to notice.

"Colonel Soulé told the jury he wasn't certain, only that there was a problem, and the problem might explain why Duke Marion—a victim of pent-up hostility—took unexpected opportunity to dispatch Edwin O. Powell to the angels."

"Lies." My throat was constricted. I couldn't raise a word above a harsh whisper.

"Or was it so unexpected, Duke? They were co-stars, those old lovebirds, so it was logical he would somehow be part of the evening, if not on the dais, a surprise appearance, like the ones they were always pulling off on that old show, what was it called? Yes—*This is Your Life.*"

I shook my head.

"That, of course, might clarify Bruno's reference to *forgive and forget*. To *trust Powell*. Bruno Guy was urging you to let bygones be bygones because his father-in-law was making a difference here tonight. Trust Powell to lead you to Bruno."

I shook my head again.

"You are a former detective, Duke, a chief of police. Wouldn't you say it all seems to fit? Why the coroner's jury might find it fit to return a verdict of probable cause against you?"

I locked my hands and set them down hard on the bar counter.

What I really wanted to do was punch out the son of a bitch.

He said, "Messy headlines, Duke. Possibly a recall election. A trial—probably a manslaughter bailout—that you know the chief of police will relish and, guaranteed, the DA will press to his own political advantage. The possibility of problems at home after your lovely wife gives some thought to what might have gone on between you and Stella, when you add that to Anny's later anxieties over Molly Deering and—"

"Fuck you!" A gritty whisper from the base of my throat. "Fuck you, Bachman!"

Bachman responded with a deploring look. Grabbed the edge of the counter and pressed forward, his eyes tight lines of malice and his tone as ugly as the rancid breath clouding onto my face.

"No, Duke. Fuck you," he said, evenly. "You are the link to Bruno Guy. You are the conduit. Get him for me. Get Bruno Guy. I don't care how. Bring him in. Quickly. Or it is most definitely you who is fucked."

I forced my voice back. "I don't know where he is or how to find him, Bachman." Calmly. My temper already had given the bastard too much edge.

Bachman eased away. He picked up his snifter by the stem and hand-stirred the brandy. "Then what else can I say?" He moved the snifter to his lips and took a gentle sip. *"Shazam!?* Yes, I think so. *Shazam!"*

Chapter 24

I got back to my office and galloped through the fifty or so phone calls I'd received since noon, then asked Rita to give me some time alone. She thanked me for the millionth time for putting her together with Molly Deering and headed out to inform some persistent lobbyists, hoping for a few minutes of my time, that they'd have to bring their sanguine smiles and snappy patter back another day.

I cleared space on the desk and compared the message Powell supposedly was to deliver to me from Bruno—

Duke—Forgive and forget. Trust the bearer of this message. Bruno.

—with Bruno's brief messages on the photo passed to me by Gustav Van Zandt—

Duke—Shazam! Bruno.

—and the photo delivered by Stella Ivers—

Duke—Keep 'em flying. Bruno.

The fountain pen ink used on the photos was the same black color and consistency, my best confirmation both notes had been written by Bruno. I had only a photocopy of the

Powell note, so there was no way of telling for certain if real ink had also been used here, although everything about the penmanship said it was from Bruno. If the note was forged, whether by hand or computer wizardry, it was good enough to pass my inspection.

The note might have been designed to put pressure on me and—if Bachman played out his threats, as I was certain he would if I did not find Bruno for him, his type knowing only how to play hardball—bring me grief.

But it was not going to bring me together with Bruno.

It lacked the road signs my old friend has put on the photos, like *Shazam!* on the Van Zandt photo, which took me to Hollyhock House.

Maybe Bruno had been at Hollyhock that night, waiting for me in the shadows, got scared off when Bachman showed up, but that thought raised a contradiction that had been attacking me like a bad case of hemorrhoids ever since.

If Bruno wanted me present as a safety measure when he surrendered to Bachman, there'd have been no reason for him not to show himself at Hollyhock on an anniversary he knew I could never forget.

Bruno could have simply stepped forward and said, *Here I am.*

Would he the next time, if I followed the sign he had left for me on the photo I got from Stella Ivers?

But there was a contradiction there, too.

Stella had delivered the photo—the message—to me at the museum, before I went up to Barnsdall.

Did that mean Bruno never intended to be there?

A dry run, was that it?

Testing the waters to see how Rupert Bachman intended to honor their agreement?

If so, as far as I could tell, the son of a bitch was playing it straight, no matter that he had to use spy tricks to track me there.

Jack Lipton had sent over two copies of Stella's freeze frame.

One I'd turned over to Fuzz.

The other was propped now against my computer screen.

I looked at her beautiful face, wondering what parts of it were left intact inside her bandages, and said, "Keep 'em flying, Stella. Keep 'em flying, Mrs. Guy."

Keep 'em flying.

If I was right about its meaning—and, of course, I was—would this be another dry run?

Meanwhile, I knew *where.*

I knew where.

Bruno would have to let me know when.

A knock at the door.

My aide, Lewis Tully, was hanging in the doorjamb.

Lewis is a tall, gangly kid in his mid-twenties who spent the first year as an intern, while he got his law degree at Southwestern. Bright, but not brilliant. So honest he'd never use somebody else's unexpired meter time at an empty parking space, always dropping in his own coins. The kind of obsessive loyalty that's more common among religious converts.

"Today's session just adjourned, boss. This a good time for your briefing?"

I waved him forward.

The couch oomphed as Lewis settled at his usual spot in the conference area. He covered the coffee table with three-ring binders and neatly labeled, legal-size manila files, carefully settled the Board meeting agenda on his lap, and began thumbing through pages in the yellow pad that bore his detailed notes and comments in a tight, minuscule shorthand of his own invention, curious letters and symbols crowding every line, leaving barely any margins at all.

"How'd the De Cordoba and Nakamura thing go?"

Lewis raised a thumb.

"I passed along your idea and Dickson added his muscle again, so it didn't even get as far as a vote. They're going to share the deed and the Olvera Street premises in a joint-venture restaurant they've decided to call *Señor Sushi* . . . Fonzy and Moki think it has real franchise possibilities. They're talking serious about going after investors."

"How much did they get from you?"

Lewis's blue eyes popped and his blush lit the room. He looked around furtively, as if someone might have overheard, finger-pulled at his nose, and swiped at his mouth. "You know I couldn't, boss. Conflict of interest. Could come back to haunt you one day."

"Oh, I don't know," I said, teasingly. "I might even put in a few bucks. Raw fish smothered in furnace-strength salsa could sweep the country if it's promoted right."

Lewis was born somber and never forgave the doctor for spanking him. He studied my face to make certain I was kidding, grunted, and started to explain a vote on an appeal by an advocacy group for parents who believed they and their kids had been discriminated against by a charter school that kicked them out with twenty-four hours notice, five weeks into the school term.

As much as I was concerned, Lewis's sentences floated innocently in and out of my head. My mind was still on Bruno. I scooped up the note and the photos and stashed them in the lock drawer.

"Lewis, feel like taking a ride?" His eyes crawled over me again, as if I had set him up with a straight line. Waited for the punch line to drop. "You can tell me the rest in the car."

Chapter 25

Within five minutes of pulling out of the garage, I sensed Lewis and I were being followed. I laughed to myself at how Bachman's tails, once you were on to them, were not, at least, as good as his forgers.

So what?

I wasn't leading them to Bruno, except in a manner of speaking.

Not now. Not yet.

Not without first hearing from Bruno that it was okay.

Lewis was halfway through his report on the agenda by the time we got off the 5 and I had navigated the Porsche along San Fernando Road to the old Grand Central Air Terminal in Glendale.

He had deftly juggled his notes and the various folders and files on his lap and was so wrapped up in his explanations that he momentarily startled, as if waking up from a bad dream, when I swung into the circular courtyard driveway created around a tall decorative fountain long ago drained and concreted over.

I ignored the parking spaces set off by faded painted stripes, chose a spot closer to the terminal, and killed the motor.

The abandoned building's stucco and tile façade and the art deco embellishments vividly recalled the Mission style of architecture in vogue during the Twenties.

The terminal tower still dominated the now-quiet surroundings, a lightly trafficked industrial park running alongside the empty L.A. River basin.

Lewis confessed he had never heard of the Grand Central Air Terminal.

I said, "They closed her down in '59, Lewis, so that doesn't surprise me. They said she had outlived her time. Too costly to operate anymore for just the private jobs and too small for the big planes, the jets. Besides, there was L.A. International now. Come on."

There was no sign of a tail car. Had Bachman's people pulled back, realizing how sloppy they'd been, or had I been mistaken earlier?

Approaching the main building, I directed Lewis to a series of mission arches.

"Passengers passed through those arches en route to the planes, TWA, American, even Mexicana, until the commercials all moved to Mines Field, which became LAX, or to the Union Air Terminal. That's now Burbank."

Lewis craned his neck and decided, "It looks familiar."

"Think *Casablanca*," I said, rounding a corner.

"*Casablanca*?"

"The movie? Humphrey Bogart and Ingrid Bergman?"

"Oh, yeah," he said, but I wasn't certain he really knew what I was talking about.

"They, Warner Brothers, filmed the final airport scene here. Maybe that's why you think you recognize it. A lot of airport scenes from a lot of movies have been shot here over the years, even nowadays. TV, too."

"Of course," he said, unconvincingly. "Is that why you know so much about the place, boss?"

I shook my head.

"Years and years later, when my friend Bruno Guy and I

were in our teens, some independent operators tried making a go of the place. We worked here. First me, then Bruno, after a kid who didn't know as much about flying as he thought got killed in an open cockpit Ryan M-2.

"It was one of Howard Hughes's planes, and the kid just borrowed it. He switched to the wrong tank, something like that, and the engine quit. He ditched in the L.A. River there. The wheels sank into the mud and the M-2 did a cartwheel and the kid flipped out and snapped his neck. He was gone in a heartbeat, and Bruno got hired the next day.

"See, over there? That's where people waited to go somewhere or to greet people. Only a couple feet from the runway. Those days we joked a lot about losing a foot under a wheel."

Lewis, humoring the boss, gave me what passed for his laugh.

We ascended the stairs to the control tower, then onto the terminal deck.

I said, "The first thing my friend Bruno did was learn how to fly. He wasn't about to make the same mistake the kid before him made. By the time he was through, he could fly anything. Anything. Then he jumped all over my back until I learned, too."

"Interesting, that's very interesting," Lewis said, trying to sound like he meant it. Something was gnawing at him. He averted his eyes every time I passed him my own glance.

I said, "Even then, like in the olden days, there was no real air control system here. A windsock on the tower. Your sock if the regular one got torn too badly. The Hollywood Hills over there? We would all follow the lights up and down. A wet finger in the sky and, if the air felt right, that was good enough, that and cotton candy clouds. At night, we would follow the lights on home, pray no tree had grown since the last time. That's what *winging it* is all about, Lewis. Where the expression came from."

He gave me a curious look. Seemed about to say something. Changed his mind.

"You'd be amazed by who we saw, Lewis."

"I suppose."

"Clark Gable. Jimmy Stewart. Robert Cummings. Robert Taylor. They were all regulars."

"Jimmy Stewart, yeah."

"Charles A. Lindbergh?"

That actually excited him.

"Lindbergh was among the last to use the strip, before it shut down for the last time. Howard Hughes?"

"Of course. The Spruce Goose."

"When he wasn't flying here, Hughes would come by just to shoot the breeze, not stuttering as bad as they say he did, and many times with some raven-haired starlet he was trying to impress. Over there, no, over to your left—that's where Hughes first spotted Jean Harlow."

Lewis's face went blank again.

"A famous actress, before my time, too. Howard said she was a model, posing for pictures next to a Thunderbird biplane. He would help his starlet into the plane and give us a thumbs up. Bruno and I would answer with our thumbs up and shout at him over the props, *Keep 'em flying!* Yeah. *Keep 'em flying!*"

Lewis listened to me ramble on and sometimes make a sound to tell me he was listening, but mostly stayed silent until we were back on the road about twenty minutes later. He seemed satisfied to stay intent on private matters until I wondered, "Penny for your thoughts, Lewis?"

He shook his head and rambled for a few minutes through the files, but finally, "Okay, sure. Penny for my thoughts."

"Fire away," I said, one eye on the rearview. I was certain a car was on my tail again; a banged-up, late-model black Camry.

"Remember earlier, boss, when you said something about *winging it*?"

"I do."

"I think that is what you've started doing on the Board of Supervisors. More and more. You are still so caught up in playing cops and robbers that you only *wing it* when it comes to the job the taxpayers are paying you to perform."

The kid almost had tears in his eyes.

"Serious words, Lewis."

He turned his head facing out the window and used his hand as a screen.

"I was thrilled when you let me come to work for you, you putting your trust in me, but I don't think I'm thrilled anymore. You miss meetings. You, you shirk your duty most of the time. You have me sit in for you, monitoring, and you count on me to do your work." He patted the work pile in his lap. "When it's necessary, when we really need you, Rita or I can generally find you over at Parker Center hobnobbing with your old buddies. Sometimes I think people have to be named Smith or Wesson to get your attention."

He blew out a stream of breath that clouded the window.

"I suppose it's too late to take back my penny?"

"I hope that's the only thing it's too late for, boss." His voice cracked. "I'm sorry. I wish you hadn't asked me."

"Never be sorry for anything, Lewis. Just keep moving ahead and hope to make it better."

The Camry had been keeping two or three cars between us, but as I slowed down to shift lanes for a switch from the Golden State onto the old Pasadena east, it closed the distance. Switched lanes and pulled up alongside on my side.

Inched ahead. Giving me a brief look at the driver and the passenger, who was having problems sighting the M-1 he had propped on the open window frame.

I pulled the wheel hard to the right, shouting, "Duck, Lewis!" and heard the sound of shattering glass.

Chapter 26

The shooter came close to sending Lewis and me off to make new friends at the morgue. The bullet whizzed through my open window and close enough to the back of my head to singe a patch of hair, grazed his forehead before bashing into the passenger window.

I would have to take him aside soon and explain that ducking is a forward motion.

If he had not leaned backward as quickly or as far as, well—

—isn't that what Fate is all about?

Or, the venerated Chinese god of good fortune, Dumb Luck?

The Camry was long gone by the time the CHiP responded to my call and I'd been too occupied keeping control of the Porsche and getting it onto the shoulder to have any chance at catching the license plate.

None at catching the shooter, but I was pretty certain that was only temporary; nothing I elected to share with the investigating officers taking my statement.

Lewis, badly shaken, was taken by the paramedics to USC-County General for overnight observation, more traumatized than he knew, urgently insisting he was fine right up to the moment his legs began to jelly wobble and he swooned into the arms of the uniform questioning him.

I got home about an hour later.

The sky was graying out, rain clouds gliding in from the coast, bringing with it a light breeze that put a chill on the mid-eighties temperature that had been slicking the city all week.

I had called Anny from the scene. She was waiting for me on the porch, pacing back and forth anxiously, and darted down the steps as I pulled to a stop in the driveway and sat gripping the wheel, finally giving in to the reality of exactly how close I'd come to exiting the planet.

She made a face at the passenger window, temporarily patched with cardboard, and had her arms around me before I was fully out of the car. Tears streamed down her cheeks.

I stroked her hair and kissed her forehead.

We stood like that for several minutes, neither of us speaking, her body quaking like a candidate for the Richter scale. Heart racing. Breath coming in short gasps of relief.

She stepped back and quietly studied my face.

After a moment, she added an enigmatic smile to match my own.

I took her hand in mine and we headed for the house.

At Marina Emergency Center, the uniformed cop sat lazy guard, halfway dozing on a chair banked against the corridor wall outside the room with a "Restricted Entry" sign taped to the door. He snapped awake at the sound of footsteps clacking toward him. His startled expression turned into a smile answering the doctor's smile.

The cop checked his watch as the doctor pushed open the door to Room 250 and entered. Verging on 3:30 in the morning.

Crossing to the bed, the doctor also verified the time.

Hovered for a minute over Stella Ivers.

She was sleeping fitfully.

Still gift-wrapped like a Christmas present, but her move out of ICU and into the private room had signaled she was off the critical list and safer, easier to reach.

A whoosh of breeze as the door opened behind him.

A yawning nurse entered the room, clipboard under her arm.

A questioning look on her face.

She didn't recognize the doctor, but she knew he didn't belong here at this hour.

He disarmed her with that same smile and a vertical finger up against his lips.

Hurried forward and slapped a hand over her mouth too fast for a sound to escape.

Gripped her to keep her from crashing to the floor and applied strong pressure to her neck until her eyes took her to sleep, then moved her gently to the bed and underneath the covers, alongside Stella.

Checked the time again—luminescent hands counting the hours and minutes—the second hand racing to the next phase of the maneuver.

Just—

About—

Now.

"Code blue, code blue. Room two-five-oh. Two-five-oh." The call charged over the loudspeaker system and down the hospital corridors, seeping into the room. "Team One respond. Code blue. Room two-five-oh. Team One respond. Code blue. Room two-five-oh."

Outside the door, a crashing sound, like the officer had tipped over on the chair and fallen. The door slammed open, banging against the interior wall. An empty gurney negotiated by a four-man team in blue wraps.

The doctor stepped out of the way as they maneuvered

Stella onto the gurney—treating her delicately—then backed out the door, chasing after them.

Past the police officer who was busy putting his chair upright, brushing himself off.

Down the corridor and onto an elevator being held in wait by another doctor, who answered his questioning look with an affirmative nod that informed him Colonel Soulé was dead.

Chapter 27

Eddie Skeffington, "Right Wing" Rappoport's clerk, was always good for a favor after I salvaged his career about eight years ago, when he was rousted and roughed up in MacArthur Park by a couple veteran patrolmen who thought I was winking when I sent down word that gay bashing was history in the LAPD.

They got early retirement that clipped several years off their pensions and the file on Eddie got lost for good, too fast for word to leak back to Rappoport, who would have been faster to forgive Eddie if he were a serial killer.

I reached Eddie in the courtroom about eight.

We kibitzed a bit before I told him what I needed and, after a few minutes on hold, Eddie clicked back on the line with Ginger Ottergo's address and, just in case, her phone number.

It was a practical thought.

When I reached the Larchmont Village area, I parked the Porsche a block away from Ottergo's street and used the cell phone.

It was verging on nine-thirty, but you would have thought it was still the middle of the night by the shaggy sound of the shooter's voice. He answered with a brain-weary, "Who the fuck?"

Satisfied I was not about to lie my way into a missed opportunity, I snapped off and took a slow walk to Ginger's place, as casually as the neighbors walking their dogs, carrying the empty cardboard box about the size of a small fax machine I had picked up on the way over, on a fast in and out to Costco, where they're generally plentiful by the checkout stands.

The dented black Camry was parked on the street, all the confirmation I needed to go with a glimpse of a woman behind the wheel and, call it cop's intuition, the notion she had to be Ginger Ottergo.

She lived in a small, unremarkable pre-war bungalow that was probably built for spit and today could bring in the low seven figures. Larchmont was a most desirable mid-city address for white-collar strivers not quite ready for Beverly Hills, Benny Ottergo's category until his divorce.

Now, Benny was just a poor lunk with a new wife and a pile of obligations to a tripped-out ex whose Evil Queen notion of getting even was to lie away custody of his son and who, lately, had come to include me on her vengeful want list.

I took the wad of gum I had been chewing and covered the spy hole on Ginger's front door before pushing the doorbell. Two notes sounded inside, but drew no response. Neither did the next two. I kept on depressing the bell, creating a silly symphony, until I heard cursing and shuffling and, finally, through the door, "Who the fuck?"

"Federal Express," I answered back.

"I didn't order any Federal Express, goddamn it!"

"Package for Mrs. Ottergo? Mrs. Ginger Ottergo?"

"Yeah, okay. Just leave it the fuck out there by the door then."

"Need a signature, sir, acknowledging receipt. Can't leave it without a signature. The package is insured."

"Then fucking shove it up your insured ass."

Conversation inside, two voices, like he was explaining to someone.

"You got a package for me?" Her voice raspier than his.

"Yes, ma'am. Federal Express. Needs a signature."

Coughing up phlegm. "Something I gotta sign?"

"Yes, ma'am. Or, if you like, I can leave a release slip. You sign the release slip and leave it on your door handle and I can come back tomorrow and leave the package."

"What is it? Who's it from?"

"Let me look; just a second." I examined the empty box. "Tiffany's, ma'am. It's from Tiffany's for Miss Ginger Ottergo."

Conversation.

"Look, fella, I'm not dressed, neither of us yet, you know?"

"I understand," I said.

I really didn't. Usually, the gag had worked by now. The door is opened, hands reaching out for something to sign, not expecting to see a .45 stuck between their eyes. Something felt wrong here, very, very wrong.

I said, "So I'll just leave the release slip here on your door handle and—"

"No, wait! Listen! That's the gift I been expecting for my daughter's wedding today. Noon. Tomorrow won't work, you unnerstand?"

The lady was a fast, fluent liar, steady with the kind of story a judge would buy. Maybe me, too, if I didn't know better.

"Yes."

Her voice dropping a fraction, trying to melt into sugar. "Jeez-o, she'll be so disappointed. I don't suppose you could make an exemption in this case?"

"I don't, I mean, it's really against the rules."

"C'mon, you dick head, do it for the fucking bride, or you got something against mothers?"

"Lance, will you shut up. Will you just shut the fuck up!" To me again, adding more molasses: "My daughter will be disappointed."

"Just throw on a robe, maybe? I promise I won't peek." Conversation. "I'll just set the package down here on the porch with the slip and a pencil on top. Take only a minute for you to sign for it and I'll keep my eyes shut."

More conversation.

I put the box in the middle of the porch, peeled the chewing gum off the spy hole so they could see it, and hid myself to the right of the door, my .45 two-handed against my chest.

"Okay, yeah, honey. Just another minute while I get something on."

A minute later, the door creaked open about a quarter of the way.

"No peeking now," she cooed coyly.

She moved onto the porch tentatively, barefooted, her full figure spilling out of a garish dressing gown meant for attention.

Looked curiously at the spy hole and shrugged.

Stepped up to the box and leaned over, hands on broad hips, exposing the deep cleavage of her massive breasts and nipples the size of quarters hardened by the brisk morning air.

Muttered, "I don't see nothing I gotta sign," as she got a grip on the empty box and lifted it. "Hey!"

Wheeled around, saw my face and the .45, and her angry confusion turned into frozen, frightened recognition.

Dropped the box.

"What the fuck's taking—?" Lance sounded like he was just inside the door.

I motioned Ginger to stay silent and start back into the house.

"You need—?" He took a step out, squinting into the daylight, swept from the look on her face to me. "Fuck it!" Grabbed a handful of gown and yanked Ginger inside, but—

I had my shoe blocking the door before he could get it shut. The pain grew intense as he kept pushing, probably both of them, trying to slice off my toes.

"Ease up now or I start sending bullets through the door," I shouted.

It felt like they didn't believe me.

I fired a shot low.

The thick door must have had a hollow core, because the shot did more damage than I intended. Lance began screaming, "My leg, my fucking leg!" and the pressure on my shoe eased.

I pulled it out, got my balance and kicked the door.

It flew open and I sailed in behind the .45.

Lance was on the hardwood floor, half lying on his right side, trying to stem the blood flowing from his left thigh with his hands, crying and moaning his *Fuck, fucking fuck it*s. Wearing a pair of red socks and red briefs with silk-screened lettering at the crotch that read "Pure Gold."

He was in his early twenties, maybe half Ginger's age, with thick blond hair styled like Brad Pitt and enough of a resemblance to Brad Pitt to make me wonder if he'd had a plastic surgeon playing with his face. A muscular body full of track marks and enough tattoos to qualify as a walking museum, including a giant heart over his heart, inscribed:

Lance and Ginger. Eternally.

Her name seemed more vibrant, fresher than the rest of the design.

Underneath I could almost make out another name.

It could have been "Gloria."

Or, "George."

Ginger stood over him, her gown wide open and half off one shoulder, dancing from foot to foot, her breasts bouncing in harmony, hands flapping helplessly, wailing unhappily. She reeked of cheap cologne that couldn't entirely mask a body stench that comes from too much sweat and not enough soap.

The whole place smelled like a brothel that was doing 'round-the-clock business seven days a week.

I flashed on an eleven-year-old boy, Rita's stepson, Coop, exposed to the scene, and wondered as I often did why judges put the law above the truth.

I kneeled on one leg and checked Lance's wound.

A lot of bleeding, but I hadn't hit any place serious.

I set down the .45 beside me and directed Ginger to find some towels, strips of cloth, cord, rope, anything I could use to temporarily medic his wound.

She stopped her St. Vitus dance, studied me while she fought to understand what I'd just asked. Her hands moved to her hips, elbows akimbo. "You're the bastard trying to help my ex-husband and his whore, getting them a fancy lawyer and all." The realization dissipated the rest of her morning stupor.

"And you're the bitch who tried to kill me last night."

"Won't miss the next time!" Lance swore.

"That's the attitude, old buddy," I said, patting him enthusiastically on his wound. "Only next time I'll see you first."

He screamed and began to cry. "You fuck! You fucking sadist!"

Ginger was still calling me names and swearing to get me and anybody who took Benny Ottergo's side against her.

She was shaking on more than a hangover.

A little morning free base pick-me-up?

Meth.

Lance's fog-saturated eyes told the same story.

I removed one of his socks and stuffed it against the bullet hole. Pushed his hand over it, told him to keep pressing hard. Pulled Ginger's gown belt free, wrapped it tightly between the wound and his knee, using my pen as a screw handle, and tied it off.

"Unfortunately, you'll live. Good enough to hold you until you get to a doctor," I said.

"I'm gonna sue your fucking ass," Lance seethed.

"You do that, fella," I said, patting his thigh.

He howled.

I patted him again.

He howled again, louder.

"That was for my passenger."

"Sue your fucking sadist ass!"

"I told you not to miss, goddamn it!" Ginger's voice was out of control. "Told you, told you, told you!"

I looked up. In the minute or two I'd been applying the tourniquet, she'd slipped off and got the M-1, which she now was trying to sight.

"See what happened, goddamn it, you and your goddamn lousy aim?" Her own was unsteady, wavering somewhere between Lance and me.

"Kill him dead, sweetheart."

"You're not being a big help, Lance."

"Fuck you, prick. Fuck you fucking dead. Shoot him, sweetheart."

He swung up an arm and caught me across the bridge of my nose with the back of his hand.

The sudden movement frightened Ginger.

She squeezed the trigger as I was grabbing for the .45 and doing a sideways roll away.

The shot powered into the floorboard, where I had been a second ago.

"You fucking missed, sweetheart. Again! Do it!"

I came up on one knee, in a shooter's position.

As Ginger, startled and confused by Lance, fired.

And scored inside his tattooed heart, the bullet entering between the Ginger and the Lance.

And began to mumble incoherently.

And released her grip on the M-1.

And draped herself over Lance, moaning his name and begging him to answer back.

As the front door kicked open and two uniforms burst inside, service revolvers ready to drop anyone who moved.

I hadn't heard any sirens.

They had probably arrived on a Code Two, silent alarm, summoned by neighbors reacting to my shot through the door.

I elevated my arms, throwing the safety on the .45, and declared, "Police officer!"

Both of them did a double take and the senior uniform, a sergeant with a gray mustache that covered half his mouth, blinking and baffled, wondered, "Chief Marion?"

Before I could answer, we were distracted by a banging racket that seemed to be coming from up the central hallway.

The sergeant directed his partner to stay with Ginger and Lance, who was staring wide-eyed into space, surprised by his own demise.

We tracked the noise to a small door and assigned roles by sign language, me on the door, the sergeant on firepower.

On a silent, head-nodding three, I yanked it open.

A cramped closet about the width of a fridge.

Dark and reeking of mothballs, and—

The kid was inside.

Coop.

Naked.

Kicking air where a minute ago he'd been kicking the door. Toes blood red and swollen. Hands tied taut behind his back with a clothesline rope that dug into his flesh. Duct tape covering his mouth. Frightened eyes, like a deer caught in the headlights; red-rimmed from crying, ringed with black circles.

I gentled off the tape.

He looked at me pleadingly. Struggled to find his voice. Promised, "I won't do it again. I won't. I swear."

Chapter 28

The uniforms got my statement and I got the hell out of there, ducking my head away from the street to avoid being made by the media trucks blitzing toward Ginger Ottergo's place, the first of what would be a half dozen or more by the time the yellow tape had stripped off boundaries on the murder scene.

Nothing like a nice murder to warm up the evening news, especially one bearing the added glamour attractions of illicit sex, child abuse, and, somehow, the participation of a *Vigilante Cop* turned *Vigilante Supervisor* already under serious attack, sitting out a coroner's jury verdict on his involvement in another killing.

"That's not all making your day," Fuzz Todd said after I reached him on the car phone to explain what had just gone down and ask for his help. "Guess you haven't had the radio on, or you would have said something."

"KJAZ, my one punch on the dial. George Shearing right now. Something about what?"

"So you don't know about Colonel Soulé?"

"What about him?"

"Colonel Soulé has bought the battalion. He's marched off to that great regiment in the sky."

"When?"

"Middle of the night?"

"I thought his condition was improved enough to get him moved from ICU."

"He suffered an unexpected case of *pillowus interruptus*."

"Meaning?"

"Someone put a pillow over his face and it permanently interfered with his ability to breathe."

"Jesus! I thought there was a uniform posted outside his room."

"There was, and nobody got past him except doctors and nurses making the rounds. Nothing out of the ordinary and he wouldn't have bothered to double-check, except for the scene down the hall with Stella Ivers."

"Are you saying she was also offed?"

"Yeah, but in a different sense, Supe. . . . Parties unknown staged a fake emergency and whisked her away on a gurney."

"What are we into here, Fuzz?"

"Whaddaya mean we, *kemo sabe?* But you? I'd say deep shit that's still rising like the tide, Supe."

I managed to make it into the County Building garage and up to my office without being spotted. Rita and Lewis were huddled by her desk, eyes riveted to CNN on the TV set in my catch-all hutch.

A correspondent outside the Ginger Ottergo home was explaining in breathless *This Just In* fashion how little was known so far:

Police were withholding the identity of any of the participants until the next of kin were notified, but—

—County Supervisor Daniel F. "Duke" Marion had been tied to the murder by an unnamed source identified only as a "Highly Placed Official."

"Crescent," I said. Lewis and Rita had not heard me come in, and the sound of my voice startled them. "Crescent's engineering one more shot at me before the coroner's jury finishes deliberating."

They twisted around, facing me with similar expressions of concern, yet with a difference. Rita was sad, apprehensive. Her hands were tying and untying knots in her handkerchief. Lewis looked glum, resigned, like I had purposely set out to confirm his allegations of the previous evening, his boss as "Unrepentant Rogue Cop."

Marion the Barbarian Strikes Again.

I said, "The victim was the shooter who tried to take us out last night, Lewis."

A breath caught in Lewis's throat and his eyes popped.

I shook my head.

"Not by me. He was taken out by the driver of the car, using the same M-1."

Another swallowed breath. His hand moved to the bandage taped to his forehead.

"How did you find them? Who—?"

"—For later, Lewis. Right now I'd like five minutes with Rita, please. You head on down to Pearce Dickson's and tell him I'll be along in five?"

"He's been calling like crazy."

"*Ranting* is more like it," Rita corrected him. "It's not just CNN. You're all over the news."

"Five minutes, Lewis," I said again, holding out a hand palm upright, thumb and fingers spread.

His curious eyes shifted to Rita and back to me, trying to read the significance behind his banishment. Failing, he shrugged, jammed his hands into his pockets, and padded out the door.

After another moment, Rita said, "Thank you for not saying anything in front of Lewis." Her hands were working furiously on hanky knots.

"Fuzz reach you?"

She nodded and sank into her chair. "Right after you

called him from the car, Fuzz said. I got right on the phone to Benny. Benny should be at Queen of Angels by now." She looked up at me, her eyes growing wet, begging for details.

"Benny was fine, Rita. Coop was fine. He was frightened and his wrists will be sore for a while, from how tightly they'd tied him, but not a mark on him otherwise."

"None you could see," she said, working the knots like prayer beads.

"Close up shop, okay? Go be with Benny and Coop."

"Too much still to get done here," she said, staring listlessly.

"It'll get handled. Go to the Queen. Benny and Coop need you more than I do."

I placed a comforting hand on Rita's shoulder. She shuddered but, as quickly, placed her hand over mine and squeezed it gently.

"Chief, you know if I had been with you this morning when you found Coop, Ginger Ottergo would be dead, too."

"If I'd found Coop before the cops arrived, I would have saved you the trouble, Rita."

I returned a call from Rupert Bachman before heading to Pearce Dickson's office. Several others were marked *Urgent*, but they were "urgent" to the callers. This one was "urgent" to me.

Whatever Bachman had to say, I wanted to hear.

Once again he surprised me.

As usual, he started with the small talk, suggesting with a jovial edge to his voice, "Duke, you're on the news so much nowadays, they should pay you the way they pay the Dan Rathers or whomever," he said, jovially.

"I was a Tom Brokaw man myself, Mr. Bachman."

"To each his own season. They all seem to have time for

you. TV. The tabloids. Now, this sad, tawdry business at the hospital."

"Who was behind it?"

"You think I would know?"

"They probably have a Betting on Rupert Bachman board at all the finer Las Vegas casinos."

Bachman chuckled. "Well, yes. If you were to put down your money on my knowing, you would not exactly lose your shirt." He paused like he was waiting out a drum roll. "Colonel Soulé's murder and the kidnapping of Stella Ivers show every sign of being the handiwork of your friend Bruno Guy."

I let the statement sink in. "Why?"

"She's his wife? Bruno wanted her back? And I have to believe Bruno discovered the good colonel was working with us in ways I won't bore you with."

"Like talking to a coroner's jury?"

Bachman ignored my sarcasm. "It could be the colonel bought a bill of goods from her and was being lured to his demise, only an unfortunate automobile accident temporarily intervened." He let me think about it for a moment. "Bruno never has been one to leave business unfinished or a precious wife behind."

"Behind? If this was all about Bruno coming in—"

"It was, yes. I don't think it's so anymore, for whatever the reasons. So, Bruno retrieved his wife, and, now, as you couldn't be more aware, Duke, we're counting on you to retrieve him for us. I don't suppose you can tell me when that will be?"

"I don't have the remotest idea," I said, lying.

"Why don't I believe you, Duke?"

"Because it's not what you want to hear?"

"Of course, that must be it," Bachman said, unconvincingly.

Chapter 29

Pearce Dickson sent the football sailing at me as I pushed open the door to his office and entered. The twister was high and to the right, and I almost bobbled a one-handed catch.

He hooted. "You're not as good as you used to be."

"Never was," I said, tossing back the ball underhanded.

He clamped it with two hands, set it down on the desk and, moving his legs from the surface onto the floor, eased his chair into an upright position.

"You never was." A cackle. "Pete DeHavilland used to tell me the same thing about you."

"Then you understand why I got to be All-America and Pete, rest his soul, was named All-Mouth."

"All-America? All-Pro Washout maybe. In this century, a bigger mouth anymore than your running mate at UCLA, our great and good late friend Pete, never was."

"Pearce, I think it's your memory I dislike the most about you."

He hefted the football. "Care to know what I dislike most about you?"

"Not really. Not in the mood."

He made like he had not heard me and jutted his chin at the dozen TV monitors mounted high on his vanity wall, tuned mutely to the news channels, where screens not filled with a remote in front of Ginger Ottergo's were airing file footage from the Nell Fontanne dinner and the museum dedication. One of the stations had even dug up tape shot when I was still in uniform, defending myself against charges of racism and police brutality raised by a cop killer's lawyer running the first lap of a plea bargain.

"You seem to have become the official poster boy for death. The first thing this morning, you're being tied into a homicide at the hospital and, now, some actor. What is it with you and actors, Duke-o?"

"Passing as a human being was his only acting job. He was a mainframe junkie into torturing kids and I didn't put him down."

"Yeah, was the girlfriend they're saying on what's become the Duke Marion Film Festival. From her pictures she looks like a pretty good roll in the hole, you think?"

"What else are they saying?"

"That Supervisor Marion is becoming a liability to the city."

"And what are you saying?"

"I'm saying I don't like the rumbles I've been hearing about a recall election."

"For you or for me?"

"Biddy-boom!" Pearce made a rim shot noise, stroking the desk with invisible drumsticks. "Frankly?"

I held out my hands and scooped air toward me.

Before he could answer, there was a rapping on the door and his press secretary, Manny Sutton, shambled in, a butt dangling as usual from a corner of his mouth, eyes dancing edgily around the room.

Pearce lobbed the football.

Manny's reaction was a fraction of a second off. The ball bounced off his chest onto the floor. He acknowledged me with a nod, stooped to retrieve it.

"I just got called from the coroner's," he said. Took the butt from his mouth and examined it. Pushed out a line of smoke. "Coroner's jury says the Powell shooting was manslaughter. Unprovoked."

Pearce pounded the desk with a fist.

"They're sending the DA and the Grand Jury a unanimous recommendation for indictment." Manny closed his eyes and snapped a smile like a rubber band at me. "What can I say, Duke, except I'm sorry. Proves as usual the only good jury is a bribed jury."

"Thanks, Manny."

Pearce said sarcastically, *"Thanks, Manny?* Here you are bringing down more shame on the entire August institution of the Board of Supervisors and the sum total of your emotion is, *Thanks, Manny?"*

"I always do better with a Grand Jury, Pearce."

He let out a shriek, and I saw he had serious anger rising, or was he just putting on a show for Manny?

"Right, the Grand Jury," he said. "The chairman here is dutifully reminded this won't be a new experience for you, facing down charges. It's like Homecoming, right? The Big Game. You're actually looking forward to facing them down. Damn it, Duke-o. You truly did not leave the police department when you came over here. You brought the police department here with you." He pushed back from the desk, popped to his feet, and stalked the room. "I was about to explain to you, before Manny got here with his news, why I didn't like what I've heard about you and a recall election." I nodded. "In my book *recalls* are pure bullshit!"

"Thanks."

He shook his head violently.

"Let me finish. . . . Maybe you should be thinking resignation."

Manny was listening intently to our exchange.

At this, he squeezed an eye shut, angled his head, stroked his lips, like me, trying to read Pearce's mood.

I said, "Mr. Chairman, I thought I was innocent until proven guilty."

"You mean like real people? Like civilians? Hell, no! Where you been?" Pearce retrieved the football and launched it at me. "Society hasn't operated on that principal for decades and equality under the law means you are guilty, even if it is only guilty of being accused."

An easy underarm catch.

"Remind me, Pearce. That the platform you got elected on?"

I heaved the football back.

"Hell, no."

He hauled down the ball one-handed.

"I lied like everyone else. Like you. Better election than rejection, I always say."

"I told the voters the truth."

"Then half the fault will always be yours, Duke-o, and the other half will always be theirs—for believing you."

"Better than buying the lie, Pearce."

He let go of another torpedo. It missed my head by six inches, caromed off the wall and shattered a large pane in his picture window as Manny called, "The televisions, gentleman!"

Half the screens were featuring close-ups of Police Chief Paul Crescent. He was in his press conference mode, shuffling papers at the podium and doing his best to look important.

Pearce found the clicker on his desk and brought up the sound on *Cable News Extra* as Crescent shook his fists at the air and decried vigilante justice.

★ ★ ★ ★ ★

The chief of police completed his formal statement in five minutes, folded the pages and slid them into an inside jacket pocket, dropped his octagonal-shaped glasses into the thigh pocket of his uniform, which he always wore at public appearances when he especially wanted to make the kind of impression he expected would one day get him elected mayor, and opened the press conference to questions. He squinted into the wall of cameras, lights, and microphones. With seeming impartiality singled out the field reporter from *Cable News Extra*.

"Chief Crescent, would you expand on your reasons for not being surprised by the coroner's decision or that it came on their first ballot?"

"Of course, Alison," he said, expecting the question. He had worked it out with her boss less than an hour ago. "Understand first, I believe in the public's right to know and, also, that I have a lot of respect for Supervisor Dan Marion."

He paused to let that sink in, nodded, and stuck out his lower lip for emphasis.

"After all, Supervisor Marion was chief of police before me, so, that's second. Third, I cannot emphasize enough, as I have all the times before now, how strongly and fervently I endorse the right of all citizens to bear arms."

Another pause, to make for an easy sound bite lift.

Make sure the point wasn't lost on the gun control goons.

"It's in our Constitution, Alison, all you ladies and gentlemen of the media, but we all know that. We also know it is not a privilege to be taken lightly or to displace those of us who are sworn to uphold the law, to protect and serve."

And, now, pause, the punch line:

"Therefore, that's why it became patently evident to the fine men and women serving on the coroner's jury that Supervisor Daniel Marion overstepped outside the boundaries of his office, his obligations and the public trust and he must be dealt with accordingly." Pause for sound bite. "Supervisor Marion left good judgment behind and his reflexes were too swift when his trigger finger cut down a man, an icon of our own silver screen, who wasn't no more a murderer than you or me or any law-abiding citizen of Los Angeles."

"But Powell was brandishing a gun," the *New York Times* correspondent called out, without waiting to be recognized. "He fired. Blanks, but Marion didn't know that. Some people would say the supervisor acted heroically."

The chief reined himself in, took a deep breath rather than be drawn into a debate that might make his animosity too evident.

Plastered a false smile in place.

"I suppose, but do our opinions matter? The will of the people has been heard once and next it will be heard a second time when the Grand Jury convenes to consider a righteous course of action and, maybe—(pause for sound bite)—also call into question Supervisor Daniel Marion being present this morning in the middle of a lovers' quarrel that ended in a murder before police could get there on the scene."

"Are you saying Supervisor Marion figures in a love triangle, Chief?"

Crescent pretended shock at the question bleated out by the *National Enquirer* reporter and mildly reproached him:

"Putting words in my mouth again, Gary? It's you who have said—(pausing for a sound bite)—Supervisor Marion figures in a love triangle . . . And that's not even the issue in front of us here now today. Here now today we are questioning if the public wants any of its leaders practicing a vigilante kind of justice that went out with . . . well—a vigilante kind of justice that went out with the chief of police just ahead of me."

Crescent nodded gravely into the camera lenses and prepared to index finger another questioner.

Bruno Guy said, "I'm telling you again, Ray. This asshole chief of police is about as sincere as a whore's love."

Bruno was watching the conference from the Burbank Village condo volunteered by a former comrade-in-arms, whose involvement in rebel causes had not aged as well as his enthusiasm after he made a pile in speculative real estate, but Georgie was available for a buck or a bunk whenever Bruno called.

"It's a performance," Bruno said, peering intently at the fifty-inch screen. "I've been on to clowns like Crescent for longer than I've been on the run."

"They're all clowns, Bruno. Anybody in uniform or carrying a badge. The reason it became necessary to defend the country against the defenders once and for all."

Ray Cream had reentered the den from the kitchen with two fresh cans of Miller's Lite. He handed off one, plopped himself down on the other end of the couch, and studied the picture of Duke Marion that appeared in a view box over the shoulder of the chief of police as the chief used his name disparagingly for the fiftieth or eightieth time.

"There's the exception to your rule, Ray, right there."

"Marion? Only because he's your friend. You say such a thing if he wasn't your friend?"

"From a rooftop, Ray."

"I mean, where anybody could possibly hear you saying it?" A smile tilted up the corners of Ray Cream's mouth.

"He was a great cop, a great chief of police. He did his thing, but only against the real bad guys."

"And never against you?"

Bruno let the question slide.

Ray Cream picked up his copy of *Paradise Lost* and, skimming for his place, said, "So if it's so, what you're saying to me, why do you got to kill him?"

"Honest to God, Ray—I wish I didn't."

"So don't then, the guy's such an ace and your old friend from the neighborhood besides."

"Too late."

"Then you do what you gotta do, Bruno."

Ray raised the Miller's at him.

"The story of my life, Ray."

Chapter 30

Manny Sutton, an anxious look on his face, was waiting for me in the garage, leaning against the passenger side of the Porsche and adding a fresh stream of second-hand smoke to the inescapable layers of exhaust fumes. His expression said Manny had more on his mind than small talk.

"I figured you'd want to get out of here early as you could after Crescent's Duke-bashing, instead of giving the news scramblers a chance to race over here and take aim again, Supervisor."

"There's nothing I could tell them now that would work for me," I said, flipping a palm upward.

"You got that piece of wallpaper hung, Supervisor. You ever gonna take care of that window?" Manny thumbed at the makeshift cardboard repair in the panel. "An open invite to car thieves shagging for parts."

"I've already talked to my car guy about it."

"Watch where and how you park until then, you know?" He gave me a knowing look.

"You didn't just happen here to talk about automotive safety, did you, Manny?"

"Well, the weather's been beaten to death."

He mashed his butt against the sole of his shoe and put it in his pocket. In another moment, he had lit a fresh one and was sucking smoke into his lungs.

"Smoking's gonna kill you one day, Manny."

"Not hanging out to talk about that, either," he said, and took another heavy drag. Smoke poured from his mouth and nose.

Manny's eyes, round and probing, seemed to be memorizing my face. We were about the same height, but he was all bones inside his double-breasted black suit and his shirt collar looked two sizes too large.

I realized my prediction might already be Manny's truth.

He stepped farther out of view by any passing cars and drew me to him with a gesture. Fished a floppy disk from his pocket and offered it. "You know the fuck from computers?"

"Better than I can program the VCR."

"For your eyes only. What you do with it after that's your decision, only don't try making a copy. I been told you try it and the disk launders clean." He snapped his fingers. "Like that."

"You going to tell me what's on it?"

"You got something against surprises?"

"Usually."

"Call it a gift."

"No red suit, Santa? No reindeer?"

"Ho, ho, ho. How's that?"

I flipped the floppy from side to side. "You discuss this with Pearce?"

He raised his eyes level with mine from an oil spot he had been studying. Grunted a laugh. "It look like a football to you?"

I laughed back. "You know you don't have to do this, whatever *this* is."

"If I did, I wouldn't," he said, his eyes shifting to the sound of an ignition lighting up nearby. "You never been but decent for me, Duke, going all the way back to the old days when I was doing beat grind at the *Times*, so I figured you were overdue for some payback." Manny turned and started away toward the exit, his steps squeegeeing on the asphalt. "Meanwhile, it's a good idea for you to watch your backside."

"Why's that?" I called after him.

He paused, his shoulders hunched over my question, and pushed more smoke into the air. "It's like the past. Follows you wherever you go," he called back.

When I pushed the key into the door lock, I noticed the small scrap of yellow paper under the windshield.

Bruno's handwriting, and all it said was:

To Hell and Back. Tonight.

I smiled, crumpled the note, and pocketed it along with the floppy, wondering meanwhile if putting it there also was Manny's doing.

To Hell and Back.

My past was not only following me, it was about to catch up.

Tonight.

I checked my watch.

In about six hours.

At about the same time, at a memorial park in Glendale, a group of twenty or so tourists, mostly Japanese dressed alike in garish souvenir T-shirts, khaki knee-lengths and cameras, were being led into The Great Sanctuary by a guide who slowed down his commentary whenever he wanted to be certain everyone understood and appreciated the significance of some special history he was sharing with them, like now—

—in front of his favorite stop on the route.

"A question I've been asked before," he said, slowly and cheerfully, after giving the group another minute to get all their pictures, adjusting his position so they could get him in some of their shots. "Perhaps more than any other in all of my years of introducing folks such as yourselves to the wonders of our fine park."

The two men flanking him bowed appreciatively and moved aside.

Husband and wife look-alikes, each toting a youngster, stepped in to replace them while a new photographer lined up his shot.

The guide angled out an arm. "It deals with the absolute and supreme mystery of this magnificent crypt right here before you."

He said it so solemnly that there was an immense wave of *aaahs* even before the group's interpreter repeated the message in an approximation of the guide's tone. "And more to the mystery, my friends, the late Mr. Archie Pratt is only recently laid to his final rest here, but his dearly precious and beloved Estelle, whomsoever and wheresoever she might be, it is still not yet right here in this remarkable repository, to this day, and no one knows if-so-ever or whensoever she ever will be. I don't know. Nobody knows. We can only appreciate that the marble of Carrerra, from whence Michelangelo broke apart one massive block to release his immortal statue of David, here culminates in a remarkable union that was and is—forever."

Appreciative *aaah*s drowned out the interpreter, but—

—one of the tourists kept a quiet smile to herself.

The tour guide picked up the bouquet of flowers at the

base of the crypt, clasped it to his uniform. "And these wilting flowers?" He improvised. "Made of eternal marble in some person's indelible dream. They come here mysteriously, to no known timetable in eternity's calendar. As a fresh, sweet-smelling homage. The sender unknown by name. A phantom intent on adding fresh leaves to the beautiful memories of Mr. Archie Pratt and Miss Estelle Ritola."

More *aaah*s, mimicking his reverence.

An undercurrent of Japanese chatter while he restored the bouquet.

"Now, if you'll head off in that direction," he said, indicating, his tone lightening as he passed through the group and into the corridor. "Our next stop along the Aisle of Eternal Dreams will be to the bronzed ashes of the silent screen comedian Huck Bacon."

The tour guide paused to shut and lock the crypt gate before trotting after them, unaware he had just locked one of the tourists inside, the one who had been smiling at his inventions. Or, that she had intentionally hung back, hiding in the half-light of the crypt shadows. Tears now streaking the makeup she had so carefully applied earlier in the day. Veined and freckled hands clutching a small, elegant crystal goblet while she studied the legend carved in the stone:

FOREVER IN LOVE,
FOREVER IN LIFE, FOREVER AFTER.

Nell Fontanne thought about it a while longer.

Moving closer to the crypt, she said rapturously, "*Forever.* How nice a thought that always was, Archie, darling," and—

—drew the goblet to her lips.

Chapter 31

I asked Anny, "How's Alicia *really* doing with it?"

"She's your daughter. How do you think?"

I smiled. "How about you?"

"We've survived worse. We'll survive this."

"I know we will, puss. I was asking about you."

Anny's eyes narrowed into slits, augmenting a firm set to her mouth. "I'd like to strangle Paul Crescent."

"He's only doing what he believes in."

"Screwing you over."

"Ratcheting himself upward at the expense of anyone. At least, he does it without showing favoritism. He's not the only one out there who's like that."

Anny was having none of it. "Breathing air a human could breathe," she said.

This might have been the perfect time to tell her about the disk Manny Sutton had given me. I had checked it out while the fresh veggies were steaming. If the documents I saw were legitimate, Crescent was a bigger fool than I ever gave him credit for being, who would be auditioning defense lawyers sooner than he could possibly finish me off, but—

—the disk came with problems, and—

—the problems made me uncomfortable.

I wanted to look some more, think some more, probably corner Manny and ask him where he got the disk and why he had passed it to me, when I saw better reasons for him to have made the disk the property of his boss, Pearce Dickson.

If I told Anny, she would want to see it for herself, immediately begin designing the noose for Crescent's neck while trying to fathom the other revelations, so I decided to wait. Besides, my mind was too preoccupied with Bruno.

My ears drifted back to her voice.

She was agreeing there were others like Crescent practicing deceit like it was a virtue.

"Like Bachman, right?" she said.

"Different. You always know where Crescent is coming from, not because he's honest, but because he's transparent. Bachman is neither. He drew me in with a lie, I'm certain of that now, and the only truth you can count on is his desire to get Bruno."

"And you don't think Bruno is cooperating, that it was Bruno's idea to begin with?"

"I won't know that until I talk to Bruno."

"Tonight."

I checked my watch. "About an hour."

"And you're certain he'll be there?"

I reached across the dinner table and took her hands.

"As certain as I was about you the first time I ever saw you? No. Somewhere south of that, but on the same map."

A smile brightened her face, then slipped into a look masking her concern.

"And you're certain it's not another Bachman trick?"

"To hell and back?" I shook my head. "Bachman can go to hell, but it will be on a one-way ticket. That one's Bruno and me."

"But if Bachman did learn what it meant and—"

"Then it would only be Bachman and me tonight, just

246

like it was up at Barnsdall. Bruno a no-show. I'd bet on it. Usual bet?"

She frowned at my wink.

"And if you're right about surveillance and Bachman's people are following you?"

"They won't be if Plan A works."

"And if it doesn't?"

"Plan B. Where he'll be, Bruno will see them coming. If he sticks, it's one story. Old Danny boy'll be there to bring him home safely. No sign of him? Confirmation about everything we've talked about."

Anny's look of concern grew darker.

"Colonel Soulé murdered. The woman, Stella, kidnapped. Promise me you'll be—"

"Careful? Who's writing your dialogue? You see how careful I am?" I leaned forward and patted my back at the belt line. "I'm still packing the .45, aren't I? Can't be more careful than that."

Anny slipped her hands away.

"Not funny!"

I grabbed them back.

"Puss, at the risk of repeating myself—one way or the other, it's over tonight. If Bruno's there, great. No Bruno there and I tell Bachman it's his time to disappear."

"Until the next message from Bruno."

Her eyes challenged mine.

I raised my hands in surrender.

She shook her head as the front doorbell sounded and a minute later Alicia was poking her head into the doorway to tell us Tobias Buck had arrived.

Tobi pushed Alicia fully into the doorway and wrapped his massive arms around her arms and waist, lifting her off the ground.

"Look at this one now. Bigger and bigger every time I see her and the supremely beautiful spitting image, thank goodness, of her mother."

"Oh, Uncle Tobi!"

"Well, you are, sweet thing," he said, settling Alicia back down.

He took a step back and nodded approvingly.

Alicia had changed into her cheerleading outfit and was about to head off for a practice session.

"And count your blessings. You could have wound up looking like your reprobate father or, worse, your Uncle Tobi."

"Oh, get out!" she said, giving Tobi a playful sock on the chest, and she sent us a *What am I going to do with him?* look when he grabbed the spot on his freshly-laundered white coveralls, fell backward in mock horror, and begged Alicia in his high, alternately whistling and wheezing sixty-something year old voice for mercy.

His voice never seemed right for his still youthful, muscular frame, the same way his thick butcher's hands with their stumpy fingers were not the surgeon's instruments you would expect to find on someone so brilliant when it came to operating on cars.

He's been ministering aid and comfort to my Porsche since before the day I had put together enough savings to purchase it from one of his customers, Jay Leno, the TV guy, who was weeding out the classics collection he houses in an industrial warehouse around the corner from Burbank Airport.

Tobi, whose garage is also in the complex, specializes in restoring classics and exotics. He's built a national reputation over the last forty-something years by personally working on every auto brought in, including high-strung formulas trucked in for tinkering and testing on the short run track behind what he thinks of as his "operating room."

"How's the time?" he asked. "We ready for this Mission Impossible of yours?"

"Let's believe it's possible," I said, rising from the table.

Alicia gave me a questioning look.

I nodded. "Time for Plan A, sweetheart."

She smiled eight thousand dollars worth of orthodontia and gave me the thumbs-up sign. I returned it and was about to answer Anny's face full of alarm when Alicia beat me to it.

"Really, Mom. Nothing to worry about."

"This isn't what I expected your father to teach you about driving when we got you your learner's permit," Anny said, making a joke of it.

Tobi said, "I taught her the driving part, Anny. Months and months of practice and she's better behind the wheel than our glorious supervisor ever will be. She'll be fine. Like a spin once around Griffith Park."

Alicia gave another thumbs up and split.

I came around the table and, placing a hand on Anny's shoulder, leaned over and kissed the top of her head.

"I'd never do anything to put her in danger, you know that, puss. Alicia is going to her practice, the way she always does. She understands she's to pull over and stop if she's hassled, but not even Bachman is stupid enough to try that."

"How can you be sure?" she whispered, nervously.

"Because he's read my file and knows me well enough to know, if he did anything that came close to harming Alicia, I'd kill him."

"After me," Tobi said, although he couldn't be entirely certain of what we were talking about. I'd only told him enough to bring him here tonight, the *what* of it, not the why.

If anyone from Bachman's team was outside, either for

surveillance or ready to wheel, over the next ten or twelve minutes they would see and hear:

—The garage door rise.

—The motor start on the secondhand Chevy we'd given Alicia for her sixteenth birthday and the headlights revealing the flatbed towing trailer Tobi had backed up the driveway and stopped dead center.

—Alicia cut the engine and dash from the garage to a window, calling for her Uncle Tobi and me to do something about the flatbed.

—The two of us emerge briefly from the garage, having used the through-door to the service porch, with Tobi complaining about the shattered passenger window before he climbs into his tow truck and eases it closer to the street, while I go into the garage and duck behind the wheel of the Porsche.

—Tobi hand signal the Porsche up onto the flatbed and cinch it down, directing my assistance while orating about his favorite driver, Juan Fangio, and the crash Fangio had survived in 1955, at Le Mans, before taking off.

—Alicia's daddy escort her to the Chevy, give her a hug and a kiss on the cheek, then go back inside the house through the porch door as Alicia snaps on the heads, turns the ignition key and gets a grind instead of a purr. Again. Again. Again. Until she steps from the car to scream at the house that she thinks she's flooded the motor.

—Her daddy poke his head out the front door and tell her to relax, give it five or six minutes.

—Alice, after not quite ten minutes and one bad try, get the car revving, gun the motor hard—

again, one more time—and barrel the Chevy down the driveway into a sharp turn up the street.

By which time I would be at the freeway and about ten

minutes closer to Bruno, having used the same time to slip out the back door, hop the backyard fence, pass to the next street through our neighbors' property, and locate the finely-tuned Austin capable of Indy 500 speeds that Tobi had parked there earlier.

Aided and abetted by Alicia's stall tactic, at best a primitive deception in this day and age, but slick enough to slow down any trackers while they tried to figure out what I was pulling and, maybe, just in case, send tails after Tobi or Alicia or both.

How well the deception worked—or didn't work—I'd learn soon enough.

Chapter 32

When I got to Grand Central Air, I waited in the Austin for about fifteen minutes, half expecting to catch some sign of Bachman, before I took the stairs two at a time up to the terminal deck, as empty as it had been the last time, when I brought Lewis Tully here. I stood at the rail and studied the clear, calming twilight sky, counting the already visible tracts of stars and grinning back occasionally at the man in the moon, having transported myself back decades, to a time when Bruno and I often stood together like this and talked about what the rest of our lives would be like.

I already knew I was going to be a cop and, maybe, he already knew the direction of his future. Bruno also would grow up to carry a weapon, but that couldn't have been as clear in his mind. He was always talking to me about peaceful change, by evolution, not revolution. He'd sometimes force-feed me page upon page from some new political tract his pop had brought home and try to convince me to join his revolution, knowing it was a lost cause, as so many other of his causes became.

"We both stand for the same thing, Danny boy. Law and order."

"You make the laws and I'll keep the order, Bruno."

"Not in the new order I see for this country, where peace is total and there's no call for a police state or police in any state."

"You are a dreamer, aren't you?"

"A doer, Danny boy," he said, garnishing the boast with a beguiling smile. "No more Vietnams. No more Nixons."

By the time I'd become a football hero at UCLA, Bruno was the ranking campus radical, always finding a cause to rally and rail against. The stunt that got him expelled was, in fact, a stunt, one they still talk about every year, when the Bruins go against our hometown rivals, the USC Trojans.

A halftime card stunt.

The night before the big game, Bruno and some of his followers, students drunk on the rhetoric of change, had broken into the field house where the multi-colored cards are stored and reworked them.

The next afternoon, when the head cheerleader exhorted the bleacher section at the Rose Bowl to turn over the cards for stunt number eighteen, what was supposed to read *Bruins Rule* instead read *Bruno Rules*.

He quit on formal education after that, telling me the only diploma he had wanted was "in *Truth,* Danny boy, something you're hard pressed to find in the classrooms of any college or university in the country, where they only teach you lies, and the lies go on to become the truths of government."

I said, "No more Vietnams or Nixons? You been smoking that funny stuff again?"

Bruno made a face. "Where the truth ends, that's where the lies begin, and soon they become the truths, only they're still lies, Danny boy, so we have to abolish the truth in order to restore the truth and bring honesty and freedom back to the government, can't you see?"

It was an argument without a winner.

And inevitable that we would drift apart, although never out of touch entirely, as if I were some meaningful ballast Bruno's life lacked.

Only a few years later, he was doing things he had always disdained, even if you believed only half the stories that pushed him to the top of the FBI's "Ten Most Wanted" list.

Some years after that, Bruno went into hiding, emerging from time to time as a name paired with the most violent of criminal acts by some group taking aim or arms against the government.

He made it to my wedding as a brief shadow on the back wall of the church.

There were gifts mysteriously left on the porch when John was born and, again, for Alicia.

Not a birthday or anniversary arrived without a card from him, mailed from some strange postmark, until four or five years ago, then—

Nothing.

Not a word.

Mama Guy said it was the same for her.

She mourned.

The best I could do was lament for the Bruno Guy that might have been.

And, now, how close was I to bringing Bruno home safely to her?

My memories were broken by the sounds of a low-flying chopper overriding the drone of traffic on the freeway. An LAPD S&R unit using the freeway as a guide path, its patrol lights scanning the horizon.

I adjusted my wrist until I found the spot where the face of my Timex was in focus.

"Like clockwork, Danny boy." Bruno's voice. "Shazam!"

I smiled inwardly. Turned around. He was invisible, yet near enough for me to hear his breathing.

"Like clockwork, Captain Marvel."

"And about time, Danny boy."

★ ★ ★ ★ ★

Bruno stepped out of the darkness and walked over to stand beside me at the rail.

We embraced for what seemed like an eternity before he pulled back and, shifting to stare out at some distant star, said, "Every week, this day, this time, we stood up here on the deck waiting for Audie to come back."

"Audie."

"There was a flyer. Audie. The most decorated flyer of World War Fucking Two. A fucking Hero. A movie star. And the best damned pilot we ever got up or got down."

"Every week," I said. "This day. This precise time."

I patted the face of my watch.

"Audie would track back over the hills, follow the L.A. river bed, come in for a perfect landing in that old Curtis-Wright Condor of his," Bruno said, mesmerized by the horizon.

"And we never missed a week."

"Not once, not so long as Audie flew here. It seems like yesterday, Danny. We tripped over each other to be the first to reach him. *Where did you go this flight, Audie?* we would ask. He would answer, *To hell and back, boys. To hell and back.* Always the same answer."

"And then Audie crashed, died, and had to be cut free from the wreckage, and we wondered, remember?"

"If it was in the same old Curtis-Wright Condor. I still wonder sometimes who it was out there, who was waiting to meet him, and whether Audie's last landing was to his own private hell or back."

Bruno pulled a cigar from somewhere, like a magician's trick. He turned to me and said, "Still off the weed?"

"Still off."

"Filthy habit, yeah." He lit up. "A Number Two Monte

255

Cristo. Cuban. One of the perks of being up in Canada, where Castro is not the three-headed beast he's always been here."

"So that's where you been hiding?"

"If you mean Canada, yeah. If you mean in Cuba, also yeah. But never hiding, Danny. Always visible among people who shared my point of view."

"But not anymore?"

He gave me a sly, non-committal look for an answer and sucked in the Monte Cristo. Filled his acne-scarred cheeks. Popped out a set of blue smoke rings. Stroked his once-taut jaw line.

Bruno still had an enviable head of hair, pepper and salt and worn long, tied in a ponytail that reached to the middle of his back; an athletic frame with the barest hint of a paunch. He still exuded the charisma of a movie star, a born leader, but his stone-etched pretty boy look was gone.

Flat, almost dead brown eyes denied the painted grin on cracked lips that hung at an awkward slant I didn't recall, and scars that had not healed properly crusted down one side of a deeply-wrinkled face gone ghostly white and fleshy with the passing years.

He caught me staring, but didn't seem to mind. "My war wounds, Danny. Some of them. Fortunes of war, but at least I still have my health, most of it." Took another hit off the Monte Cristo. "Anny still as beautiful as ever?"

"Do angels ever change? She sends you her love."

His smile showed missing teeth, others stained a gross yellow or gone black with decay.

"Alicia?"

"Spitting image."

Another giant smile, but fractured at once by his next remark.

He said, "I cried when I heard about Johnny."

After a moment I managed to answer, "Thanks."

"Went to church. Lit a candle. Said a prayer."

"Since when are you Catholic?" Trying to make a joke of tragedy.

His eyes knew it. He said gently, "I wasn't doing it for me, Danny boy." I patted his shoulder appreciatively, not trusting my voice. "Also went to the service. Graveside, too."

That was a revelation. I looked at him incredulously.

He reached over and pressed a palm against my cheek.

"Something I had to do. The whole damn country was on my ass, fingering me for the embassy bombing that took out that rotten bastard Amir, but I was bleeding for you, knowing how much Johnny meant to you and to Anny. And to me. He was as close as I'll ever come to having a son of my own."

"Me, too, Bruno."

"I never did get the whole story. Tell me."

"Nobody did, only a few who had to know."

"Share it now?" Bruno's eyes seemed to be pleading. "What say, dear friend?"

My eyes bent inwardly and my mind regressed as the scenes of my worst dreams played themselves out, how I'm called away from a crime scene with an urgent message to get to the hospital, something about Johnny, something about Johnny being in ICU.

I get there, to ICU, and there's Johnny plugged into modern medical science.

There's Anny, hollow-eyed, rushing into my arms, her silent alarm switching into babble as she hugs me desperately. Her tears spilling onto my face as I lead her out into the waiting room. Still babbling. Stuttering out something about Johnny on drugs, a dark secret we'd never even suspected— not our clean-cut, model student, super athlete, son of a cop kid. Something about Johnny overdosing on LSD, speed, or something. Something about Johnny going out of his mind.

"I was asleep, Duke," Anny says, "and I feel something, sense something, at first thinking it's you finally home. I opened my eyes and there Johnny was, just like all those years ago, my little boy, when he'd appeal to me with a look to crawl onto our bed, and I told him, *Okay, baby.*

"He kissed my cheek and headed right for the foot of the bed, like he was a little boy again. It was so sweet . . . he was so sweet . . . I dozed off, but something woke me up later. Something made me look. John was gone. Only that old sensation remained, like some heavy winter blanket warming my feet.

"It got to feeling so wet. Too wet. It was seeping through the covers, so I switched on the lamp. I saw blood. Where he'd been sleeping. Johnny. It had to be his blood, Duke. It had to be Johnny's blood.

"I ran to his room. He wasn't in his bed. I went running through the house and couldn't find him. I woke Alicia and told her we had to look for her brother. We both went calling, *Johnny . . . Johnny . . .*

"I don't know what made me go to the closet, except that's where John used to go when we played Hide-and-Seek. We'd inch open the door and he'd be there with his face buried in his hands, remember?"

I start to say something.

Anny looks up from her lap and glares at me.

She doesn't want interruptions.

She says, "He must have come straight to me from the kitchen, Duke . . . it was one of the good dinner company knives, the Henckels stainless steel . . . when I found Johnny there in the closet, the steak knife was still sticking out from his stomach . . . his stomach. I don't—I think Johnny is going to die, Duke."

Before he can, I wake up. Always at this point, escaping my nightmare, but aware it's pointed me to spend another day living life without my son. I try not to think about it or speak about it, never even to Anny or Alicia, whose own mourning is also perpetual. I can see that on their faces, no matter how they try to hide it, as both of them can see it on mine. The not speaking about it is easy, but there's too much that makes the not thinking about Johnny's death impossible . . .

I shook my head to Bruno's request as I snapped back to the moment.

He said, "Some things are better left secret, huh? Even from best friends?"

I had no answer for him.

"Then just this," he said, understanding. "What's it like to lose a kid, Duke?"

I said, "God's worst punishment."

A corner of his mouth flicked upward. "Then maybe a good thing I fell out of that habit a long time ago."

I said, "Johnny never wanted to believe the worst about you, Bruno."

"And you?" When I didn't answer at once, he said, "Only some of the worst?"

"Some of it."

He made a laughing sound.

"I wondered if you were going to lie to me. I could always tell, you know? You never were very good at lying."

"I always gave you the benefit of the doubt, Bruno. You always deserved that from me. That's what I told Johnny anytime he asked. Alicia, too."

"Anny?"

"Nobody tells Anny anything."

Shared laughter.

"That's always been so, yeah. I once told her I loved her and you know what she said? Anny said, no, I didn't. It was just that you had her, not me, so I wanted her. Get your own girl, she said."

"And you did."

His smile disappeared and his face became taut. "Yeah. I did."

"Stella."

"Stella."

"Kids?"

"Just Stella."

He turned from me. I could see he was holding something back.

"What, Bruno?"

He shook his head.

We were quiet for a few minutes, each exploring a patch of convenient sky, until he questioned, "You've seen my mama lately?"

"To tell her you might be coming home."

He nodded. "Brave lady, Mama. I miss that damn garden of hers, you believe that? You remember, Danny? For sure we figured I would turn orange from the carrots and you'd turn green from the peas."

"But I only peed green from the peas."

It was our old joke and Bruno laughed loudly into the still air, the way he used to when we feasted on Saturday morning cartoons. It lapsed into a grunt, and we were quiet for a few minutes, finding reference points on the fire-damaged Griffith Park landscape catching the last orange and golden flickers of daylight savings time.

"Are you coming home, Captain Marvel? Did I tell Mama right?"

"You tell me one, instead, Danny." Bruno studied the

cigar. Finger snapped a half inch of ash. "Is Stella, is my wife, is she okay?"

He saw my confusion.

"After they snatched her from the hospital, then what? What have they done with her, Danny? With Stella. Rupert Bachman and his government assassins."

I gasped audibly. "Bruno, what the hell are you talking about?"

Chapter 33

Bruno made a broad gesture and said, "Come on, Danny boy. If you're playing Bachman's game, you know the score."

"Bachman told me you took Stella out of the hospital. You and your people. He said—"

"My *people?*" Bruno laughed uproariously. "Hiding out for seventeen years is not the best way to keep *people*. You get old while they get on with a revolution that is not *your* revolution anymore. They're your clod-brained reactionaries and those splinter movements that aren't ever going to be as good as my worst bowel movement." He shook his head in disbelief. "No, it wasn't me and my *people* who snatched my wife. It was him, Bachman, behind it. Grabbing Stella was his asshole way to keep me from changing my mind, I suppose."

"Change your mind? Why? You agreed to come in. You had a deal. You got me into it to guarantee your safety, or are you saying that was one of Bachman's lies, too?"

Bruno shook his head, began nodding vigorously.

"That was Bachman's idea and for a while I wished it was mine. It capped a long, sometimes violent negotiation, but I should have known he was already scheming. Get what he needed from me, then I was fair game." He made a hissing sound as he pinched a thumb and two fingers together, as if putting out a candle flame. "Goodbye, Bruno."

"The deal is for your freedom."

"Danny, Danny. The deal's anything the government wants after the government gets what it wants. My information is vital. Necessary—or a whole lot of federal buildings are going to go boom soon and leave a lot of bodies lying on the ground. But Bruno Guy? Try and picture Bachman having to explain my amnesty to a Senate committee or some White House bozo as a fair trade. I don't think so. Having me disappear afterward saves him a lot of potential embarrassment."

Bruno couched his cigar on the railing, looked at his fingers and, seeing my curiosity, pushed them at me, for me to take my own look. The tips had been scarred beyond any reasonable print ID.

"Ask me why I deluded myself into thinking otherwise," he said.

I gestured for him to go ahead.

"Because I was ready to come home and because Stella was, too. More for her than for me. There is genuine evil out there today, terrorists who kill indiscriminately, for kicks, not for a cause, and joke about it among themselves. Mass murderers in the name of revolutions not worth our snot. I am as against them as anything I ever protested in my life, but there is a world of difference between a revolutionary and a reactionary. Worth the try, I told myself. Convinced myself . . . I was wrong."

"The Freedom Militia?"

"Sick souls powered by ignorance, but they're not the only ones. There's almost as much evil working 'round-the-clock in Washington. An entire army of Rupert Bachmans. Once Bachman drip-dries me of whatever I know, the only way he'll want me is dead. I am Bruno Guy, for Christ's sake. I am his Cracker Jack prize. His box top. I am Rupert Bachman's route to his next promotion. Bottom line, his worst nightmare, who can make his impossible dream come true."

"You don't know that."

"I do," Bruno said.

I challenged him, "Tell me how."

Bruno tossed me an arrogant look, like I was a beggar in need of a bone.

"Bachman got what he needed to know about the bombs, dates and places, from Gus Van Zandt," he said matter-of-factly. "Gus was as tired as me of the revolutionary life, Danny boy. When I sent him off to deal with Bachman on my behalf, he dealt for himself.

"Bachman roped Gus with promises of a new name, a new face, a new country. A fresh start. All the same shit I was ready to buy for myself. For Stella. For Gus and one or two others who feel the way I do and, as it turns out, are a damn site more loyal than Gus Van Zandt."

"And you killed Van Zandt for dropping the dime."

"Van Zandt was executed for treason."

"Which you also were ready to commit."

Bruno drew a *score one for you* line in the air.

"But not against my friends. Not against comrades. Treason, maybe. Yes, treason. But betrayal? No. Never betrayal, Danny."

"You make a fine distinction."

"One of the perks of leadership," he said after a moment, not comfortable with the remark or his response. "Why do you think my name was never attached to criminal acts anywhere near your authority, either as the chief of police or as a supervisor? You don't tread on friendship."

"The Satterfield Massacre?"

His head drove left and right. "They put my name to it, but it wasn't me, so help me, God."

"You never believed in God."

"I still don't, but that's never stopped me from asking for His help, giving Him a chance to prove me wrong. Where I could always ask for your help, Danny boy, and never have to worry about the consequences."

A grin lit his face, failed when I suggested, "Maybe Bachman got to me, the way he got to Van Zandt."

"Are you telling me it's so?"

I changed the subject. "What about Colonel Soulé?"

He hand-patted an easy rhythm on the wooden railing for a moment or two, almost dislodging the Monte Cristo.

"Another Bachman tool, deluded into believing it was in the best interests of your darling Nell Fontanne. The night of the accident, Stella was taking Soulé to me to deal with."

"And he was willing to go with her because she was Edwin O. Powell's daughter."

"Something along those lines. Poor dear old, wonderful Eddie. If only he'd stuck to the plan, instead of dreaming up a new one for himself and the love of his life." A new sadness lit his eyes. "If Eddie'd stuck to it, there could have been a different ending to all of this."

"And would Colonel Soulé still be alive?"

"You see how he's dead anyway?" he said, ignoring a direct answer. "Bachman's doing, Danny boy, not mine."

"What about Nell Fontanne?"

"What about her?"

"She's disappeared."

"Not me. Not us."

Bruno seemed genuinely puzzled. I let it go.

"Why would Bachman bother murdering Colonel Soulé if Soulé was cooperating?"

His palms turned upward.

"Constructed for Bruno Guy to get the blame. A murder

that's not covered by our amnesty agreement. So, he would have me for that, if word about the amnesty leaked, as I'm sure he'd have it do. He needed to put a public face on my death. Didn't Bachman tell you that?"

I said to the sky, "Again he accuses me of playing Bachman's game."

Turning back to Bruno, I said, "Why? Have I changed that much in your eyes?"

"It would be easier it was true."

"What would be easier?"

Before Bruno averted his eyes from mine, turned his face away, I saw he had no intention of answering the question.

"Bachman tried," I said. "Lots of threats and what ifs if I didn't help him get to you."

"And that's why you're here?"

"I'm here for you, Bruno, not for him, but there's a bigger question. Why are you here? If you know Bachman is out to get you, why?"

"Like I said, Stella makes the difference." His voice faltered. "If Bachman didn't have her, he wouldn't get me. You see? I'd be out of here already. Forever. And when the bombs went off, blasting those seven federal buildings to smithereens, it would teach him a lesson. Serve him right for playing his games on us."

"I'm not tracking you."

"Meaning?"

"You said he got the dates and places from Van Zandt."

"And names. Gus also had names to give him."

I grasped at once his expression of crisp contentment. "The information he got from Van Zandt. It's no good."

He gave me another chalk mark. "Like Gus himself. Like Bachman probably has found out by now."

"And you would let those buildings blow and hundreds of

people die, just to teach Bachman a lesson?" He shrugged. "In my mind that makes you no better than the fanatics you disdain for spoiling your goddamned revolution."

"War is hell, Danny boy, especially when the enemy is ourselves."

"All this time and you're still quoting Pogo."

"Can I help it if a comic strip possum has more common sense than the so-called leaders of the so-called greatest society in the history of man? Like Pogo, I have seen the enemy and he is us."

There was a rustling sound behind us and Bruno called, "It's okay, Ray. Come on out."

A man half-stepped out from around a terminal wall, an Uzi 9mm semi-automatic cradled in his arms, finger at the trigger, and took up a position behind Bruno.

"Danny, say hello to Ray Cream. Ray, say hello to my best friend, Danny Marion."

Ray grunted to my nod.

There was something familiar looking about him.

I couldn't place it at first.

He was a six-footer, in his mid to late forties, his bulk stretching his huntsman's jacket; jeans tucked inside lumberjack boots. Shaved head. A heavy, blue five o'clock shadow. Hard eyes lurking dangerously behind steel-rimmed oval frames.

"Been eavesdropping, Raymond?"

"As a matter of fact." He kept his eyes on Bruno while addressing me. "It's all the truth you been hearing. I was the one what disposed of that traitor Van Zandt, what sold out to the Feds and Bachman, gave up a lot of names, even Stella's daddy, Eddie Powell, and that got them onto that jerko Colonel Soulé." Ray Cream pronounced the name to rhyme with *fool*.

267

I threw away a hand. "Why you look familiar! You bumped into me that day. A minute before you put the knife to Van Zandt." He rolled his eyes like I had missed the punch line to a joke. I slammed my forehead. "The woman who was there! It was Stella."

"Stella was keeping Ray company, Danny boy. She was ready to make a diversion if it became necessary."

"Got away nice and clean, that one. Same as you never saw me when you and that maggot food that goes by the name of Bachman had your rendezvous up in the park." He mispronounced *rendezvous*.

"The homeless guy."

"Right on. And thanks for the fiver. I think it should have been more, though, you being a public servant and all?"

He was drop dead serious.

"Next time," I said, but Ray missed the sarcasm.

Turning back to Bruno, I said, "So, what now? Where are we now?"

His face sagged. "I have to honor a promise I made to Stella, what became the damn real reason for us getting together tonight."

"Not to connect with Bachman?"

"Not for old times sake, either, Danny boy, although it's been nice as far as it went. As far as it can go."

Bruno had about half a Monte Cristo left. He doused the cigar on the tower railing and dropped it in a pocket of his safari jacket. Eased out an HK P7 automatic pistol from his shoulder holster and held it with the barrel facing up.

"I have to do you, Danny."

I looked at him incredulously.

Shifted my eyes to Ray, who had the Uzi aimed at my belly and was nodding agreement.

Back to Bruno.

"I expect you still carry, Danny, so I'll need your piece. And it wouldn't hurt to keep your hands where we can see them."

Ray kept nodding as I slipped the .45 from the holster at the small of my back and, gripping it by the barrel, gave it to Bruno, then reached up for the sky like we did when we were kids playing cops and robbers.

Bruno said, "Believe me, Danny, this is nothing that gives me pleasure, not another Gus Van Zandt thing, but a promise I made to Stella after you killed her father."

"Accidental. An accident, Bruno."

"I know, but try convincing a dutiful daughter who is whacko with anguish and begging me to revenge his murder by executing his murderer. So, I promised Stella. Gave her my word. Told her we needed you to come in. Told her we'd get settled in our new lives and then—" He drew the P7 across his throat.

"You can do it?"

"Danny, Danny. Been doing it for years. Don't you read the newspapers? The only differences—those were casualties of war, the revolution business, and this was revenge Stella was demanding. This time the victim would be like part of my own family, have a name and a face, and I'd grieve and light a candle and say a prayer for you, the same as I did before for Johnny."

A pained look crossed his face.

"I tried talking Stella out of it, believe me. She was not hearing a word I said. Brains in a basket. So, I said fuck it, I would, figuring give it some time. Let the truth take over. She'd meet you, hear you out, come to her senses, call it off. Only there was that accident first, and then Bachman stole her from the hospital and here we are."

"You kill me and then what?"

"Into the wild blue yonder, old chum. Remember the poem we had to learn in Mrs. Fernandez's class?" He recited, *"He who fights and runs away may live to fight another day . . ."*

I finished it for him. *"But he who is in battle slain will never ever fight again."*

"You got it, Danny," he said, leveling the P7 at my chest in a marksman's grip. "I don't remember who wrote it, though."

"Me, neither. I could go look it up. Be back in about an hour?"

He laughed loudly, the forced gaiety of someone who is trying to cover another emotion.

Ray sensed it, too. "You rather me, Bruno?"

"S'okay, Ray. I have to do it myself now, for Stella."

Ray mumbled something I couldn't make out, sounding disappointed, and restored the Uzi to rest.

I said, "Without Stella, Bruno?"

He narrowed his eyes, forming deep furrows between his brows, and eased the sight line. "Explain."

"You asked me before where Stella was. What Bachman had done with her. You said it like you meant it, like you meant to get your wife back."

"I did. Once I'm out of here, we'll reopen dialogue. I get Stella, he gets what he wants. Original deal in place. I find out Stella is—" He swallowed hard. "Then I would have no reason to deal and Bachman is marked."

My mind shifted to overdrive.

"Kill me and live to fight another day, you'll never get her back."

"Meaning?"

"Bachman will lose her out of existence, all the way back to Stella's birth certificate, the same way Soulé's death will never be connected to Bachman."

270

"So you did know after all."

"I did," I said, lying. "Bachman recognized he had no reason to shut me out of his game plan once he was satisfied I was still law and order."

Bruno probed my eyes, his own plagued by doubt.

Finally, "She's okay?"

"She's fine," I said, hoping it was the truth.

"You're saying you can get Stella back?"

"I'm saying—"

"He's shitting you, Bruno. Blow him away and let's us get the hell out of here."

Bruno eased an arm back to quiet Ray. The look on his face told me he was trying to understand if I was lying to him or inventing a wild card that might buy some time and possibly save my life.

Rivulets of sweat trickled down my brows and into my eyes. The salt stung, but I didn't dare wipe at it or call attention in any way, or Bruno might notice the slight give in my knees and know the truth for certain.

"Explain."

"You were right about Stella being Bachman's bargaining chip, and he counted on me, our friendship, to convince you your deal still stands. Bruno—he put it on paper for me. I wouldn't take the bastard's word anymore than you. He hears what he has to know from you and, guaranteed, you and Stella live anonymously ever after. You, too, Ray."

"Where's the paper?"

"Secure. Lockbox in my office."

"Why didn't you tell me this before?"

"I had to know for myself where you were coming from."

I saw Bruno wanted to believe me.

Christ! I wanted to believe me.

Only Ray Cream wasn't buying.

"Oh, Jesus fuck!" Ray said, not fooled at all, and he took aim at me with the Uzi.

Bruno understood the look on my face. He swung around to face Ray, at the same time telling him not to fire. The suddenness of the command startled Ray, disrupting his aim.

A series of shots scattered into the floor of the deck, and—

—a bullet smashed through Ray's left lens, splashed out the back side of his head.

Another cracked into his forehead.

Their force rocked him onto his heels, up five or six inches, like his spine was made of elastic.

He surrendered his grip on the Uzi.

It hit the floor before he did.

Bruno and I dove for cover as more bullets zinged overhead, sailing harmlessly through the tower or lodging in a wall. Then—

Silence again, except for the clatter of animals and birds in the park complaining about the noise.

Rupert Bachman said, "You are certain it was not Bruno Guy you took down?"

"Positive, Mr. Bachman. Take a look for yourself," the SWAT team commander offered.

Bachman accepted the high-powered rifle and sighted it through the scope, across the two hundred or so yards separating the control tower from the roof of the eight-level storage garage built on the perimeter of the old airport.

Except for a chunk of body, the leg tricked awkwardly, and what was likely a puddle of blood, Bachman saw nothing. Nobody. No movement on the deck.

"Don't see a damn thing, Commander."

"Those spare shots from my men were meant to push the

others up there out of the way, especially if they had ideas about returning fire."

"But you're positive it wasn't Bruno Guy."

"Not unless he lost all his hair since the briefings. Male we took down was bald and about to tick off your man, Supervisor Marion, when I gave the command."

"Cream," Bachman told himself. "Raymond Cream."

"He was brandishing an Uzi, 9mm semi-automatic rifle, high impact, sir. I expect it fell within reach of Bruno Guy, who was already fielding what appeared to be an HK P7 automatic pistol."

Bachman nodded and handed back the rifle.

"It breaks down now as a standard hostage situation," the SWAT commander volunteered. "My men are ready to either infiltrate or, given a reasonable sighting, take out Bruno Guy before he possibly wastes the supervisor, sir."

Bachman's head began shaking furiously. "Do nothing, Commander."

"I believe, sir, if you were to give me and my men the freedom to free fire—"

"Believe in Santa, you choose to, so long as you know I'm not interested in your beliefs," Bachman barked. "Chief Crescent put you under my direct command, that so?"

"Correct, sir, yes."

"Then hear me. Do nothing. Nothing happens unless I say it and, if Supervisor Marion catches one, well—that's just too damn bad."

The SWAT commander looked at him in disbelief.

He thought better of responding and instead turned back to sighting the airport through the rifle scope.

"Speak of the devil," he announced. "Sir, I believe that's Supervisor Marion coming out of the tower building now."

Chapter 34

In the half light that precedes nightfall, I searched for defini-
tion in the shadows surrounding me as I marched cautiously
from the building to the courtyard fountain, my arms out
forty-five degrees from my body, my fingers splayed, showing
any snipers I was unarmed and no threat.

Except for the sound of my footsteps crackling gravel, an
eerie silence surrounded the area.

There were about a dozen vehicles in the lot, run-of-the-
mill cars and mini-vans parked at the far end, in front of a row
of industrial storefronts, horizontal to the tower. They had
been there when I arrived and I had figured they belonged to
people working late.

I sensed the presence of others, tracking me.

I glanced upward and played the sky like I was counting
the armada of pillow clouds that had sailed in over the past
half hour, my eyes settling briefly at the top of the eight-story
storage warehouse, attracted by a speck of movement.

It was in perfect alignment with the tower, the right height
to get off the shot that killed Ray Cream, and I was ready to
bet that's where the shooters were.

I was confident they didn't want me, too. Bruno, yes, but
not me. Yet, I was not about to do anything to test the theory.
No sudden movements, no words that might be heard as
threats.

I strolled around the fountain until it was between me and

the tower, eyes and ears sucking up the territory. Then, slowly sank to the ground one knee at a time and raised my arms.

At once I was descended upon. In a series of swift movements, I was slammed to the ground, my hands pulled behind my back and cuffed, lifted by hands latching onto various body parts, and transported like a gunny sack through a building door that was flung open as six pair of stomping boots hit the sidewalk behind two mini-vans.

The door pulled closed behind us and I was maneuvered into a standing position as Rupert Bachman's familiar voice echoed in the stairwell.

"Duke, glad to have you join us and in one piece."

He wagged an index finger and one of the flak-jacketed SWATs undid the cuffs. They had done all the work, but I was out of breath, too. I leaned forward, hands on my knees, and gulped air.

"How's your old friend Bruno?" Bachman inquired, moving off the steps and approaching, his ever-present cigarette holder held casually, empty, in his left hand.

"Better than Ray Cream."

What passed for a smile flashed across Bachman's face, and he fortified it with a nod. "That is good news. We do need him in one piece, you know?"

"So far so good."

"And so are you, I see. Until you stepped out from the tower building, I deeply feared Bruno might have decided to put aside his personal feelings toward you and taken your life in retaliation for that idiot Cream."

All the while he was finding a cigarette to plug into the holder. A filter tip. An extra measure of safety. Lit with serene pleasure.

"It's still a strong possibility, Mr. Bachman," I said, rubbing my wrists where the cuffs had bitten hard and left red-skinned bracelets. My expression told him nothing. "I thought I got away clean from you."

"Imposing on the great Tobias Buck I can understand, but involving your darling young daughter in your scheme, shame, shame on you, Duke."

I let it pass. "How did you manage to track me here?"

"Tricks of the trade," he said, dismissing the question with a gesture and a thin trail of blue smoke. "If you must know, we were here before you arrived. I have had this location staked since your earlier visit with Mr. Tully. Call it professional intuition. Same as I have kept Hollyhock House under constant watch. You appeared and an immediate call for tactical reinforcement went to Chief Crescent."

"My tax dollars at work."

Another improbable smile. "You haven't said yet, Duke. Did Bruno spare you for old time's sake or are you the harbinger of good news or is it both? Here to blaze the trail for Bruno himself to step out and join us, keeping his end of the bargain?"

"Here to transmit Bruno's demands, Mr. Bachman."

"Demands? We have our deal in place, so what is there to demand?"

"Stella Ivers."

"Stella Ivers?"

"Bruno wants to see her, know she's well and alive, before he comes in."

He cocked his head and crunched his eyes, like he had encountered an impossible word in the *New York Times* double-crostic.

"I told you before, Duke, we didn't take Stella Ivers. Bruno Guy took his wife. So whatever his game now, I can't play it. We'll have to go in after him and take our chances that we get him alive."

He looked to the SWAT team leader on the stairwell, as if he were about to issue the command.

I said quietly, "Even if you had somewhere to go with your bluff, Mr. Bachman, Bruno will be dead before they get within fifty yards of him, maybe sooner."

Bachman bit down hard on the holder. He didn't like hearing that. He gripped my elbow and steered me away from the others, whispering so we couldn't be overheard.

"Spill it out, Duke," he said, on the edge of losing his temper. "The rest. Every damn word of it."

I said, "Bruno believes you took Stella for insurance, right after you killed Soulé. You killed Soulé because he's not covered by the amnesty agreement. Bruno comes in, gives you your information and—instead of sending him and Stella to Happily Ever After Land—you rape them both with a murder charge."

He liked hearing that even less.

I said, "Bruno is giving you an hour to show him Stella is alive and well."

"And after that he'll surrender himself?"

"Not quite," I said, embroidering on what I had told Bruno. "He expects me to get something on paper from you acknowledging he had nothing to do with Soulé's murder."

"Right," Bachman said, blurting it out like he'd just heard the funniest joke of his life. "You Boy Scouts never do take off the uniform, do you?"

I shrugged indifferently. "No paper, no Stella—no Bruno Guy."

"He thinks he can get out of the tower and away? The murdering fool has another thing coming. And as for his wife? He can kiss goodbye any chance he'll have of seeing her alive."

"Bruno knows he's trapped in the tower and knows the odds against seeing Stella again, assuming she is alive, are nil if you don't agree to his demands."

"And you say Bruno will be dead if the SWATs move in on him because . . . ?"

"You know that, too, Mr. Bachman." His eyes locked on mine. Blinking rapidly. "You have an hour to produce Stella. After that, Bruno eats his gun. Blow his brains out and with them any chance you'll have of stopping the Freedom Militia before it blows up seven federal office buildings in seven locations—" I checked my watch. "—forty-eight hours from now."

Bachman glanced at his watch.

"He would let that happen, wouldn't he," he said, not as a question, erasing any doubt I might have had that Bruno was wrong and any list Bachman had gotten from Van Zandt was a good one.

"No, the way he sees it, you'd be letting that happen. Bruno doesn't want another Oklahoma City or World Trade Center or anything remotely like that, Mr. Bachman. He wants to save the lives of innocent civilians as much as he wants to make a new life for himself and for Stella. Maybe more, but only on his terms."

He wagged a fist as if getting ready to ram it through the plaster. "Bastard!"

"His pet name for you is *Prick*."

Bachman kicked the wall instead, as if he were going for a field goal. His highly-glossed black wing-tips left a gaping hole near the baseline.

He kicked it again.

Turned back to me, his face a furnace of frustration and anger.

Said, "I suppose he also knows exactly how he wants us

278

to—*produce* her?" Making "produce" sound like a word that carried its own germs.

"As a matter of fact, yes."

Chapter 35

Bachman couldn't have been hiding Stella Ivers too far away, because, forty-five minutes later, the sun not quite ready to leave the burnished gold and orange horizon line, an LAPD emergency rescue chopper landed in the airport parking lot, ten or twelve yards from the Austin Tobi Buck had loaned me. It was a modified two-seater, the area behind the pilot and passenger seats redefined for stretchers and gurneys.

The cabin door slid open as the rotors quit.

A medic jumped down, looked around anxiously and waited with his hands on his hips, as Bachman advanced from our spot behind the parked vehicles, where the SWATs and some of his sunglasses-wearing Brooks Brothers boys had taken at-the-ready positions with orders not to fire at Bruno save on direct orders from Bachman, whose heels I dogged.

Upon reaching the chopper, I stepped up to the cabin.

I checked inside while Bachman and the medic exchanged a few words.

The medic whirled and hurried to join the others behind the automotive barricade.

Stella was strapped down securely on a stretcher belted to a pull-down bunk, her head and shoulders visible above the covers. Fewer bandages than I remembered from the hospital. Seemingly asleep inside the oxygen mask. A few monitor hookups. Taking an intravenous feed.

Her eyes opened tentatively, then wider, perhaps with recognition.

"Satisfied?" Bachman said, not bothering to hide his ongoing annoyance.

I held him back with a hand while I moved closer.

Her large brown eyes were as remarkable as I remembered them, but etched in pain where last time they were full of dancing merriment.

I smiled and told her, trying to forget she blamed me for her father's death and wanted me dead, too, "Bruno will be here in a few minutes. You're going to be fine, the both of you."

Stella's lips parted, as if she wanted to say something, but all that came out was a gargle from the back of her throat.

I eased back and, turning around to Bachman, told him, "Satisfied."

"And now you signal your friend, correct?"

"Correct," I said, taking the steps to the ground.

I turned away from the chopper and raised my hands, as if I were about to guide in a jet.

A minute or two passed.

Bachman stood with his arms settled across his chest.

His fingers strummed anxiously on his arm and side while a foot tapped out an impatient rhythm of its own.

After another minute that played like an hour, the door that I had passed through earlier opened slowly and Bruno stepped into view, pausing to check out the scene. Feet astride. The Uzi cradled in his arms. Right hand gripping the P7.

He was a Rambo ready for instant action.

I gave him another high sign.

He nodded, but eyed the situation one more time before

starting for the helicopter with slow deliberation, stopping when he was about two feet from us.

Bachman emptied his cigarette holder and slid it into his handkerchief pocket, crushed the butt under foot.

He said, "So here we are at last, Mr. Bruno Guy," his light-hearted manner unable to overcome the contempt in his tone.

Bruno acknowledged him with a derisive look and turned to me.

"She appears to be fine," I said. I pulled a folded paper from my inside jacket pocket, held it out to him. "The agreement absolving you of Soulé's murder."

Bachman had angrily scribbled it on a pad borrowed from the SWAT commander, who added his own signature, as a witness, in a fine hand full of swirls and curlicues.

Bruno nodded.

Briefly loosening his grip on the Uzi, he snatched the document from me with his free hand and jammed it into a jacket without bothering to check. "Stella," he said. "See her for myself."

"Of course, but why don't you hand over your weapons first?" Bachman said, as if he were offering to hang a coat in a guest closet. He extended his arms. Bruno didn't react and he said, "I'm certain you understand."

Bruno gave Bachman a thin-eyed sideways glance that suggested he understood a lot of things and swung his face across the row of vehicles.

The SWATs and several Brooks Brothers were partially visible, lined up like they were at a firing range and Bruno was their target.

"See her for myself," he repeated, but passed off the Uzi and the P7.

To me.

Clipped my shoulder with a friendly punch, hoisted himself up the three steps, and disappeared into the compartment.

"I'll just relieve you of those," Bachman said.

I gave up the weapons, remembering too late that Bruno still had my .45.

Bachman shrugged at the news. "Not a match for these babies." He examined them. "Excellent choices," he said, strapping the Uzi to his shoulder and examining the P7 for its load. "I'd wager there are hundreds more where these came from, wouldn't you, Duke?" He sighted the automatic using his forearm for balance. "At least ten times that number of innocent victims."

He expressed the thought in a way that said he blamed Bruno for all of them. The malicious glint in his eyes sent out a signal I knew. I'd felt it myself facing down thieves, drug slugs, rapists, murderers. Worse than that. I had never acted on the emotion without cause, answering force with equal force, but nothing here suggested this was Bachman's rule.

The Freedom Militia threat didn't matter now. Maybe it never really mattered.

Bachman intended to pull the trigger on Bruno.

The SWATs, the Brooks Brothers, they were all for show.

Bachman was going to be a hero today.

Had I heard and seen things along the way that should have warned me?

"You and Bruno have a deal, Bachman!"

"Of course," Bachman said, breaking out a fast, phony smile, as solicitous as an upscale maître d', "but my first deal is always with the American people."

Just then, Bruno came into view in the chopper doorway.

He appeared more relaxed, resigned to the moment, all the tension he had been wearing like a shroud gone from his face and shoulders.

I shouted his name and flew at Bachman.

Bachman sidestepped me like a matador, but he was off balance and his series of shots missed Bruno by a foot and ripped into the side of the chopper.

I stumbled forward, tripped over my own feet, and fell headlong onto the asphalt.

Pushed back onto my feet and twisted around as Bachman fired again.

Saw one of the bullets had caught Bruno in the thigh.

Rushed Bachman from behind.

Trapped his arms by his side.

His next shots thwanged uselessly into the ground.

Bruno was grappling with the pilot, maybe half again his weight. They danced around and around in a frantic foxtrot of elbows and fists.

The pilot yowled and fell backward from the chopper, landing hard on the asphalt.

Knocked cold.

Bachman brought his heel down hard on my instep. The pain coursed through my body, causing me to ease my hold on him. He broke free and took aim.

But Bruno had already pulled my .45 from his belt.

He squeezed off three fast shots.

They caught Bachman in the chest and stomach and blew him backward. His own last shots before the P7 clattered to the ground put invisible holes in the darkening sky.

Bruno pulled the door shut and, before it closed all the way, fired two shots at me.

"For Stella!" he called out.

The first shot zinged past my ear by an inch. The second

ate into the asphalt, as did two others as I dropped and rolled quickly under the chopper, out of Bruno's sight line.

"Shazam, Danny boy!" he hollered over the rotors while pulling shut the chopper door. "If Stella ever asks, I can at least tell her I tried."

The SWATs had decided it was time to disobey Bachman's orders. Bullets zinged as the chopper powered up and the blades began rotating. Some from behind the parked vehicles. Others from SWATs racing forward, trying to close the gap before the chopper could get off the ground.

I rolled away and backed off in a crouch, dragging the unconscious pilot with me.

The chopper began a slow ascent into the night, and—

—a SWAT shot deflecting off the sponson cut into my back.

I yowled. Lost my grip on the pilot. Felt the searing pain. Looked up to see the chopper breezing past a three-quarter moon—Bruno en route back to hell—before sinking into a black hole of my own.

Chapter 36

A fraction of an inch to the left, said the doctors, and the deflected bullet would have severed my spine and crippled me for life. Instead, the slug veered right and passed through my body, missing everything that mattered.

To the doctors.

The holes would heal eventually, leaving me with two more scars, more souvenirs of life as we live it today, my first scars as a county supervisor, maybe the first ever on a county supervisor wounded in the line of duty, joining a scar collection built on two wars, one foreign, one played out on the streets of L.A.

Physical scars, I mean.

The kind that includes the aches and pains that come back whenever the weather grows cold.

Mental scars are something else.

They also last a lifetime, but they have no respect for the seasons.

I was patched up and after a twenty-four-hour period of observation, sent home with handshakes all around, vials of assorted painkillers and sleeping potions, and the news that I was no longer a blood-lusting vigilante.

In the intervening hours I had become something of a national hero.

"Marion the Barbarian" was history.

The story delivered to the media and in turn to the gullible public could not have been farther from the truth than the Pacific Ocean is from Palm Springs.

Make that another twenty miles east, from the ocean to Rancho *Mirage;* better, more appropriate, because a desert of fantasy was being irrigated by an oasis of lies.

Of course, the bad guy was Bruno Guy.

Bruno had killed Rupert Bachman in a calculated act of pure aggression while making a successful getaway from the abandoned Glendale airport, where he had lured the renowned "Bug Man" with that intent.

A politically-motivated killing (it was suggested) underwritten by a foreign power with an (unspecified) complaint against the United States. Plans were underway to give Bachman a hero's military funeral at Arlington National Cemetery, with the President in attendance.

L.A. County Supervisor Daniel F. Marion had gone to the airport, he understood, to negotiate Bruno Guy's surrender.

While bravely trying to save Bachman's life, Marion was shot in the back by the morally bankrupt revolutionary, a former childhood friend who has been on the run and the FBI's "Most Wanted" list for most of seventeen years.

Supervisor Marion was successful in saving a helicopter pilot from the savage fugitive, disobeying orders that had kept a crack L.A. SWAT team from moving on Guy, for reasons the government agent heading the press conference said he was not presently at liberty to divulge. For reasons of national security.

Members of Bachman's unit, meanwhile, had successfully brought down a Guy confederate, Raymond Cream—the name he used more often than the dozen others on his rap sheet—who earlier had been linked to the politically-motivated murder of a bedridden hospital patient, the aide to one-time movie great, the missing actress-now-princess Nell Fontanne, identified as Col. Karl Soulé.

Cream was killed in a blazing shootout with the federal agents, and—

—on and on, *ad nauseam.*

There was just enough truth to make the story play.

Enough lies to guarantee that Bruno was never coming home again.

Or so I thought at the time.

Incorrectly, as it turned out.

The Freedom Militia?

Not a word.

And twenty-four hours after I got home, when no bombs had brought down seven federal buildings in seven states or anywhere in the country, I had to wonder if any of that had been true.

Or had that been Bachman's lie?

Bachman's ruse to get Bruno?

Or, Bruno's lie?

Okay, consider, Duke, consider:

Maybe Bruno originally bought the concept from Bachman or, in fact, offered it to Bachman as a trade for amnesty, for the chance at a new life with Stella.

But along the way Bachman learned from Gustav Van Zandt what he needed to prevent the wholesale slaughter planned by the Freedom Militia.

Contrary to what Bruno told me, Van Zandt did have the legitimate locations.

Jesus!

I had questions inside questions inside a conundrum.

I howled and wanted to call my own press conference.

Put the whole truth and nothing but on the table for a change.

My whole truth, anyway.

I was talked out of it by—

—everyone.

Charlie Temple led the pack.

"America needs its heroes and villains far more than it needs the truth," he said, grumbling breath into the phone while I stated my case. "You can be one or the other, kid, but you can't be both."

"And what do you think the truth makes me, Chief?"

"In this particular case?" He pretended to give it a moment's thought. "Stupid would be my guess. Don't waste it on Bruno Guy, the truth. The son of a bitch tried to waste you."

"He meant to miss, Charlie, goddam it."

"The same way he meant to spill his guts to Rupert Bachman instead of spilling Rupert Bachman's guts all over Rupert Bachman?"

"Bachman shot at him first."

"I think Bruno would have shot him anyway. I think that was his idea all along. *Do unto others before others do unto you,* isn't that how it goes? A signed paper getting him off the hook for Soulé? Camouflage, pure and simple. Why he had you order up a helicopter? Setting it up for a fast getaway with his wife. He told you as much, Danny boy."

"That's not the way I heard it."

"Of course not. My way makes you a dupe, where the way you heard it is the way you share with his mother. Why not? She needs something to hold onto. All I need is a golfing partner who can get us a good starting time on any public course in the county."

Pearce Dickson was equally pragmatic when he came to visit.

"You are a first class fucking hero," he said, offering a

snappy military salute before marching into my bedroom and lobbing a small potted plant at me.

Instinctively, I reached up to grab it, pulling my back muscles, and yowled with pain.

"A fucking hero!" Pearce repeated, swiping back the plant and clearing a place for it on the night stand. "By the way, I spared every expense on this expression of my deep affection for you. Some newbie lobbying for the gas house gang sent it to me a day or so ago, like he's on a budget for getting on my good side, kissing supervisorial ass."

"You have no good side."

"And you also can kiss my ass, but I do have what you now have, that being a clean slate and a renewable future in politics."

"Meaning?"

Pearce sat on the bed with his feet on the carpeting and patted my cheek.

"Your sterling performance in trying to subdue the forces of evil at no small and I might add stupid risk to your own life and limb has inspired the Grand Jury to dismiss examination of the coroner's jury opinion of your recent foibles with firearms. In other words, your neck's off the block."

"The DA?"

"Concurs. Case closed."

"Crescent?"

"Not happy, but lacking the support necessary to hold up as much as one of his balls, he's putting on a happy face."

Pearce leaned forward and surprised me with a kiss on the lips.

"A fucking hero!" he shouted at the window, his hand at one side of his mouth.

I told him about my conversation with Charlie.

Rising from the bed, Pearce adjusted his jacket and tie, patted my cheek again, and announced, "The score is Charlie 1, Dumb Fuck a giant-sized zero. Duke, stay a hero. Not a zero."

"I am what I am."

"No, that's Popeye. Duke Marion is a damned fine leader who has a lot more to give a city that can never have enough Duke Marions. Stay a hero. Shooting off your mouth now would only give Crescent and everyone else with a personal agenda a fresh excuse to come after you again."

"Before that happens, Pearce, I can nail Crescent to the cross."

He slicked back his hair with both hands. "I know you think that sounds like a bad thing, but try and remember it turned a carpenter into a king."

"Aren't you curious to know how?"

Maybe it was the way I asked, but Pearce hesitated for a moment and gave me an uneasy look before dousing his chest with palms of air.

"I fell into a floppy disk," I said. "It's full of scans. Documents. Contracts. Private correspondence. Receipts. Memos. Photographs . . ."

"From whence?"

I swept away the question with the back of a hand. "It doesn't matter. Only that it exists. I take it public—Crescent is gone for good."

"What's the bad news?"

"He goes, the way the disk reads he automatically takes other people with him. People in high places."

Pearce's face darkened. His eyebrows danced up, then merged into a furrow deep enough to tell me he suspected he was one of them. "How high is up?"

"In your case, eye level."

Infected silence before he said, "That serious."

"You ever hear of the Ebola virus?"

You could almost see his mind doing cartwheels. He had to be certain. "Anybody I know besides Crescent?"

"Intimately."

"Why didn't I like that answer?"

"For the same reason you knew it was coming?"

"Sounds about right. . . . The source? Did I miss that name?" He cupped an ear. "Nobody I'd call my friend, I suppose."

"Not anymore."

"Are you still a friend, Duke-o?"

His gaze struck me like a Santa Ana and when I didn't answer fast enough to suit him he said, "So, where are you going with the disk?"

I considered the question. "If you were in my place, what would you do with it?"

Pearce looked away from me and made a show of thinking about it. "Under other circumstances, I would assemble the media hordes and blow the motherfuckers out of the water."

"Under these circumstances?"

"You have every right to take Crescent down, Duke-o."

Pearce passed the remark so easily, I wondered for a moment if he did, in fact, know his fingerprints were all over the damn disk.

"And the other *goniffs?*"

"Gah-niffs, Gah-niffs," he corrected my pronunciation. "Moses H. Fuck! You don't get it right by the next election and you're certain to lose at least half the Fairfax Avenue vote."

"Stop evading the question. Do I also take down the other thieves, Pearce?"

"Evading? That's the difference between a politician and a statesman, Duke-o. A politician gives you an answer you can't hear. A statesman gives you an answer you don't understand."

"Which one does that make you?"

"A damn fine supervisor by any name. One of the Five Kings who's done this county a shit load of good. Year in and year out."

"And yourself, too, I'm learning."

"Never at anyone's expense."

"Not even your own?"

"I've never done anything to be ashamed of."

"Then, maybe, you have a higher threshold for tolerance than I do."

He shook his head. I couldn't tell if it was for me or for himself. A thought played across his face. "You mention this yet to Charlie?"

"Only to you."

"Then, maybe, call up Charlie and ask him, too?"

"It doesn't touch him, Pearce."

"Lucky Charlie, but he might have an opinion."

"I'd still like yours. What would you do with the disk if you were in my place?"

After another moment, he threw out his hands like the Pope greeting the masses from his Vatican balcony. "But I'm not in your place, Hero. I'm not." Turning to leave, he opened an overripe smile and said, "The minute you're up for it, you and the lovely Anny will have to come on over for one of Jeannie's deluxe briskets, pan broiled potatoes, the whole schmear, the way you like it."

"And I'll bring the pies," Anny said. She was standing in

the doorway, arms folded across her chest, beautiful in a form-hugging magenta wrap dress. I had no idea how much of the conversation she'd heard. "Apple cobbler and maybe a nice peach for a change?"

"Works for me, you gorgeous thing," Pearce said.

He gave her a light kiss on the lips, urging, "Take care of our boy," as he passed through into the hallway, unnecessarily reminding us that he could find his own way out.

Anny waited a minute before inquiring, "Am I right in thinking the disk you were talking about doesn't have Sinatra singing songs in the wee small hours of the morning?"

I hadn't had a chance to tell her about it before this.

When I was finished, she added some deep sighs to her somber expression, and wondered, "No question that Pearce is one of those people in high places?"

"Only until you click on the files."

She thought about it. "As bad as I'd like to see that bastard Crescent go down . . ." The thought drifted to nowhere.

"Yeah," I said, so quietly I almost didn't hear my own answer.

"So! Where are you going with the disk, Sailor?"

I gave her a reluctant smile. "I suppose to hell and back."

"Didn't you just make that trip?"

"A bumpy ride," I said.

Anny grinned adoringly, trying to free me from a quiet of conscience that wasn't going to lead anywhere today. "You want me to come over there and talk about it?"

"Will we get a lot of talking done?"

"Probably hardly any."

"Will we reach any conclusions?"

"In a manner of speaking."

I patted the space next to me.

She stepped into the room, closed the door, and clicked off the overhead, slowly, seductively unfastening the waist cinch that held her dress together.

"Shazam!" she said, and flew onto the bed.

Chapter 37

A few days later, Fuzz Todd called to say Nell Fontanne was no longer missing, adding, "The rest of it you and Anny may not like hearing."

He was right. Her body had been discovered locked inside an elaborate crypt at a Glendale memorial park. Judging by its condition, Fuzz said, Nell had been there several days.

"Like Beethoven in his grave," he added unnecessarily. "Decomposing. . . . Nothing official yet, but the ME thinks it'll come down as suicide. He found evidence of poison, physical and eyeball, so you can almost count out natural causes."

"How positive is the ID, Fuzz?"

"I've seen your princess looking a whole lot better, but, yeah, certain as a fox in the hen house. A tour guide said he could remember her because she was one of the few Caucs in a fleet of Japanese tourists, but he had no idea she might've been Nell Fontanne, just another one of them old ladies who drop by occasionally and visit their future."

"Next of kin notified?"

"One of the reasons for calling, Supe. You've been elected."

"What's that mean?"

"Got the ballot right here in my heavy little paw."

Fuzz meant a letter the lab boys found among the incidentals in Nell's handbag, in an envelope addressed to me. It was the clearest link to her identity. He got a photocopy over to Lewis Tully, who dropped it off that evening.

I read it and cried.

I handed it over to Anny to read, and she cried.

We cried together.

After Alicia fled to another one of her interminable slumber parties, we decided to try putting a smile on our mourning by watching one of Nell's old movies in our video collection. We chose an early Technicolor epic, Nell at her most beautiful, in love with a dashing and debonair Edwin O. Powell.

The print must have been minted from a negative on the edge of disintegration. It was full of scratches, jump cuts, and a disjointed soundtrack that often lagged behind the picture, but none of that mattered to us.

It was Nell Fontanne, and Anny and I were young again, cuddling on the couch over hot buttered popcorn and tall tumblers of fresh cold lemonade.

Edwin O. Powell locked Nell in an embrace, and I clicked on freeze and muted the sound. I wanted to hear her letter again, and this seemed to be an appropriate place.

"Go ahead," I told Anny.

"I read it the last time."

"It feels better coming from you."

She made an *Oh yeah* face at me, reclaimed the letter from the coffee table and made a modest adjustment in her eyeglasses, pushing them an inch higher up her high-strung nose.

"My dear Daniel," Anny read, trying to match her voice to the flowery script of a bygone era. "I write with fond regard and an explanation to precede a request I trust you will be good and gallant enough to grant me, considering the understanding and beauty you showed me following the moment of singular tragedy we so recently shared, each in our own way.

"I speak, of course, about my darling Archie Pratt, who you know better as Edwin O. Powell, the kind and gentle soul who has had my undivided heart, although marriages prevented us from ever enjoying the single union we would have wished. By saying this, you will readily understand that my emotions of grief the other evening were a sham, a message intended for my aide, Colonel Soulé, to report back home to his prince, my husband in name.

"It had been our intention, mine and Archie's, to leave this veil together in a spectacular manner that united us forever in the mythology of Hollywood, a unity in eternity that we lacked in life. Some would call it ego and foolhardiness. We called it love and devotion.

"Our precious Stella, the love child I was never able to proudly declare mine, became a willing co-conspirator. So did Colonel Soulé, or so I thought then, but no longer. Quite the pretender, the colonel, loyal to a fault, but not to me.

"Yet, how our plan went amiss we may never know for certain, except that it so cruelly did. Instead of the real bullets we wanted, somebody—Stella? The colonel? Both, neither wishing our deaths for reasons of their own?—substituted one more act of make-believe into our lives. Harmless blanks. Thus, you, dear man, came to suffer because of your brave act, undertaken for the bravest of reasons, believing in the truth of the moment as I and Archie intended for the truth to be.

"And, so it shall be, for I have chosen not to allow fate to deny us each other any longer. If you are reading this, I have already joined my precious love, and I ask you, I beseech, beg you and authorize you to take on the task our daughter Stella is now not able to see to fruition—commit us to our final rest here on earth also together.

"Our crypt was carved from stone years ago and Archie is

already there waiting for me. Give him his Estelle. As for Nell, she was never real anyway, so the prince need only know she lost her glass slipper.

"I thank you from the bottom of my heart and, this time with greater certainty, preparing to join my precious love, I leave you, dear Daniel, with words . . ."

Tears were spilling over Anny's eyes.

Her voice had cracked several times.

Unable to continue, she pushed the letter at me.

I read, "I leave you, dear Daniel, with words you may already know: 'The web of our life is of a mingled yarn, good and ill together. Our virtues would be proud if our faults whipped them not, and our crimes would despair if they were not cherished by our own virtues.' So—God bless and keep you, too."

I put the paper aside and thought about the quote.

"*Romeo and Juliet?*"

Anny shook her head. "*All's Well That Ends Well.*"

I glanced at the TV picture.

Nell Fontanne and Edwin O. Powell frozen in time.

And shortly caught myself wondering about Bruno.

Knowing there was every reason to believe I'd be seeing him again.

And then—

what?

Chapter 38

Bruno looked up from the paper, an *I'll be damned* expression doing contortions on his face, wondering if he should tell Stella; knowing already the answer had to be yes.

He had been surveying the *Times* obits daily in the two weeks since rescuing her from that treacherous lying bastard Bachman, looking for a sign that Ray Cream's family had him back for a proper burial.

Otherwise, Bruno knew from history, lacking claims from any next of kin after six months, the coroner would free up refrigeration space by cutting out and storing the jawbone, then cremating the body and consigning it to a common, toxic waste dumpsite.

Ray had been too good a soldier for that, and he deserved better, why Bruno made it an issue with the slur-brained fanatics who picked them up at gunpoint when he landed the chopper inside their camp site northeast of Bakersfield, in the isolated flats of the San Bernardinos.

They were on him like liver spots, pointing more heavy artillery in his face than he had evaded twenty minutes ago, flying low and on the ground before the law had time to even set up a search, and probably would have wasted both him and Stella if the trading cards hadn't been dealt in front, the chopper for temporary safe harbor and a getaway van with clean out-of-state plates.

They called him "Dude," but treated him with a sullen respect for his reputation, "brand name recognition" their leader termed it, even while arguing against his demands for a doctor as they moved from the weed infested airstrip to a small, remote bungalow at the compound, insisting it was not part of the deal.

"She'll die if she's not looked after," Bruno said, but the bald headed, jug-eared freak in camouflage fatigues wasn't swayed to oblige until Bruno agreed to map out a hit that would turn a spotlight on their cause.

The leader called it the New Millennium Crusade, but he was unable to describe or explain it to Bruno's satisfaction.

Fuck! He was another scumbag savior from the Evelyn Wood School of Speed Revolution, whose nuts had traveled from his pants to his brain.

Bruno recognized arguing was useless, so he agreed and sketched out one of the Freedom Militia plans he'd originally invented for Bachman.

A few adjustments and it fit this asshole's intended target, a storefront orthodox synagogue in Palm Desert, and won him no little awe and a snappy salute that bounced off the leader's pimple-stained forehead.

The doctor, an intern at some privately-owned hospital in San Berdoo, still in work clothes, a green smock stained with someone's blood, pronounced Stella relatively fit and probably able to travel in a week to ten days. He dished out a small vial of pain-killers, swallowed a handful of blues from another container that he offered around, and shuffled off after accepting a hug and a hundred dollars in twenties from the leader.

Stella was on her way back to bed from the bathroom when Bruno walked into the room wagging the newspaper at her.

She was increasingly ambulatory, the residue pain ranging from subtle to severe, depending on how she moved.

Bruno knew from her vague stare that she was hopped up, taking too many pills at a time, not ready to surrender a habit she enjoyed too much to ever quit entirely.

"Ray's notice?" she asked, gritting her teeth as she adjusted the bed to a forty-five degree angle backstopped by three pillows.

Bruno shook his head. "Better. You want some coffee?"

Stella waved him off. "I'd rather have some sweet, slow loving from you, baby, but I think it'll be a while longer." A pouty-lipped frown. Her voice a fuzzy monotone. "What's better?"

"A memorial service for your mother."

Bruno's declaration jarred her into a painful outburst, a sound somewhere between a whimper and a whine. "For Mommy? You shitting me?"

"Here in the notices section by the obits, honey."

Tears crowded Stella's eyes as they had regularly any time she was reminded of her mother's death, four columns of news, including an old photo from her Hollywood days, that Bruno had brought her last week.

"It's at the crypt, the way she wanted. Let me get you that coffee?"

Stella signaled for him to stay.

He read the notice to her.

"The fucking prince is doing this for her? Letting her be buried with my daddy?"

"Not the prince."

She stroked her cheeks dry as he again read to her the part that said the services would be conducted by Sterling Morris, who was identified as president of Amalgamated Broadcasting Company.

An ouchy shrug. "Maybe this Sterling Morris guy knew my mother in the olden days. Before Daddy?"

Her slur thickening. The damn pills.

"I don't think so, honey. He's a comic book character, Billy Batson's boss."

"Comic book? Billy Batson?"

"You know—The boy newscaster who says Shazam! and becomes—"

"Captain Marvel. Yeah. So, who?"

"Danny Marion."

Stella's eyes blurted open. "Now you're shitting me!"

"It has to be, honey. A million to one."

"Whatever you say, baby," she said, further interest dulled by the pain-poppers. "I have to be there, though, you know? No matter who this Morris Marvel is. Say goodbye to my mommy."

"Of course."

"Not a problem?"

"Not a problem," he repeated, although he didn't mean it. Getting in would be easy. Getting out—

—another story.

And Danny, what was that about, sending him a signal like that? They'd done all the talking that had to be done that night at the airport. What was left to say? That it was safe for Bruno and Stella to be there? Yeah, that had to be it. God damn friends. What friendship is supposed to be all about. Taking care of one another, no matter what. No matter fucking what.

Bruno moved across the room and adjusted the covers up around Stella's neck, leaned over and gave her a soft kiss on the cheek.

Stella pulled an arm out from under, reached up for his arm, pulled him onto the bed.

Settled her hand on his crotch and began fondling him.

"I'm missing that something fierce," she said hoarsely, suddenly alert.

His smile sent back the same message, not entirely meaning it. He wanted her to get more rest, conserve her strength for the trip to Los Angeles, but he didn't resist as she undid his fly and set him free, and moaned her way into an awkward position that let her take him in her mouth.

Moments later, Bruno was moaning, too.

And when they were both satisfied, Stella, a groggy goner, asleep with her eyes open, said in slow motion, "He still gotta die, you know, baby? Fucking friend of yours killed my daddy and he gotta pay the piper."

"I know, honey, I know. Danny boy is there, I won't screw up again."

"Won't screw up again, make Stella happy," she agreed, passing the words through a blender. Eyes closed now, unable to see the look of extreme pain on her husband's face. "Love you, baby. Love you."

Chapter 39

The morning brought with it a light drizzle.

The sun couldn't make up its mind where it wanted to be, slipping in and out of cracks in the black-bottomed cumulus clouds that hung overhead like a fleet of blimps, covering the memorial park in patterns of gray light, and I wondered if Bruno also would be coming.

I checked my watch.

Nine-forty and still no sign of him.

Twenty minutes to curtain, to show time.

How I thought of Nell Fontanne's memorial service, although Nell already had given the final performance of her life.

Here she was cast in the role of "Estelle Ritola," for that's how her name read in the *Times* notice. Only her real name used, but first among details, as befits the movie icon Estelle became.

I had done it like that rather than risk the presence of media hordes and star-struck gawkers. This wasn't meant to be a star-studded gala honoring lifetime achievement, and so what if future visitors to the Great Sanctuary and this elaborately conceived monument to love never learned that a princess was sleeping eternally alongside her one true love, a lover truer than the prince she had abandoned?

I checked my watch again.

Nine-forty-two.

Eighteen minutes to show time or no-show time.

Which will it be, Bruno?

A stage cough echoed in the corridor and I turned my head to the four neat rows of folding chairs arranged in front of the crypt, facing a handsomely carved podium. All but three of the twenty seats, counting mine, were empty.

The cough had come from Anny, who was giving me one of her Whaddaya think? looks and tapping her Dopey face watch, the Dopey of Walt Disney Seven Dwarfs fame, the case shaped like the little guy's face, a gift Anny was unable to deny herself during a weekend prowl of the Glendale Galleria.

She had an aisle seat in front of Bruno's mother, whose own aisle seat would make Mama Guy the first thing Bruno saw when he arrived.

If he arrived.

He'd be less inclined to disappear at the first sense of an empty hall, a chapel of deception meant to draw nobody but him.

Nine-forty-two and a half.

Bruno, Bruno, Bruno.

Mama Guy sat patiently, hands folded one on top of the other in her broad hipped lap, looking a bit like Whistler's Mother in a rich black dress with a white collar, her eyes closed and her mouth working inaudibly as she rocked forward and back in what could be silent prayer.

"Why can't Bruno just come straight home?" she had asked me when I phoned her yesterday.

She'd accepted my answer without argument, only the noisy burst of anxiety still playing on her face when she arrived with Anny in the station wagon an hour ago.

I'd gone on ahead to the memorial park, to check out the arrangements and make sure the other people I'd invited arrived and settled in where I wanted them to be, where they could not be easily spotted by Bruno, who was sure to check out the scene before he stepped foot inside the building.

Charlie Temple was outside exploring grave markers. His left hand clutched a bouquet of carnations wrapped in green tissue, leaving his right hand free to grab the .38 snub he always holstered under his armpit.

Fuzz Todd was not far away, like Charlie dressed for a day at the country club, looking like a ripe plum underneath his shades and a duck-billed cap. He'd insisted on being here with us, and Charlie agreed having someone with bankable authority around was a good idea, in case anyone had plans for Bruno they were not sharing with me.

Clem McAllister thought Fuzz or anyone was unnecessary. "The arrangement will hold," he said, after we had come to terms and I'd expressed concerns for Bruno's safety. "He and the girl, Stella, have nothing to fear."

"Even if Bruno doesn't buy the proposal?"

"Bruno and Stella will be able to leave untouched by human hands."

"You're so positive of that, even before you make the call?"

"With all due modesty, Duke, this is Clem McAllister you're dealing with." A facetious grin. "The higher the mountain, the louder the echo."

"How high is up?"

"When I'm dealing with Washington? As high as it has to be, my friend."

We'd had the conversation the day before I placed the notice in the *Times*.

McAllister didn't hesitate to invite me out to Malibu when I phoned and by mid-morning I was passed through the electric entrance gate without having to identify myself to a smiling guard, who gave me a high sign and offered to take the Porsche off my hands if I ever decided to part with it.

A bodyguard led me to the patio, where McAllister was taking late breakfast with a dark-skinned woman in a skimpy bikini, who silently excused herself and disappeared with an ass-pat from McAllister while he gestured me to a seat as he cinched his terry cloth robe tighter around his fit, otherwise naked body.

I passed on the food platters, but let him pour me a cup of coffee. He refilled his cup and stirred in cream and a heaping spoonful of sweetener from a sterling silver service, and we passed the next few minutes admiring his sweeping view of the Pacific, before he inquired pleasantly, "So, to what do I owe the pleasure of your company?"

"I think you know."

McAllister looked up, pointing his chin at me, and squinted into the sun while he pretended to think, humming a Broadway tune that could have been "On the Wheels of a Dream."

"MacMurray," he said, finally, smiling for a treat.

"MacMurray," I agreed. "It comes up for a vote next week."

"Yes," he agreed.

"I'm prepared to vote for it," I said, trying to sound like it was a new intention.

"And, remembering my position in the matter, you'd like some encouragement from me?"

"I only mention it in passing."

"Of course."

"But there is something you might be able to help me with, Mr. McAllister."

I felt uncomfortable, like a criminal, guilty just from mouthing the words.

He leaned forward, propped his elbows on the table and swiveled his palms up, his smile as bright as the reflection beating off the glass-topped table.

I said, "Bruno Guy."

"Yes?"

Over the next fifteen or twenty minutes, I told him everything. When I finished, he motioned to a bodyguard lurking in the shade, who hurried over with a canister of cigars. He selected a mammoth Havana and let the bodyguard light it for him after clipping it with a pocket-sized gold scissors he pulled from his robe. The bodyguard moved back to his post.

"You see people licking the cigar first, either they don't know what they're doing or they're about to rag on an El Cheapo," McAllister said, pushing a lean trail of smoke out the corner of his mouth. "Sure you won't have one?"

"Thanks, no. So what do you think?"

"Not to speak ill of the dead, but I think Rupert Bachman was a bona fide asshole, particularly if all you say is true. Even half."

"As true as I know."

"And you'd like to try it one more time, let your old friend hit a home run, get amnesty, although it looks like he doesn't have the Freedom Militia and seven bombs to trade with?"

"If he ever did."

"Understood." More smoke. Another show tune hummed. Something Cole Porter. "But you don't know where he is or the girl, his wife, or even if she's still alive?"

"That's right."

"Supposing what you're asking for is possible, how do you propose getting the news to Bruno?"

I told him.

"You're assuming he's somewhere close, where he could be reading the obituary page."

"The chopper never made it onto a radar screen. That tells me he landed fast and probably within a hundred miles. I saw the shape his wife was in. No condition for Bruno to risk too much ground travel."

"Maybe he crashed and they're both lying dead somewhere out in the desert."

"Maybe."

"Okay, supposing they're not. Explain how you can be so sure Bruno will check the obituary pages."

I looked him straight in the eyes. "Bruno will—unless he's lying dead somewhere out in the desert."

A grin cut into McAllister's face. "I definitely like your style, Supervisor Marion." He played some finger games with his nose while smoke drifted upward from the corners of his mouth. "Only one thing." The grin broadened. "I don't happen to need your vote on MacMurray."

I looked at him with something between amazement and disbelief.

"I didn't say you could have it," I finally managed to say.

He leaned back in his chair and locked his hands behind his head. "Of course, but let me tell you something anyway. Even if you were inclined to vote my way before you came on up here today, and I believe you were, it no longer matters. Since our last chat the balance has swung that way with or without you anyway."

"You know that for a fact, I suppose."

His face said as much.

"Something else I know." He paused for a swallow of coffee. "Say I was mistaken and MacMurray goes down for the count." He threw away a hand. "Shit happens. Only it doesn't end there." He arched an eyebrow. "The Board'll immediately vote to reopen their consideration, only this time

310

the members will be appointing a brand new committee with a brand new committee chairman, all predisposed to act favorably on the issue."

"So what you're saying is, you can't help me with Bruno."

"Not that at all. I'm saying I don't need your help with MacMurray."

"Why did you let me carry on about Bruno?"

"You said so yourself. One thing had nothing to do with the other. What you want for Bruno? You got it. Done. A done deal." A smile to sweep the world.

"But there is something else." I saw it in his eyes.

"Duke, there's *always* something else." There was more than a good three-quarters left to his Havana. He doused it in his coffee cup anyway. "We have a mutual friend, you and me—Pearce Dickson."

Jesus!

"It's the floppy disk," I snapped.

"No wool over your eyes."

His voice had flattened out and so had his face, giving away nothing, like a poker player who could be bluffing on a hole card.

My head began shaking involuntarily. "He's dirty, Mr. McAllister, Pearce is dirty, although I don't suppose that comes as much of a surprise to you as it did to me."

"You can say that about everyone and, where you doubt it, go check under their toenails. Even your friend Bruno Guy. You desire to put Bruno in a better place. I desire to keep Pearce where he is."

I could give McAllister my vote on MacMurray because it was there to begin with. I would have been playing a white lie that left me with most of my morality intact. This was something else.

"You've never seen my toenails, Mr. McAllister."

"I'm trying for a peek now, Duke."

"And if I say no?"

"My answer about Bruno is still yes."

"Why?"

"Maybe you'll say yes next time I'm looking around for an echo."

Which is how McAllister came to be sitting in the back seat of his powder-blue Rolls Royce, CLEM WON, outside the Great Sanctuary of the memorial park, about ten yards from the main entrance, in front of his other Rolls, CLEM TOO.

The two cars had arrived about a half hour ago, in front of Anny and Mama Guy.

Sharing the back seat with McAllister was a man in his fifties, whose hawk nose and high cheekbones gave importance to his deeply-tanned face, who was introduced to me as Perry Little Sky and shook hands like he didn't care for me or what was happening.

McAllister's lawyer, Thom Ehrlichman, was in the back seat of the other Rolls, as officious as ever, and did not bother identifying the man with him; early thirties, heavy sweat, and a chronic twitch in his right eye that suggested he was one of the firm's four-hundred-dollar-an-hour gofers.

A pair of drivers and bodyguards were pooled curbside by the cars. I recognized two of them, including my Porsche fancier, who gave me an eyebrow salute when he noticed me on the entrance terrace, looking around anxiously for any sign of Bruno at—

—checking my watch again—

—nine-forty-seven.

As Duke turned to go back inside the Great Sanctuary, he was unaware of the cream-colored van that eased up the road

312

and glided into a parking space parallel to the grass island across from the building, giving it a clear view of the entrance about fifteen or twenty feet away. The brown lettering splashed across the side paneling identified the InternetWorks & Techknowledge Company of Redlands and promised "Solutions Instead of Problems."

The leader of the New Millennium Crusade was behind the wheel, dressed for a prayer meeting, as was the woman in the passenger seat, similarly dressed, although their nose rings and the mismatched rings rimming their ears, as well as the head she'd shaved to match his, seemed better suited to a mosh pit than a memorial service.

The woman, who was in her early twenties, lifted her Lolita lollipop shades and squinted past the two Rolls Royces at the entrance, then let her eyes roam the grounds, hardly pausing to examine the two old geeks who had stopped to chat amidst the grave markers.

"What do you think?" the Leader wondered.

"Smells like beaver bush to me."

"Why?"

"Count the cars."

"She must've known rich fucks," he said. "Two-a them anyway."

"She must've known a lot of other people also, so what did they do? Walk up that goddam fucking hill?"

"Down below, the lot across from the gift shop?"

"The guy at the gate sent us on up here straightaway, so why wouldn't he do the same with everyone else?"

"They're late? Goddam freeways!"

She backhanded his arm. "Dumb fuck! Who made you boss anyway? See the time? Starts in ten more fucking minutes. I don't think everyone's as late as my period."

"You want to go then, get the fuck out of here?"

"We promised her, didn't we?"

He giggled at the concept. "She wasn't so good a three-way, though, so why we have to kill this Duke guy for her?"

"Because that was the deal. Don't you have any, what's it called? Integrity. Don't you have any integrity?"

"Shit, no!" he said. She slapped him on the arm again. He exaggerated his pain and punched her tit. "Neither does the Dude, either, or she wouldn't be so worried about him doing it that she wanted us for backup."

"Don't matter why. The Duke guy walks out that building and it means it's our turn. Ka-bam!, and get the shit out of here."

"What the hell. Been needing some more target practice anyway. Show me his picture again."

She opened the glove compartment, pulled out the photo they had been given last night by Stella. Bruno Guy was the guy on the left, twenty zillion years ago, but he hadn't changed so much she didn't recognize him, and neither had the guy on the right, the Duke guy, who she knew right away anyway from all that shit on the television.

She handed it over.

The Leader studied it. "Yeah, okay, then. Cocksucker on the right. Soon gonna be as dead as my old daddy's dick, not to mention a whole lot of scrambled kikes out in the desert." He handed her back the photo. Eased up the short-barreled, semi-automatic rifle from the space between his seat and the door panel. "Go ahead, check it out."

"Anybody looking?

"Unh-unh."

She put the photo back in the glove compartment, adjusted herself in the seat, hefted the rifle, and scoped across the drive. "Guys by them Rolls Royces? Tough mother-fuckers and I think they're packing. Two, anyway."

"What is it with you, Kayla? First about the damn cars not being here, now you got guys packing?"

Kayla laid the rifle across her lap and studied the upholstery. "It don't feel right, Andrew. Maybe we should just up and get the fuck."

He made a sharp laughing noise and slapped the top of her head. "What's with you, girl? You lose your fucking—" blowing the word out of proportion— "integrity? We got the fuck last night, remember?"

"It just don't feel right."

"Yeah, okay, but now you got me in the mood for target practice, so don't start causin' me out, okay?"

Chapter 40

Back inside the Great Sanctuary, I saw that Bruno had somehow managed to slip in. He was hugging Mama Guy, who was kissing him hungrily and stroking stray hairs off his face. I didn't spot Stella until she stepped out from the courtyard of the crypt and, cautiously using surfaces for support, limped to a seat in the first row, directly in front of the podium.

Anny, who had moved away from Mama Guy and was on her feet, seemed to be studying Stella, who still had bandages covering various parts of her, but none on her swollen face, a mess of healing cuts and massive bruises; what was going to be a jagged scar in the hollow of her right cheekbone.

Bruno caught me in a glance.

"Excuse me, Mama," I heard him say. "Anny, keep an eye on my mama, please, while I talk with Danny."

At the mention of my name, Anny turned in my direction.

Something was disturbing her. It showed on her face.

Stella was shooting me a hard, unforgiving look.

It said she still blamed me for her father's death and wanted me dead, too, but—

—that's not what was bothering Anny.

What that was became clear shortly after Bruno took my hand tightly, followed the shake with an arm around my back and a push that took us down the hall, where we could speak without being overheard.

"Some things don't ever change," I said, over the clatter of our footsteps, proud of myself.

"What's that, Danny boy?"

"How we'd check the obits everyday, looking for names we knew and inventing histories for people we didn't. I do it to this day, read them, and I counted on the fact you would, too. The best way I could figure to connect with you if you were still around."

"Still around, didn't want to travel Stella too far in her condition, but as for the other—I took the obits off my reading list a long time ago, when I became responsible for a lot of the names that were there."

"So, how—?"

"Poor Ray. Was hoping to see his family had come for him. Otherwise, you'd have been out of luck, Danny boy. Just me, you still would have been out of luck, but Stella was another story. I couldn't deprive her of being here for her mother's memorial service."

"I was counting on that, too."

"Except—" He held me to a stop and coaxed me against the corridor wall. "—it's bullshit, isn't it, the memorial service? You did it to draw me out, using the name of Billy Batson's boss. Knowing I'd know it was a message from you."

"Yes, and I counted on you still trusting me enough to show your face."

"And my mother?"

"A reason for you to stick long enough to hear me out and, if this is as close as I get to bringing you home, at least Mama Guy will have had time with you."

"Let me tell you something first. I trust you, but not the people chumming you, so I took precautions. You wander out the side—" He pointed down the corridor. "—you'll see a van parked in the red. Black. Nevada plates. I'm not back there by ten to flip a switch, the van goes boom. Powerful enough to turn this place into oatmeal. A regular population explosion."

He screwed his face into a serious smile. Checked his watch. "Eight minutes and counting," he said.

I didn't believe him and told him so.

"Bluffing? Blowing my brains out at the airport, that threat was a bluff. Our bluff. This one is for real, Danny boy, so if you have a lot to say I suggest you talk fast."

His hole card was buried too deep in his eyes for me to find, but I said anyway, "You'd kill your own mother?"

"Not to mention Anny," Bruno answered, so calmly my skin did a double-boogie. "And me and Stella and you. Solve all our problems at once, won't it?"

"You're full of shit, Captain Marvel."

"Who made you the King of the Guessers, Danny boy?"

"Fuck you, too," I said. I could see his mind ticking off the seconds. I said, "Your deal's back on."

He said, "Seven minutes and counting."

I drew from a jacket pocket the document delivered to me early this morning by one of McAllister's messenger boys and rushed through a reading.

In exchange for testimony, Bruno and Stella would receive full and unconditional amnesty and, if they wanted it, the government's witness protection program.

The document was authorized and signed by the Attorney General of the United States. Countersigned by a couple high-ranking Congressmen.

By now Bruno's head was going a million miles an hour.

"What's the catch, Danny boy? Where they drill for oil in my asshole? There's an old Indian proverb—The cobra will bite you whether you call it cobra or Mr. Cobra."

"Read it for yourself, no catch," I said, offering him the two-page, single-spaced document. "You talk, you walk."

He took it, but only to hold. "And if the government doesn't hear what it thinks it's going to hear or wants to hear from Stella and me?"

"You talk, you walk."

"Soulé?"

"You're covered like mold on a Swiss cheese, across-the-board through today. All your sins washed away, real or imagined." I shook my hands hallelujah style. "Or, putting it another way—You're home free, Captain Marvel."

"Who did you have to fuck?"

I snorted out a laugh.

"Myself," I said, and told him about Clem McAllister.

He seemed to go gooey-eyed, just stood statue still looking at me. "Was I really worth it to you?"

"Not to me, to the lady over there," I said, indicating Mama Guy, who had sat down again and was studying us with a puzzled expression.

"You always were a sucker for good home cooking."

"Speaking of whom—" I held up my watch at Bruno.

"Oh, yeah." He dug what looked like your basic pager from a pocket. Snapped the switch. "There we are." Checked his watch. "Not a minute to spare."

"You said you had to do that at the van."

"I forgot to mention the remote backup? Precautionary. Stella's not too slick on her legs right now."

"The explosives were a bluff, weren't they? You were bluffing?"

He donated his face to a grin that told me nothing and dropped the pager back into his pocket. "What now?"

I gave myself a minute, and counting, to pull myself together.

"Out front. McAllister's waiting to say hello to you. An assistant attorney general is with him, who expects to deliver you to the Federal Building in Westwood, and so is McAllister's personal lawyer. McAllister's idea, to make certain there's no deviation from his blueprint."

Bruno poked a finger into my breastbone. "You did good, Danny boy. You're a regular Picasso."

I shook my head. "Sometimes, a Norman Rockwell is good enough."

"Stella," he called, "You place the bouquets?"

"Yes, baby, and said a little prayer." Her voice broke.

"Time to go then, honey."

"What about the service, baby?" Stella asked. Her eyes were flashing pinwheels of pain, and I saw what it must have been bothering Anny a few minutes ago, and now.

Stella was brandishing a small automatic, which she had aimed at me, using the top of a chair to steady her nervous grip. From here, a .22, tough to target at this distance, but nevertheless deadly. I stopped and automatically brought my hands out and shoulder high.

Bruno put a hand to my back and said quietly, "Let me handle this. She's half out of her mind on pain killers, so don't do anything foolish."

"Better you should convince her."

"And don't be so cute about it. You can't begin to know that kind of hurt."

"Of course, I can."

"Yeah. Shit. Sorry." To Stella, "Wonderful news, honey. Danny has arranged for us to go free. Total amnesty."

She digested the news and spit it out. "Doesn't change anything, baby."

"Honey. I told you I would take care of it. Let me take care of it, okay, baby?"

"Then you come and take care of it, you hear me?" Stella demanded, her voice climbing on every word. "I want you to do it right this time or I will!"

"Okay, honey. I'm coming to you now, to get the gun."

Anny started to rise from her seat in front of Mama Guy, with a look that signaled her intent to try something stupid.

"Don't!" I shouted.

Stella snapped a glance and ordered, "Get your ass back in that chair."

Anny froze in a half crouch, shut her eyes to the fear, and sat down.

Stella swung the gun back at me.

Mama Guy had been paying attention.

She said, "Such a thoughtful daughter-in-law you gave me, Bruno. She brought such nice roses over there where she put them, you see, for her mommy and daddy?" She pointed at the crypt. "Come and sit here by me, Stella, sweetheart, so we can say a prayer together." She patted the seat next to her. "Oh, I know you hurt, so, maybe it'll be better I come over to you."

Stella appealed to her, "Please don't, Mama."

"It's okay, Stella. Just because my joints make funny noises don't mean I can't still get around fine and dandy."

"Mama!"

"Bruno, it's okay. Stella and me, we're going to say a prayer together. We also got to thank God for bringing you back to me." Mama Guy had now moved so that she was standing directly in the line of fire. "And you, Stella, maybe even a little one soon, to make me a grandmother?"

Stella urged her, "Move aside, Mama."

"What's that? A gun? You gonna shoot me, Stella? What's that all about?"

I said to Bruno, "I don't know who's crazier, you or your mother."

"Stella," he said, and called, "Stella, honey. Don't do anything silly, baby."

"Then you do what you're supposed to!" she said. Every word hit the ceiling and careened in two directions.

Mama Guy was blocking our view of her, but not of Anny, who was poised to try a lunge.

Before I could scream at her not to—

A shot.

Chapter 41

My first thought was for Anny, the possibility Stella had turned the gun on her. I heard myself going crazy, frantically shouting her name, louder than Bruno was begging Stella at the top of his lungs not to do anything stupid.

I was certain it was too late for that, and—

There was a second gunshot.

I charged ahead in what felt like useless slow motion. My heart was drumming in double-time, bouncing Anny's name off the walls, Bruno a half step behind me, and—

Mama Guy wheeled around and held out the gun, which she had snatched from Stella, who was sinking to the ground, her legs no longer able to support her, and—

Anny was reaching down to help her, calling back to me, "I'm okay, I'm okay, I'm okay."

In another eternal instant, Bruno took the gun from Mama Guy, who eased into a sitting position and moved Stella into her arms, cautioning her, "Don't cry, darling. Don't cry. Mama is here to take care of you."

Stella was crying uncontrollably, blubbering through an ozone layer of drugs, "He has to die, he has to die, he has to die."

"Why, darling? Who?"

"Him. He. Him. Danny. Danny. He. He killed my daddy. He killed—" She saw me behind Mama and reached a clawed hand toward me. "He. Him. Killed my daddy."

"Honey, darling, sweetheart. Think on it." She placed her fingers over Stella's lips. "Your mama, may she rest in peace, your mama she entrusted Danny to look after her, to see she got buried next to your dear father, may he also rest in peace. If she trusted Danny, she must have forgiven him, you see? So, you can also, in honor of your precious mama, can't you, Stella? Can you, darling?"

The noises pouring out of Stella that could have meant anything.

Bruno checked to be certain she was all right, knelt, and kissed her forehead. He swept to my side, jaws flaring; a look on his face so intense I could feel it, the question self-evident.

"I don't know either," I said. "I'm going out to look."

"We're not waiting to find out."

I pushed my face into his. "Don't do anything crazy." We hung in the moment. "Give me a minute to go out and see."

It was clear by now the gunshots had happened outside.

Bruno said, "If it's supposed to be a military burial, they're nineteen short."

"A minute. Do yourself a favor. Do Stella a favor."

As I pushed off, he stopped me with my name.

I turned and reached out in time to catch one-handed the automatic Mama Guy had swiped from Stella, a .22.

"I owe you one," Bruno said.

"For a .45, you owe me two," I said, stashing it inside my belt, then, pulling back the jacket enough for him to see the .38 I was packing in a hip holster.

"The minute I'm giving you, that's the other one."

"Then two minutes!" I called across my shoulder, dashing down the corridor.

The gunshots had been backfire from a power-driven

lawnmower sailing up and down the aisles of slick grass across from the Great Sanctuary, on Island of Love XVIII, where Charlie Temple and Fuzz Todd, who were examining adjacent headstones, sprang off their haunches after the first shot, drew their weapons, and with cold, wide-eyed alarm began searching for the source.

So did all four of McAllister's men, who were standing by the Rolls Royces and now carouseled out of their gossip circle, each brandishing a Glock and a *Don't fuck with me!* look of certainty, and—

—who did not go unnoticed by either Andrew or Kayla inside the van.

Both also had reacted to the first backfire. Kayla had the short-barrel steered out her window and looked like she relished the concept of using it. Andrew had yanked a Magnum from the same place he'd stored the rifle and was acing the front windows like an anxious hunter.

They noticed McAllister's men about the same time the four men spotted them, attracted by glints of sunlight dancing off Kayla's barrel.

And Charlie had seen it all by the time of the second backfire.

He rapped Fuzz Todd's arm, trying to remember the last time he'd felt so much fear sweat jumping off his forehead, used his head as a pointer to direct Fuzz's attention to the van and the Glock exhibit in front of the building.

Fuzz nodded, motioned for him to stay behind, and crouched into a roundabout maneuver over the grave markers that kept him out of the sightline of the van occupants.

He reached the side of the van and used it as a brace, his .45 pressed against his broad chest, barrel up and cocked.

A few seconds later, Charlie was alongside him, panting

like a car running on gas fumes, his .38 snub also ready to fire.

The gardener on the power lawnmower saw Charlie and Fuzz, howled something Charlie figured was Japanese for "Shit!" and went racing down Island of Love XVIII as fast as his stumpy legs would carry him. He stumbled over his sneakers, plunged forward, and rolled out of sight.

Charlie turned to Fuzz with a questioning look.

Fuzz shrugged, then used the .45 as part of his sign language telling Charlie to ease himself over to the driver window while he inched around the back of the van to the passenger window.

The shooters across the street? Charlie motioned.

Fuzz, his eyes reflecting the puzzle and deep furrows forming between his brows, fished for his badge wallet and turned it so the gold badge was showing, held it aloft so it showed over the roof of the van. He mouthed, *This will have to do,* and began his move.

Charlie stepped cautiously toward the driver window, unable to see that I had emerged from the building entrance and now stood looking around, the .22 dangling indifferently in my right hand.

It was a sight that didn't escape Kayla.

"Andrew, there's that son of a bitch now!" she said, loud enough for Charlie to hear.

Andrew said, "He brung an army with him. We got bigger wars to fight than him. We're getting the fuck out of here!"

"Gimme a chance, Andrew! Gimme a fucking shot!"

An instant later, too fast for Charlie to react, the van's motor gunned and it pulled out from the curb.

Hit the brakes loud in front of the building.

Stayed only until a shot fired, then sped away, but—

—not before Charlie got off one that exploded the left rear tire and—

—I dropped to the concrete.

Fuzz was heading for the bodyguards, waving his badge and identifying himself with scatological fury, demanding they put down their weapons, and—

—Charlie, with what energy he had left, wondering if he was meant to suffer a heart attack on the goddam steps of a cemetery building, was pressing toward me, as—

—both doors of the van flew open and the driver and his sidekick rushed off at a diagonal across the lawn of the Great Sanctuary building, ducking and zigzagging as bullets from four Glocks zinged into the lawn, zipped overhead, and dinged into the sculptured marble walls, and—

—I was on my stomach.

I wasn't moving.

I sensed somebody kneeling behind me.

I rolled onto my side, blind aiming my .38.

Charlie said, "Pull the trigger, asshole, and you are really gonna fuck up my golf game."

I didn't have time to answer Charlie.

I leaped to my feet, shouted to everyone to stay where they were, and raced back inside, fearing the latest gunfire had convinced Bruno and Stella to flee. Charging down the hall, I saw Anny and Mama Guy sitting together, holding hands and trading words, but not Bruno and Stella. There had been enough time for them to get to Bruno's van.

Anny called out as I whizzed by.

I ignored her, racing to what I hoped was the entrance Bruno used earlier, bolting outside in time to see a van caroming down the drive. Black. Nevada plates. Bruno's van.

I cursed the gray sky for a minute, cursed Bruno for running, then wandered back inside, in no hurry to explain to Mama Guy, to Clem McAllister or anyone, to the Feds, that Bruno was gone again, this time possibly for good.

Only, he wasn't.

He said, "I might have given you more than your two minutes if the Civil War hadn't broken out."

I turned in the direction of Bruno's voice.

He was behind me and to my right, leaning against the building, his arms folded around Stella's waist.

She was a limp doll, facing him with her hands locked behind his neck, half asleep with her head on his chest, unable to support herself, a marathon dancer who wouldn't be around for the last go-round.

"In fact, I think it was more like three and a half minutes," he said.

"Is Stella all right?"

"Nothing fewer poppers and better health won't cure. Am I right, baby?" He asked the question like he didn't expect an answer and got none, except for a faint moan.

I hurriedly sketched in what had happened.

"The two of them only tried to kill you, Danny boy. Me, they stole my goddam getaway."

"The good news is, the ride I planned for you is still out front." A wistful smile. "Danny Boy's Delivery Service."

He made a gesture of compliance. "Gets you where you want to go, whether you want to go or not. You hear the man, honey? Danny boy has us where you wanted to be—out from under."

He stroked Stella's hair, kissed the top of her head.

Stella answered him with a deep-throated moan.

I asked, "The people who shot at me, friends of yours?"

Bruno understood what I was driving at.

"Couple Number One? Of course. I'm large on bald-headed morons, especially the babes . . ." His head wagged. He shamed me with his look. "The New Millennium Crusade, and now you've experienced them first hand. Children of the revolution, the new order of murdering assholes that I told you about. Probably trailed us down here. Either they had a duplicate set of keys or they hot wired the rig. They're pretty up on grabbing wheels off the street."

"Why would they follow you?"

A shrug. "Maybe to get high on being in a boneyard? Who the hell ever knows with people like that, who get off on blowing up synagogues packed with Jews when they're not being equal opportunity killers, killing innocent people to make a statement regardless of race, creed or color."

Bruno shook his head and grinned at some private joke. He fished the beeper from his pocket and tossed it at me.

I caught it high, one-handed, and gave him a questioning look.

"You're a believer in the system, a purveyor of good government, Danny boy, so do the world a good turn. Click that switch and make go-boom, rid the planet of the two lower than lowlifes."

Bruno was playing out some moral, the way he did when we were kids, making me uncomfortable, something else he was always so good at.

"No, thanks," I said, and flipped back the beeper.

He made a one-handed catch.

"Don't be so quick. Think it through. They die and how many lives do you save as a result? In the long run? I'd say a lot. Also in the short haul." Bruno nodded affirmatively and tossed back the beeper. An easy palm-of-the-hander. "Switch it on and press on the arrow. Do the good deed. Be a hero."

"Tell the Feds about them. That's good enough."

"And there's what's always been the difference between us, chum. You, a tool of the law. Me, a tool of justice."

He hardly had the words out of his mouth when there was a large explosion, followed by a trail of black smoke, maybe a mile away.

"Shazam," Bruno said, quietly. "Justice speaks."

I stared with disbelief at the beeper switch, then, at Bruno, whose eyes glistened with satisfaction.

"Never fear," he said. "It wasn't you done the dirty. They did it to themselves. I turned off the timer, but not the safety backup. Another ten minutes on the clock. Better than a club on the steering wheel."

"Did they know you'd wired the car?"

"You know, I forgot to ask."

"Murder, Bruno. In the first."

"Amnesty, Danny boy. Remember? Or, do you plan to tell on me and spoil the party?" He fished out a Havana from his jacket and popped it unlit into his mouth.

Before I could answer, he looked past me and said, "Well, well, well. Company."

Turning, I saw McAllister's men had rounded the corner of the building and were standing in an erratic row a few feet from the base of the stairs, their Glocks aimed at us, all four seriously considering their options. The one with a broken, off-center nose looked ready to translate the twitch in his eye to his trigger finger.

Charlie and Fuzz, both struggling for breath, skimmed the same corner and almost bounced into them a moment later, at the same time that Anny and Mama Guy stepped cautiously from the building, Anny first, holding Mama Guy back with a hand. At once, relief replaced Anny's look of apprehension, and Mama Guy broke into desperate tears of joy.

The two Rolls Royces sailed around the corner, followed

by a black stretch limo I hadn't seen earlier. It screeched to a halt and dumped out three men in Brooks Brothers black, reflective shades, and assault rifles.

A McAllister bodyguard had McAllister's door open in seconds. McAllister eased out with an eager smile and jaunty wave, sending greetings to Bruno and me, explaining, "Hello to both of you, Mr. and Mrs. Guy. I thought the stretch would be a nice touch for your drive to Westwood with Mr. Little Sky and your new lawyer, Mr. Ehrlichman, while I personally deliver your mother home in the Rolls."

Bruno read him in a blink. "And the cavalry?"

"Apart from my people—" He snapped his fingers and the bodyguards holstered their Glocks, as did Charlie and Fuzz. "Mr. Little Sky is with our government and he has certain rules he must follow."

McAllister looked at the assistant attorney general, who had stepped from the second Rolls.

Perry Little Sky frowned and nodded.

Bruno asked indifferently, "Another Rupert Bachman?"

"No, Mr. Guy. Unlike Mr. Bachman I'm still alive, no thanks to you, and I plan to stay that way," Little Sky said, spitting out the words.

"I have the same plan for me and my wife," Bruno said. "Little Sky. You Indian?" Little Sky stared back coldly. "So not the cavalry to the rescue. The Indians. Why do I find more than a little irony in that?" A teasing smile. "Y'know, Little Sky, the country could still be yours if your ancestors bothered to understand what Sitting Bull's victory meant. Instead you got fucked over, fenced in and the agonies of Wounded Knee."

"Thanks for explaining that to me," Little Sky answered sarcastically. "I'll give it to my ancestors when I make it to the Happy Hunting Grounds. Now, if you don't mind?"

"Yes," McAllister said, retaking control. "We should be on our way." His hand swept the air. "After you, Mr. Guy?"

I quickly stepped forward to help Bruno down the steps with Stella.

Her disturbed eyes twitched open to my touch, and when she recognized me—

She said haltingly under her breath, in a distressed tone that made me understand I was not in anyway forgiven, "I won't forget you."

The look of certainty was still on her face as she turned to me for one final, harsh stare before following Bruno into the stretch.

Some people hang onto revenge like it has a value in antiquity.

From the sound Stella was one of them, but—

—she never got a chance to prove me right.

Or, wrong.

Chapter 42

By all accounts theirs was an easy death, if such is ever really possible, so swift there was barely time for surprise, much less pain.

The terse announcement out of the Attorney General's office identified Bruno and Stella among the eight persons who died, including the Marine pilot and navigator, when a light military transport exploded in mid-air on takeoff from Edwards Air Force Base in California's Antelope Valley.

The plane's scheduled stops included Spaulding, Iowa, where the Guys were to testify before a special grand jury convened to consider government allegations of a dozen or more treasonous acts of malice or murder by a group of local extremists not identified by name.

Bruno Guy, especially, the news release went on, was considered the key witness in the government's case, as he had been already over the past three months, testifying in front of other grand juries in other states.

A statement by Assistant Attorney General Perry Little Sky credited him with "meaningful testimony that substantially disrupted or led to the conclusion of criminal activities of subversive outlaw groups like the Freedom Militia, the True Children of the Revolution, and the New Millennium Crusade, although the return of Mr. and Mrs. Guy to basic principals espoused by our government, the true American Way, does not excuse or in any way condone their own wrongful acts in past years."

And blah, blah, blah.

The government playing "Protect Your Ass," as Bruno had predicted it would.

Damning with the faintest of praise, and not even the simple letter of condolence I had urged them to send Mama Guy, to give her something besides this deep new pain to hang on her heart.

"It's time to face up to it, Sailor, you can't blame them," Anny said about the thousandth time I complained. "You strip away your buzz words like *friendship* and *loyalty* and go to one like, for argument's sake, *truth;* you come to grips with another word, *reality.* Bruno devoted most of his life to—" She sucked in her breath, appeared anxious not to hurt me with too much of a word like *honesty.* "—really bad stuff."

"Stuff?"

"Stuff. He turned into a bad guy who came to like what he did not as a cause but—because. Because he was good at it, he liked it, and after awhile it was all he knew how to do. And you know the worst part of all?"

"Twenty years ago he tried to steal you from me."

Anny put on the face my mother used whenever I failed to clean up my room. "Twenty years later, you still retreat by turning everything into a joke."

"Not how I feel about you."

"You make everything a joke, especially when you know you're wrong and—that is the worst part. How wrong you've been about Bruno. Not your boyhood friend, who died a long time ago. I'm speaking of the Bruno who forgot what he was fighting for but kept on fighting anyway. The Bruno Guy who could blow up a van and the two people in it with the flip of a switch, laughing and joking about it immediately afterward, ignoring the possibility other, innocent people could have being killed by the explosion."

"But none were, and that pair, they were stone killers in their own right."

"And you're still Dirty Harry." Anny released a sigh of exasperation. "God, I hate it when you sound that way."

So did I.

We were sitting up in bed, watching Leno and not paying attention to his opening monologue.

I wanted to tell her she was right.

I wanted her to know I meant it.

I was not agreeing to agree, to make her feel good or to terminate an argument that, if allowed to continue, could create days and days of black brooding; the two of us maneuvering the house like subs in enemy waters.

I leaned over to kiss her, but I was too late. She moved away, turned on her side and at once started breathing soundly, pretending like she had fallen asleep, so I clicked off the set and rolled in the opposite direction, and played out in my mind how I wanted to tell her my words had slipped out before my mind processed them.

Anny had been right, of course, as she so often was.

I wanted her to hear me say it.

I had been defending Bruno out of habit, because in a way it justified my own blind actions on behalf of a friendship carried on in name only for most of the past two decades.

Because of Bruno I'd entered into a devil's trade with Clem McAllister, trading hard evidence about a bad cop and a double-dealing, money-grubbing supervisor, among others, in exchange for another chance at life for someone who had made graveyards of death wherever he settled.

Or so I was still trying to convince myself. The truth is, not Bruno, not anyone, could have made me do anything I didn't want to do, anymore than I was susceptible to the quiet, self-serving, manipulative urgings of Pearce Dickson.

But, I was.

I did something I thought myself incapable of doing.

And, I didn't understand why.

Three months later and I was still plagued by the black hole of doubt I had fallen into, wondering what I might find when I reached bottom.

If I reached bottom.

Had I committed first degree murder or manslaughter of my soul?

I was reminded of the question any time I passed Pearce Dickson in the hall or turned from one of the begging stares he laid on me during Board meetings.

I didn't have to tell him for him to know that we'd never again be the friends we had been, anymore than I had ever considered following a bad guy into a cell and turning an arrest into a relationship.

I'd miss his friendship and the closeness our families had shared, but it was not a place I could go anymore, not if I wanted to hold onto what was left of my own, formerly unimpeachable honesty and integrity.

I don't know if that's the same conclusion that was reached by Pearce's aide, Manny Sutton, who'd slipped me the floppy disk, but Manny was no longer around. He'd resigned and gone to some small town in Oregon, where he purchased and was running a weekly newspaper, I heard, something Manny had dreamed about for years.

It made a nicer story than the one I heard from Charlie Temple:

How Pearce had fired Manny after tracking the floppy back to him.

Charlie didn't have a problem with Pearce, urging me to

measure his greed against the good he'd done for the county, the same argument Pearce had once tried on me, and I couldn't help thinking Pearce had put Charlie up to it.

Charlie denied it, insisting his only concern was with what he termed my "willful destruction" of a perfectly good golf foursome. "Give the guy a break," he urged. "Maybe this experience will convince him to turn over a new leaf."

I swiveled my head left and right.

"Charlie, a day after the Board approved the MacMurray project, one of Clem McAllister's people delivered me a thank you note and a beautifully framed and mounted Picasso wash drawing on zinc, 'The Dove.' One of Picasso's great images, a worldwide symbol of peace. Worth somewhere in the middle-to-high six figure range, minimum."

Charlie let out a whistle. "It must've been a peace offering. McAllister certainly wasn't giving you the bird." He winked.

"I think he was. He knew I was going to vote his way on his pet project, but he sent it anyway. To remind me we had done business and could do it again. I didn't want any part of it. I told his guy to take it back with my sincere *Thanks but no thanks.* The next day, I had to be in Pearce's office for a committee meeting. The Picasso print was hanging on his wall, in a place of prominence above the couch. This is no sign Pearce learned a lesson or is going to change his ways, Charlie."

He made light of it. "I might have taken it, too, you know? Anything worth six figures can go a long way toward a more comfy-cozy retirement."

"I do know, Charlie. That floppy disk put your name on my monitor screen once or twice."

His silence fit the melancholy expression that froze on his face.

Finally, he said, "I been wondering a long time if you ever intended to get around to mentioning that."

"Another reason I bargained with McAllister. It wasn't just for Bruno."

"For what it might be worth, Danny boy, I never made those same mistakes twice."

"Three times, by my count."

"Four." He said, raising a rogue smile on his face. "So, how come we're still talking like this and I'm still welcome in your house. Or, am I?"

I didn't have an answer for him.

Or for myself.

Then or now—

—as I begged my mind to turn off and give me a chance at a few hours sleep; continued to struggle with the question after a comfortable position until—

Anny rolled over and nestled against my back.

Her breasts pushed into me.

Her hand massaged my thigh before it inched over and quickly found, expertly grabbed onto what she was looking for.

"I was wrong," I said hoarsely, my voice growing with a desire for her.

"You saying that just to get back on my good side?"

"You don't have a bad side," I said, and rolled over to face her, pulled her closer in, and pressed hard against her. Kissed her eyes and her nose. Slid my tongue into her mouth in search of hers and grew harder with the connection.

How I loved this woman.

I told her so and heard my pulse roar when she echoed the thought.

I began massaging her buttocks, circular patterns of desire, ran my hand up and down her back to experience the electrifying softness of her skin, then onto her buttocks again. She made a birdlike sound and, lightly kissing and licking my neck, grazing my cheek with hers, she whispered in my ear, "Bruno never stood a chance with me, twenty years ago or ever."

"You're saying that just to make me feel good."

"Yes. Now it's your turn to make me feel better."

Rather than risk another disagreement, I did as I was told.

Chapter 43

The government said there was not enough left of Bruno or Stella for one decent funeral, much less two, so Mama Guy invited all her friends and neighbors in to pay their final respects.

That's how Anny and I came to be at her home on a rain-threatening Saturday afternoon a few days after their cremated remains were finally released and delivered to her in a securely-sealed, double-strength plastic bag inside a thick, brown cardboard container hardly big enough to hold one average-sized cantaloupe.

Mama Guy had transferred the ashes into a single multi-colored ceramic bowl she'd used until now for arrangements of flowers selected from the garden that stretched out back along the fence line and given the bowl the place of honor on the mantle.

Next to it was a framed photo of Bruno with Stella I didn't remember from other visits, one of those oversized color enlargements you get in a shopping mall photo booth, maybe because Stella back then held no significance for me, or because it was lost among all the other photos that tracked Bruno's life.

Happier times.

Other girls.

The prom.

A cheerleader he was serious about for a year, who had

other ideas and other beaus.

Me, of course.

Happier times.

This photo appeared to be a year or two old.

Bruno and Stella looked much as they did the last time we saw them, disappearing into McAllister's stretch limo for the ride to the Federal Building in Westwood, except for the uncertainty clouding their eyes and the pinched corners of their mouths telling a truer story than their smiles.

Not how they would look to me a short time from now.

Anny and I were stationed at the front door, welcoming arrivals and shuttling them to Mama Guy, who sat with quiet, queenly authority in a straight-backed chair just inside the living room, then pointing them past the dining room archway to a table that was set with heaping platters of cold cuts, all kinds of breads and rolls, fresh diced fruit and vegetable salads, and an astonishing assortment of desserts, mostly home-baked pies and cookies brought over earlier by neighbors. Many of them had known Bruno as a boy, including some who also remembered me as a neighborhood kid and had special words of condolence for the pain they assumed in Bruno's best friend.

Radio music drifted over the tangled conversations in the crowd, which varied at times from a few to a few dozen. The station was spinning the kind of jazz Bruno and I had grown up with and made our own, and I smiled at the notion today's programming was dedicated to him.

None of the guests knew Stella, except from the news stories, of course, and now Mama Guy's description of her and the photo on the mantle, not the threatening, revenge-bound Stella I knew, but rather a princess of a woman, who loved her son as much as her son had loved her.

I was amused by Mama Guy's use of the word *princess,* sometimes casual, sometimes emphatic; and how she took care not to mention that Stella's mother was sharing her own kind of mutual eternity in a memorial park crypt in Glendale.

Forever in Love, Forever in Life, Forever After.

Now, Bruno and Stella, too.

I dumped another load of winter coats and jackets in Mama Guy's bedroom and was turning to go when I saw on the dresser a framed photograph that I could swear had not been there on my last drop-off.

Someone must have come into the bedroom and put it there in the last five or ten minutes.

It was next to a smaller, browned by age, photo of Mama Guy's husband in a less expensive frame.

It was an eight-by-ten in an elegant, highly-polished sterling silver frame.

Bruno and Stella.

Their faces had been worked on, drastically altered, but it was Bruno and Stella. I saw it again in their eyes and the set of their mouths, just like in the photo on the mantle.

Enough difference to fool everyone.

Almost everyone.

My breathing became stuttered.

My heart was thumping inside my chest.

I grabbed up the picture and raced from the bedroom, threaded my way through the guests clogging the hallway and pushed to Mama Guy's side. She looked away from old Mr. and Mrs. Rosenbaum and caught the question on my face, first, then the framed photograph.

At once her smile evaporated into a sheepish look that answered one of the questions I had for her.

I squatted and, holding the photo in her direct line of vision, pressed my mouth close to her ear and asked it anyway.

I wanted to hear it from her.

"Bruno and Stella?"

She said nothing to offset the guilt flushing her face.

"Are they still alive?"

Her eyes clouded and she looked away.

Her lips moved in and out, shifting between a pout and a grimace.

"They're still alive, aren't they, Mama Guy, or tell me the picture was taken before the plane crash."

She pulled the frame from me and pressed it against her bosom.

Shook her head.

"He said they was bringing a surprise for me today," Mama Guy said, barely able to work the words out. "I told him not to come, but he said he needed to see me one last time." Her explanation trailed off into a husky sigh.

"Did he?"

No answer.

A breath caught in my chest.

Bruno had been here.

Maybe Stella.

They might still be here.

I bolted up so urgently I almost lost my balance.

Surveyed the room, checking faces for anyone who looked like either face in the photo.

Worked through the crowd, earning angry looks whenever I twisted a back around that might put me face to face with Bruno or Stella.

The dining room. The hallway.

The bedroom again.

The bathroom. The kitchen.

Another storm through the living room and, past the shoulder of a bald, bulb-nosed man my age, who'd correctly identified himself earlier as someone I wouldn't remember from junior high.

I saw Anny. She was trying to attract my attention with something she held aloft in her left hand.

I pushed my way to her, ignoring complaints about my rudeness.

"Two people leaving just gave me this for you," Anny said, a question mark screwed between her brows. She handed over a thin, rectangular package clumsily wrapped in butcher paper. "Danny boy" printed in large letters. I ripped away the paper, exposing a copy of Audie's autobiography, *To Hell and Back*. Inscribed on the flyleaf in fountain pen ink: "Shazam!"

Dated today.

Unmistakably Bruno.

"Jesus!" Anny blurted out.

"Stay put!" I called, already pushing out the door and onto the porch, getting there in time to see a black four-wheeler pulling out from the curb halfway down the block.

I charged down the path, past Mama Guy's garden, aiming for my Porsche.

It was parked almost in front.

I jumped in.

Anny pulled open the passenger door and angled half her body inside.

"Don't!" she demanded.

"I thought I told you to stay put!"

"He could have the car rigged, like he rigged the van!"

"He wouldn't do that to me." I stuck the key in the ignition.

"He's doing it for her, for Stella! She's his wife."

"I'm his best friend."

"I'm your wife and your best friend!"

Anny settled onto the seat beside me.

Yanked her door shut.

"Get out!" I yelled.

"Let's go!" she yelled back. Then, quietly appealing to me, "He rigged the car, Sailor. You know it and I know it."

I hesitated for a lifetime of thought before I pulled out the key.

"Doing it for you," I said.

She rested a hand on my arm.

"I don't care why," she said.

Less than a month later, a car bomb took the life of a Colombian drug cartel leader and his family on their way home from a World Cup elimination match. News reports drew similarities between this bombing and car bombings that terrorist Bruno Guy had taken credit for during various federal grand jury appearances.

A statement by Assistant Attorney General Perry Little Sky acknowledged the similarities in denying any complicity in the successful assassination attempt, although admitting the cartel leader was high on the Justice Department's most wanted list. The statement included a reminder that Bruno Guy and his wife had been killed in a mid-air mishap.

By then I was driving the Porsche again.

About the Author

Robert S. Levinson wrote the best-selling thriller, *Ask a Dead Man*, as well as the best-selling series of novels starring Neil Gulliver and Stevie Marriner: *Hot Paint*, *The John Lennon Affair*, *The James Dean Affair*, and *The Elvis and Marilyn Affair*. His short stories appear often in *Ellery Queen Mystery Magazine* and *Alfred Hitchcock Mystery Magazine*. Two were voted back-to-back "Ellery Queen Readers Award" honors, while others were included in the annual anthologies, *World's Finest Mystery & Crime Stories* and *The Year's Finest Crime and Mystery Stories*. A former newspaperman, television writer-producer and award-winning public relations executive, Bob is an immediate past national director at-large of Mystery Writers of America, past president of the MWA Southern California chapter, and a past board of directors member of the Writers Guild of America. He and his wife, Sandra, reside in Los Angeles. Read more at www.robertslevinson.com.